LET'S NOT BE FRIENDS

PHOEBE MACLEOD

Phoebe xx

B
Boldwood

First published in Great Britain in 2022 by Boldwood Books Ltd.

Copyright © Phoebe MacLeod, 2022

Cover Design by Leah Jacobs-Gordon

Cover Photography: Shutterstock

The moral right of Phoebe MacLeod to be identified as the author of this work has been asserted in accordance with the Copyright, Designs and Patents Act 1988.

All rights reserved. No part of this book may be reproduced in any form or by any electronic or mechanical means, including information storage and retrieval systems, without written permission from the author, except for the use of brief quotations in a book review.

This book is a work of fiction and, except in the case of historical fact, any resemblance to actual persons, living or dead, is purely coincidental.

Every effort has been made to obtain the necessary permissions with reference to copyright material, both illustrative and quoted. We apologise for any omissions in this respect and will be pleased to make the appropriate acknowledgements in any future edition.

A CIP catalogue record for this book is available from the British Library.

Paperback ISBN 978-1-80426-272-6

Large Print ISBN 978-1-80426-273-3

Hardback ISBN 978-1-80426-271-9

Ebook ISBN 978-1-80426-274-0

Kindle ISBN 978-1-80426-238-2

Audio CD ISBN 978-1-80426-266-5

MP3 CD ISBN 978-1-80426-267-2

Digital audio download ISBN 978-1-80426-268-9

Boldwood Books Ltd
23 Bowerdean Street
London SW6 3TN
www.boldwoodbooks.com

To Chris, without whose encouragement this would have been a very short adventure

PROLOGUE

'I therefore proclaim that they are husband and wife!'

I can hear the vicar's words, but he seems far away, as if he's in another room. All I can see are James' piercing blue eyes gazing into mine and, as he leans in for our first kiss as a married couple, my heart feels like it's going to explode with love. I can barely hear our guests clapping and whooping over the blood rushing through my ears. It's taken us just over three years to get to this point from the day we met. I'd been dragged along to a rugby match by one of my school friends, who was mad keen on one of James' team mates but didn't want to go on her own. I was a bit pissed off when she abandoned me in the bar afterwards in order to give Harry her full attention, but James noticed me sitting on my own and came over. We got chatting and that was that. We dated for two years before he proposed over dinner at Wiltons in Jermyn Street, and pretty much every spare moment in the last twelve months has been taken up with planning our wedding.

I wouldn't call myself a Bridezilla, but I have put a lot of work into making sure that everything is perfect today. Organising weddings and events is my day job, so it wouldn't have looked very good if my own wedding wasn't up to scratch, especially as many brides could only dream of the budget I had. We kneel down and I can hear the vicar saying some words of blessing, but my mind is now working through the schedule for the rest of the day, going over it to make sure there isn't anything I've forgotten. It's pointless, I know; there's nothing I'd be able to do to fix any problems now, but I just find it reassuring to run through the checklist and not find any gaps or pinch points.

James leads me over to our seats and the vicar starts his sermon. It's not bad, actually. He's repeating some of the stories that we told him about how we met and what we enjoy. I'm relieved, as I was worried it would be a long religious rant like we used to get in school. I'm not religious at all, and most of our guests aren't, so that would have been wasted on us. In fact, I would have been quite happy getting married at a castle or some other picturesque venue, but James' parents insisted that a church wedding was the only way to get married 'properly'. To be fair, it does look very pretty in here with all the flowers, and the ancient church building will make a lovely backdrop for the photos after the service. I relax and glance down at the wedding ring glinting on my left hand. I can't believe I'm actually married!

After the sermon, we traipse into the room at the side to sign the registers, and I beam with delight as the photographer takes his shots. I was lucky enough to be able to book Toby Roberts, who does the photos for quite a few of the celebrity weddings you see in magazines like *Hello!* He was much more expensive than any of the other photographers I looked at, but he's the best, so it was a no-brainer. Once Toby has all the shots he wants, we form up into the procession for leaving the church. James' hand clasps mine firmly as the vicar asks the congregation to put their hands together for Mr and Mrs Huntingdon-Barfoot, and we step out into a barrage of flashes as everyone tries to get a picture of us. I feel that I could literally explode with happiness.

As Toby takes more pictures after the service, I find myself thinking about what's to come. The reception should be amazing; we've got a Michelin-starred chef in charge of the food, and Dad's wine merchant has worked hard with us to get the right pairings for each course. And then, tomorrow, we're off to the Seychelles on honeymoon. Two weeks of sun, sand, and delicious sex before we move down to Devon, where James' family owns a substantial amount of land. I've already seen the house we're going to live in, a perfect little cottage on the farm. It's a bit run down at the moment, but I've got big plans to renovate it.

I can't wait to start my new life.

1

FOUR YEARS LATER

It's official: I hate the bloody Aga.

I know most people who have them swear by them, but I seem to spend most of my time swearing at mine. I wasn't exactly an experienced cook when I moved here, but the Aga has had it in for me from day one. After my first attempts resulted in food that was either burned to a crisp or still raw, I bought various Aga books and tried to get my head around the mysteries of this completely uncontrollable cooker. It steadfastly refused to be tamed, despite my efforts, and has become ever more temperamental to the point we're at now, where it's impossible to predict whether it will be hotter than the sun and burn everything, or so cold that you can't even boil water on the hotplate. To be fair to it, I suspect it needs a good service, but James tells me there's no money for luxuries like that, so one of the farm hands comes and pokes and prods it for a bit every time it goes wrong, and it limps on.

Except for today. Today, when I have to bake and deliver two Victoria sponges to the Women's Institute for the village fête tomorrow, it's decided to go out completely and it's stone cold. Bastard thing. There's no way that I'm prepared to incur our WI president's wrath by letting the side down, so I reluctantly lift the phone handset and dial my mother-in-law.

'Hello Sophie, this is a surprise! Is everything okay?' she trills.

On the surface, I get on fine with her, but there's an uncomfortable undercurrent; I'm convinced she doesn't really like me, but every time I've brought it up, James says that I'm imagining things and that she adores me. Nevertheless, I'm always wary around her.

'I'm really sorry to bother you, Rosalind, but the Aga's gone out and I really need to get these cakes baked so I can deliver them to Pauline. Is there any possibility I could borrow your oven for an hour or so?'

'Of course, darling! I've just taken my cakes out, so it's all yours. What a bore for you, though. Have you told James? I'm sure he can get Tony to look at it for you.'

Tony is the mechanical maestro of the farm and, to be fair to him, he does seem to understand how the Aga works. Unfortunately, he's also a grade-A letch who thinks addressing every sentence to my chest or crotch is perfectly acceptable. I change into my baggiest jumper whenever I know he's coming round, but it doesn't seem to make any difference to his blatant ogling. He's also a little too hands-on for my liking. James says he's just friendly, but I think he's a creep.

'James is next on my list, if I can track him down,' I tell her. 'If you don't mind me dropping the cakes round in a few minutes, I'll go and look for him while they bake. It'll take hours for the Aga to get back up to temperature once it's going again, so it'll be a microwave dinner.'

'Poor you. I'd invite you both over, but I haven't got a thing in!'

She's a terrible liar. I saw the Ocado van lumber past with her latest delivery only yesterday afternoon. I'm not quite sure how she can afford to keep the big house going, employ a cleaner, and shop at Ocado when James tells me the farm is on the brink of bankruptcy and we have to save every penny we can, but I try very hard not to think about it.

'That's so kind of you,' I lie in return, 'but it'll just be James on his own tonight.'

'Of course it will,' she purrs. 'I'd completely forgotten that you're spending the weekend with your *friend*.' She emphasises the last word, as if I'm up to something unsavoury. I'd lay good money, if I had any, on the odds that a supper invitation will be forthcoming to her beloved son as soon as I'm on the train.

I'm looking forward to spending the weekend with my friend Di. I like the sense of space that living in the country brings, but I miss the buzz and hubbub of London sometimes, so a weekend in the capital is going to be a real treat, and well worth the seven-hour return train journey from Down St. Mary. When we first moved down here, James suggested I should have regular weekends in London so that I didn't feel completely cut off from my old life and, although I don't go as often as I used to, it's a tradition that's persisted. Dave, the only taxi driver in the village, is collecting me at four o'clock to take me to the station. I glance at my watch; it's two o'clock already, so I'd better get a move on.

'I'll see you in a minute,' I tell Rosalind, and hang up the phone. The cake mixture is already in the tins, so I bundle them into a box and set off up the track to the main house. The Huntingdon-Barfoots, as well as being minor nobility, used to be one of the wealthiest land-owning families in Devon, and the main house reflects their previous status. It's huge, with twelve bedrooms, enormous formal reception rooms, and servants' quarters in the attic. It must have been quite a spectacle back in the day but, like everything on the farm, it's suffered as the money has dried up. As I understand it, James' ancestors used to get most of their wealth from tenant farmers. The world wars and increasing mechanisation of farming drove the tenants away to other work, and James' grandfather found himself having to farm the thousand or so acres on his own. To begin with, he did well and the money continued to flow in, but increasing bureaucracy and foreign imports, along with some disastrous financial decisions, have left the coffers bare. When James and I married and moved down here, we had no idea how bad things were. It was only when his father died unexpectedly of a heart attack two years ago and James got his first proper look at the books that we realised the gravity of the situation.

I let myself in through the kitchen door and call out a greeting. It's never locked during the day, even when Rosalind goes out. Her view is that there's nothing in there worth stealing, and any burglar who could make it all the way down the half-mile of farm track from the lane, across the yard, and back again without someone spotting them deserves to help themselves to whatever they want. She's not wrong. Anything that had any value and was easily moved was sent to auction years ago in various attempts to keep the farm afloat. There's still quite a lot of furniture here, but it's mostly things that either have sentimental value or just wouldn't fit in a normal house. The dining-room table, for example, is a beautiful piece of furniture and is theoretically worth a fortune, but you can easily fit twenty-four people around it. Not really suitable for a semi-detached in the suburbs. The floors on the ground floor are mainly polished wood with tapestried rugs that would have been stunning years ago, but are now faded and more than a little threadbare. It's also cold, even in summer. I don't know how Rosalind stands living here, but she's resisted every attempt to move her to somewhere smaller and more practical.

There's another Aga in the kitchen here, but Rosalind also has the ultimate luxury – a fan oven. I make a beeline for it and turn it on, savouring the ability to set a temperature that I know will cook the sponges perfectly in the twenty minutes the recipe recommends. I've brought everything I need for the filling, so I'll just have enough time to let them cool enough for me to finish them off and drop them round to Pauline before I leave. I notice that Rosalind's own cakes, a carrot cake and a coffee and walnut, are already in their Tupperware boxes ready to be delivered, so maybe I can earn some brownie points by offering to take them as well.

'Help yourself to whatever you need,' Rosalind says to me as she walks through from the hall. She's immaculately turned out, as always. I'd love to know how she does it. I only have to walk across the yard to get mud halfway up my jeans, even with wellies on. Rosalind, on the other hand, is wearing polished brown brogues with tassels, immaculate dark-blue jeans, and a white shirt under her quilted body warmer. If there was a definition of 'rural chic', she would be it.

'Thanks so much for this. You're a life saver,' I tell her, and a small smile flits across her face. 'I'm just waiting for the oven to get to temperature, and then I'll pop them in and go and see if I can track James down. I'll be back before they need to come out.'

'It's not a problem, really. I'm glad I could help. If you tell me how long they need, I'll take them out for you if you're not back. Let's just hope he's not on the other side of the farm!'

'If he is, then I'll have to leave him a note. Dave's collecting me at four, so I haven't got hours to spend searching, but if I'm not back in twenty minutes, I'd be really grateful if you'd check them and take them out if they're done.'

The light on the oven goes out to indicate that it's up to temperature, so I hastily shove in the cake tins and make for the back door. I hate being indebted to Rosalind. She's always very gracious when I need something from her, but I get the feeling that she's storing it all up in some mental balance sheet to use against me later. I check my phone as I cross the yard. One of the downsides of living here is that the mobile phone signal is pretty much non-existent, so I'm surprised to see that I do have a tiny bit of reception. I dial James' number, praying to the mobile phone gods that he's also somewhere with a signal, but it's not to be. The call goes straight to voicemail. There's no point in leaving a message, as he might not get it for days, so I will have to continue my search on foot.

I notice Tony with his head inside the engine of one of the tractors, so I walk in his direction.

'Hello Sophie, you're looking nice today. Off anywhere special?' he says, as he fixes his eyes on my chest, as normal. Annoyingly, I'm wearing a fitted white shirt, so he's getting a better view than I'd like him to.

'I'm off to spend the weekend with a friend later. Do you know where James is?'

'Yeah, he went off to help Becky with something at the stables about twenty minutes ago. I expect he's still there.'

'Thanks.' I can feel him watching me as I set off down the track. He really is a disgusting pervert.

It's only recently that the stables have been brought back to life. James' father was violently against the idea of keeping horses on the farm. He felt strongly that farms were no place for 'toy' animals that served no agricultural purpose and, in his time, the stables were mainly used for storage. One of the first things that James did when his dad died was get rid of all the crap in them, clean them out, and bring them back up to standard. We have stalls for sixteen horses, and we charge handsomely for their care. The fees not only cover the cost of employing a groom to look after them, but they're one of the few parts of the farm that actually make a profit. A selection of horse boxes appears every weekend to take the animals off to various events, and they're generally back in their stables by Sunday evening. As I stride down the track towards the stable yard, I can see that I'm in luck; James' farm truck is parked outside. I pause next to it and make a brief fuss of the dogs, who are waiting patiently in the pick-up bed. The stalls are arranged in a U shape, and I pat the noses of some of the horses as I make my way around them, peering into each one to see if it contains my husband. As I approach the hay store and tack room at the far corner, I can hear faint noises coming from within. The door is closed but, from the gasps and grunts coming from the other side of it, it sounds like James and Becky, the groom, are struggling with something heavy. However, as I get closer and I can hear more clearly, I start to suspect something far worse. I know what that sound is, and it's not the sound two people would make if they were struggling with something. Very much the opposite, in fact.

My heart is in my mouth as I gently pull on the door to open it.

2

I'm speechless, probably because I seem to have stopped breathing. The scene I've just walked into has literally knocked all the air out of my lungs and I'm temporarily paralysed. The small part of my mind that hasn't shut down from the shock is frantically searching for the appropriate action to take after walking in on your husband having sex with someone else, but it's coming up blank.

This isn't even the 'traditional' method of catching your husband cheating, either. The way it's supposed to work is that you come home unexpectedly, husband and lover hear the door, and you walk in while they're frantically trying to get dressed. At least, that's what the TV would have you believe. The scene in front of me is nothing like that. Instead of a bedroom, James and Becky are hard at it on a hay-bale, which looks rather uncomfortable and scratchy to me. They also have no idea I'm here, so they haven't even had the decency to stop.

Another part of my mind unlocks and, even more strangely, I find myself critiquing my husband's technique. There is nothing here that would fit the term 'making love'; this is raw and animalistic. It's fucking, pure and simple. They haven't even undressed properly. Becky, the groom, still has her fleece on, although her boots, jodhpurs and knickers are carelessly chucked to one side and the fleece has ridden up to expose her pale, toned stomach. James is still wearing his boots, with his trousers and underpants pulled down to his ankles. I'm no expert but, from what I can see, there can't have been much in the way of foreplay before they got down to the main event.

The rest of me is totally shut down. It's like I'm observing something that has nothing to do with me. I'm almost expecting David Attenborough to start narrating it: *'The dominant male senses her receptiveness and wastes no time in mating with her. It's a brief and functional encounter, which will be repeated several times while she is in heat.'*

Well, you've got that one wrong, David. It may be functional, but it seems to be going on for a bloody long time. To be fair, I've probably only been here for around thirty seconds, but time has a weird way of stretching and compressing when you least want it to, and it seems determined to stretch this so that it feels like I've been standing here, motionless, for hours.

After what feels like half of my life, but is probably only a minute or so, James gives a couple of big thrusts, bellows like a bull in pain, and slumps on top of her. This seems to be the trigger to unfreeze my body and, without thinking, I turn and start running back up the track towards the yard. My breath is coming in great ragged gasps, partly from the exertion of running, but also from the shock of what I've just witnessed. I keep glancing behind to see if James is following me, but the truck is still parked outside the stables. As I near the yard, I slow down to a walk. My mind is in complete turmoil, and I have absolutely no idea what I'm going to do next. I've only just noticed that my cheeks are wet with tears.

'Did you find him?' Tony's voice is enough to snap me back to reality. Whatever is going on, the last thing I need is Tony sticking his nose in it. I hastily wipe my cheeks with my sleeve and say, 'Yes, thanks, Tony,' in as normal a voice as I can muster. To reinforce the sense of normality, I continue walking purposefully towards the main house. Rosalind glances up from the newspaper as I enter the kitchen.

'Did you find James?' she asks casually, and then her face drops. 'What on earth is the matter? You look like you've seen a ghost!'

'I found him,' I tell her, and suddenly the tears start to flow again. I swipe at them angrily with my sleeve; I really don't want to talk about this with Rosalind.

'Oh, darling!' she coos, as she comes over and puts her bony arms around me. This simple act of kindness is more than I can bear, and the tears turn into full-on sobs. Rosalind lowers me gently into one of the kitchen chairs and sits facing me, with her hands on my thighs.

'What's happened?' she asks gently.

It takes me a while to get any words out through the sobs, but eventually I manage to utter 'He was at the stables. He was with Becky. They were...'

I can't get any more out than that, but I see the look of comprehension dawn in Rosalind's eyes. She moves her chair round so she's sitting next to me, wraps her arm around me and pulls my head on to her shoulder. It's extremely uncomfortable, partly because I'm not used to displays of affection from her, but also because the bones in her shoulder are digging into my cheek and the arm of the kitchen chair is pressed hard into my side. At least the discomfort is giving me something else to think about. My mind is replaying the scene with James and Becky over and over, like one of those annoying GIFs that people post on social media, except this has high-definition audio and video.

The sobbing fit appears to be subsiding a little, so I gently detach myself from Rosalind and head for the downstairs loo to sort out the worst of the mess. I've been proper, ugly crying this time, so first I blow my nose and wipe away the river of snot that has run down over my top lip. Thankfully, I don't tend to bother much with make-up these days, so I don't have to worry about my mascara running or anything like that. I splash cold water on my face and dry it carefully with the towel before returning to the kitchen, where Rosalind hands me a cup of tea. She's also taken the cakes out of the oven and put them on racks to cool.

'I've put sugar in it, to help with the shock,' she tells me as she passes over the mug. 'It stings, the first time, doesn't it?'

'I beg your pardon?'

'His father was just the same, you know. Sexually incontinent. I had hoped that Edward wouldn't have passed on that particular trait to James, but it seems he has. The first time it happened, I was just like you are now. We had an almighty row and he promised he would never do it again. I wanted to believe him, but deep down I knew he was lying. In the end I just accepted it as part of his nature. I don't think men can help themselves. They're like children, always distracted by something new.'

'Why didn't you leave him?' My voice is barely more than a whisper.

'Where would I have gone? Things were different in those days. I had no means of supporting myself; I'd never had a job and wouldn't have had the first idea how to go about getting one. Although he was continually unfaithful, he did love me, and I would have thrown away a comfortable life here for something much worse. I also had James to consider.'

'But he broke his marriage vows! How can you stay with someone who does that?'

'Marriage, my dear, is so much more than love and vows. It's also a business merger, where you each bring something that the other needs. He needed someone who understood him, and in return he made sure I had the lifestyle I wanted. You and James are the same. Why else do you think we were so happy for him to marry you, when you're from such different backgrounds?'

'What do you mean, different backgrounds?'

'Oh, come on. You can't possibly be that naïve. Yes, you had a private education and you speak very nicely, but your family has no pedigree, does it? Your father is a self-made man, a market trader made good, essentially. He may be rich, but he has no class, no breeding. By marrying James, you gained a level of social respectability, as well as a title, that your father could never have given you. Surely you see that?'

I'm horrified. I didn't realise such ridiculous attitudes still existed.

'And what does James get out of it?' I ask her, although I think I already know the answer.

'Money, of course. If he can just keep this place going until you inherit, all his problems will be solved.'

'Is that really all I am to you? A cash cow?' I ask, acidly. I'm not sure what's more upsetting at the moment, the video of James and Becky that's still playing in my head, or the brazen way that Rosalind is trashing me and my upbringing.

'Certainly not, darling! We liked you too, and we could see that he was very smitten with you. We did worry about how you'd adapt to life in the country, but you've done splendidly, on the whole. It's a pity about your fertility problems, but James tells me you're addressing those.'

'I'm sorry?' I interrupt her, sharply. While it's true that James and I have been unable to conceive and we're due to start IVF when we get to the top of the waiting list, I thought we'd agreed not to say anything to Rosalind about it, mainly to spare his blushes.

'Don't worry,' she continues blithely. 'Your secret is safe with me. James just happened to mention that you were having some difficulties, and you might need to spend some time away having treatments. I wish you every success, dear. James needs an heir. If you can't produce one, that will be an issue. Unless...'

She stops dead. An idea has obviously come to her, and I can see she's decided it's best not to share it with me. Frankly, I can't see how she can come out with anything more awful than she's managed already, so I might as well hear it all.

'Unless what?'

'Well, don't take this the wrong way, but if you're not able to have a child, and Becky is... it would be a cuckoo in the nest, of course, but it would be his, nonetheless.'

My mouth falls open. I cannot believe what she's just said. If I thought things couldn't get any worse, I was spectacularly mistaken. I've always tried to be polite and deferential around Rosalind, but she's just made it abundantly clear what she really thinks of me, and something snaps inside.

'So, if I understand you correctly,' I begin, 'you and Edward gave your blessing to our marriage, despite the fact that I'm evidently far too common for James, because I'm going to turn into the goose that lays the golden eggs and bail you all out of the financial mire at some point in the future. However, until that happens, my role here is essentially that of a brood mare, producing babies to carry on the family line. Because I've failed so woefully in this apparently simple task, you're proposing that James carries on seeing Becky with my blessing, and we enter into some kind of fertility contest to see who can fall pregnant first. Is that it?'

'I think you're being a little melodramatic, darling! I'm just considering the options, that's all.'

She's unbelievable. I'm so angry I can feel my fingers tingling.

'There's just one little flaw in your plan,' I tell her, 'beyond the fact that there is no way on earth that any sane person would sign up to it. The reason we haven't conceived has nothing to do with me. I haven't fallen pregnant because there are tractors on this farm with a higher sperm count than your son!'

I can see the shock in her face, and I'm glad that I've managed to deliver at least one retaliatory punch. Before she can say anything more, I hear the sound of a car crossing the yard. I glance at my watch. It's not time for me to leave yet, but I need to get away from Rosalind.

'That'll be Dave, coming to take me to the station,' I say, and I can hear the tremble of rage in my voice. 'I think we're done here. You'll have to give my apologies to Pauline.' I don't wait for her response, slamming the door behind me as I leave.

* * *

'Give me five minutes,' I call to Dave, as I let myself into the cottage. 'I'm all packed, I've just got to grab my stuff.'

'No rush, Sophie,' he replies. 'I'm fairly early and your train isn't for another hour and a half, so we have plenty of time.'

The lack of warmth in the kitchen reminds me what started this horrible chain of events. I never even got to tell James about the Aga in the end. I grab a piece of paper and scribble on it hurriedly.

James,
The Aga has gone out. Please fix it. You'll have to microwave something from the freezer for your dinner.

I pause for a minute, the pencil hovering over the page. I'm seething with rage after everything that I've just been through. The red mist descends and I add, in a shaking hand.

By the way, I SAW you and Becky this afternoon. You utter BASTARD.

I turn on my heel, sprint upstairs, and collect my overnight bag from the bedroom, before grabbing my phone and purse from the hall table and throwing myself into the back of Dave's battered taxi.

'Let's go,' I tell him, and he starts to make his way gingerly down the farm track. He doesn't know it very well and falls into a couple of the potholes that I avoid without thinking now, but I'm so focused on getting away from here that it doesn't occur to me to warn him about them. As we near the turning to the stables, my heart goes into my mouth. James' farm truck is on its way back, and there's no option but for us to pull into the side and let him pass. As he draws alongside, he stops the truck and winds down the window. He's smiling, as if nothing is wrong.

'Drive on,' I say to Dave.

3

James has obviously stopped at the cottage and seen my note, because the first call comes in before we've even reached the station. I press the reject button and turn my phone off. I'm nowhere near ready to have a conversation with him. I need time to process everything that's happened this afternoon. Rosalind's revelations have shocked me almost as much as what I saw in the hay store, and I feel desperately alone all of a sudden. Nothing is what it seemed to be. I think back to the first time that I met James' parents, and how nervous I was. Although most of my friends came from similarly wealthy backgrounds to mine, this was the first time I'd been introduced to a baron. I'd spent ages looking up the correct forms of address (Lord and Lady Huntingdon-Barfoot) and trying to work out whether I should curtsey or not. Thankfully, they had gone out of their way to make me feel at ease, or so I'd thought at the time, and I'd been so grateful to them. Now, I reimagine the scene as a cartoon, with pound signs flashing in their eyes every time they look at each other. They didn't care about me at all. In fact, it's worse than that, because Rosalind made it perfectly clear that they would probably never have accepted me if my father wasn't rich.

Who the hell is she to sit in judgement on my background? Yes, my dad was raised in a council flat in Shoreditch, but he's a billionaire because he works hard and is good at what he does. At least he earned his fortune, rather than just expecting to inherit from the previous generation like James and his father did. I make a resolution to myself: even if James and I manage to get through this and stay together, not a single penny of my father's money will go into that bloody farm.

I think of the cheque Dad gave us as our wedding present – two hundred thousand pounds 'to get ourselves set up'. Within weeks of our return from honeymoon, James was spilling out a sob story about some temporary financial hole that he and his father had to navigate, and I gladly agreed that he could take it to tide them over until things improved. All the things that I had planned to do to the cottage, including renovating the kitchen, were put on hold. Every time I asked about it, there was some new delay, but I was assured the money would be repaid very soon. And then, of course, when Edward died and we saw the true extent of the problems, it became obvious that it was long gone. There was no way the farm would be able to pay it back.

The train to Exeter is quiet, and I stare morosely out of the window for most of the journey. It's a beautiful autumn day, and I'd normally be enjoying looking at the rich golds and reds of the trees as they change colour, but today it's all a blur. I'm overwhelmed by the events of this afternoon, and my mind is just an amorphous fog. As I get further from the farm, I even start to wonder if any of today has been real. Maybe this is just a dream; I'll wake up in a minute in our bed in the cottage and none of it will have happened.

By the time I've changed trains at Exeter, any hope of waking up to normality has faded, and I have to stare out of the window so the other passengers can't see the tears gliding silently down my cheeks. Darkness is falling, and I contemplate my reflection in the glass as the train speeds eastwards.

I must have drifted off at some point because the next thing I know, we've arrived and everyone is rushing to get off the train. I retrieve my overnight bag from the rack and join the throng heading for the barriers. It's a while since I've been to London, and the crowds and the bustle take me by surprise at first. Di has promised to meet me at Paddington, even though I'm quite capable of getting the Tube on my own to Parsons Green, where she and her husband live in a pretty terraced house. I scan the concourse for her but can't see her to begin with, so I start to thread my way through crowds to our agreed meeting point under the clock. I'm just about to reach it when I hear her calling my name. I turn, and I'm instantly enveloped in a huge, bosomy hug.

'It's so good to see you!' she exclaims, squeaking a little in her excitement. 'I can't tell you how much I've been looking forward to this weekend.'

'It's good to see you too,' I reply as she loosens her grip. 'It feels like ages since I was last here.'

'We're going to have so much fun,' she continues. 'Richard's away with his golfing mates, so we've got the place to ourselves all weekend. I've stocked up the wine rack and there's a stew waiting for us in the slow cooker. Come on!'

She grabs my hand and practically drags me into the Underground.

'I can't stand the Tube normally,' she tells me as we head for the District Line platforms. 'It's so stuffy and airless, and there's nothing to see. I much prefer the bus, but it takes a lot longer and we have wine to drink and gossip to catch up on, so time is of the essence.'

Her natural effervescence is infectious, and I feel my spirits rising a little. If anyone can help me to navigate my current crisis, it's Di. On the surface, she's easy to dismiss; she's short, curvy, and loud, with a mess of curly brown hair. But there's a core of steel running through her, and she's quite capable of putting you firmly in your place if you step out of line, as a couple of her past boyfriends discovered to their cost. A train arrives at the platform, and we cram ourselves in somehow. I'm pressed up against a man dressed in tracksuit bottoms and a vest; he's holding on to one of the overhead grab handles and my nose is uncomfortably close to his armpit. Thankfully, I can't smell anything untoward. Di is in front of me, but conversation is impossible without everyone around us listening in, so we travel in silence.

As we move away from the centre of London, the train starts to empty and we're able to grab a couple of seats opposite each other for the last couple of stops. During the ten-minute walk from the station to her house, she fills me in on her life. Richard, her husband, is still working incredibly long hours as an investment banker, but it's obvious that she's devoted to him. His income, combined with her earnings as a solicitor, mean that they're able to live quite comfortably. She's telling me all about their upcoming trip to the Maldives when we reach the front door, which she throws open and ushers me through before double locking it behind her and turning off the burglar alarm.

'I know it's all very genteel around here, but it's still London,' she explains, when I raise my eyebrows at the level of security.

'I'm sorry,' I tell her. 'I guess I've been in the country for so long I've forgotten what it's like.'

'You certainly have, your Ladyship!' she laughs, grabbing my jacket. 'I can't believe you're actually wearing tweed, and it's not even ironic! Is it a landed gentry thing? It suits you, don't get me wrong, but it's still funny. Now, let's get a bottle open and you can tell me all about you.'

She leads me through into the kitchen, which is filled with the most amazing smell. I don't know what she's put in the stew, but my stomach growls with hunger. The sandwich I had for lunch seems a lifetime ago. It certainly belongs in a different world, a world before I found out my husband was cheating on me and his mother told me that I wasn't good enough for him anyway. The sudden reminder of this afternoon's events unlocks something inside, and the tears begin to fall fast and heavily again. Di is occupied opening a bottle of prosecco and doesn't notice that I've crumpled, so I grab a piece of kitchen towel to try to mop up the worst of it.

'Here you go – dear God, what's the matter?' Di places the full glasses on the counter and wraps me in another of her hugs. I don't know how long we stand there, but I just let the tears come as she holds me, telling me that she knew something was up as soon as she saw me. Eventually, after a couple of large gulps of prosecco, I'm able to start telling her the story of my day. She doesn't say anything as I fill her in on all the details, from our money worries and the Aga, through the scene at the stables, to the extraordinary conversation I had with Rosalind.

'What a bastard!' she cries when I'm done. 'And who the fuck does his mother think she is? Does she know that this is the twenty-first century and shit like that doesn't matter any more? James may be a baron, but the days of the nobility expecting to have shagging rights with everybody who works for them are long gone, thank goodness. And look at Prince William! He's much posher than James, yet he married a commoner and nobody batted an eyelid. Everyone knows that the only reason we persist with this feudal bollocks is because it's good for tourism. What are you going to do? I hope you're going to cut his balls off, force-feed them to his mother, and then divorce the hell out of him!'

As I mentioned before – Di doesn't suffer fools.

'I have no idea what I'm going to do yet,' I tell her, pathetically.

'I rather hoped that some time away would help me get some perspective, and that you'd be able to give me some advice.'

'Of course I will! I can't guarantee to be objective, but I'll do my best. I suspect I may have already laid my cards on the table with my previous remarks, but I'm willing to listen and we'll figure it out somehow, okay? Let's have a top-up and then I'll look at the stew.'

Her no-nonsense approach is just what I need, and I feel lighter somehow now that I've shared everything with her. I settle myself at one of the stools at the breakfast bar, hand her my glass, and she tops us both up from the bottle. I watch her adjusting her sleek induction hob as she puts a pan of potatoes on to boil and feel a pang of envy. If I didn't have such a bloody unreliable cooker, I might be sitting here in blissful ignorance of James' infidelity. I can't help wondering if I'm better off knowing about it, or whether I'd have preferred to stay in the dark.

'There's something I don't understand,' she says, as she turns back to me.

'Go on.'

'Why haven't you got any money? Your dad is literally a gazillionaire.'

'Partly because I haven't asked him for any, but also because that's not how Dad works. He's always been worried about spoiling me, that I'd grow into some bratty princess who didn't know the value of anything. So, even though I lived the high life when I was growing up, going on amazing holidays and stuff with them, he never just handed me money for anything. If I wanted something, I had to earn the money and pay for it myself.'

'He bought you that sports car, though, didn't he?'

'That was a birthday present, but it's a good example. I know most people don't get brand new cars for their twenty-first birthdays, okay? I get that bit. But it didn't come without conditions. He taxed and insured it for the first year but made it very clear the costs of running it were down to me after that. He always expected me to get a job and be financially independent from him. Why on earth would we have lived in that shitty flat if he'd been bankrolling me?'

Di and I shared a flat with two other girls for a couple of years before I got married and moved down to the country. It was a really happy time in my life; I had a job I loved and that paid enough to allow me to cover my part of the rent, put petrol in the car on the rare occasions that I used it, and enjoy nights out and the occasional shopping trip. The flat itself was tiny and very run down, but we filled it with odd things that we picked up at markets and junk shops, and it had a kind of shabby chic feel to it. We loved it, but it was a bit of a shithole, especially compared to the immaculate house that Di lives in now. Even our little cottage on the farm is a considerable step up from that flat.

I can see Di processing what I've told her. On one hand, it would be easy to dismiss my dad as cruel for allowing his only daughter to live in relative poverty when he has so much, but I don't blame him at all, particularly as he did give me a pretty impressive wedding gift and I've never had the courage to tell him where it ended up. In a funny way, I'm pleased that he didn't just give me handouts whenever I needed them; it made me work harder, and I still remember the sense of achievement I felt when my first month's salary landed in my bank account.

'Have you heard from him?' she asks, suddenly.

'Who, Dad?'

'No, James.'

'He tried to call while I was on my way to the station. I turned my phone off.'

'Nice. He's probably going round the bend. Serves him right. Shall we see?'

'I'm not sure I'm ready.'

'Don't answer it if it rings. Let's turn it on, see whether he's left any voicemails or texts, and then turn it off again. You don't have to listen to anything or read anything until you're ready. Okay? Would you prefer me to do it?'

I reach into my handbag, pull out my phone, and hand it to her.

'What's the code?' she asks, after she's powered it up.

'Two five oh nine,' I reply.

'Your wedding date. Nice.' She enters the code and the phone immediately starts to ping with notifications.

'I think we can assume he's panicking,' she tells me when the phone eventually falls silent. 'Twelve calls, three voicemails and five text messages. Good.'

She turns the phone off and hands it back to me. 'Let's give him a little bit more time to stew, shall we?'

4

I wake the next morning with a belter of a hangover. I'm not surprised, really. As well as the prosecco, Di and I polished off two bottles of white wine while we sifted through the debris of my marriage to see if there was anything worth saving. My memories of where we ended up are a little hazy, but I think she was still very much of the opinion that I should do him some sort of permanent injury and then get the hell out of there. I crawl out of bed and pad down the corridor to the bathroom, where I spend much longer than usual under a shower as hot as I can bear. Once I've washed and dressed, I head downstairs to find Di devouring the largest slice of toast I think I've ever seen. The kitchen smells of fresh coffee, which is normally one of my favourite aromas, but today makes my stomach heave queasily.

'How come you're not hungover?' I ask her.

'Oh, I am. Carbs and coffee are my go-to hangover cure. Do you want some?' She indicates the coffee machine and a loaf of bread on the side.

'I'm not sure I can face food yet,' I reply.

'It'll be a lot worse if you don't eat anything. Sit yourself down and I'll fix you a piece of toast. You'll be right as rain in no time, I promise. I thought we'd go into town for some retail therapy today. That always used to cheer you up in the old days. We'll do all our greatest hits: Harvey Nics, Selfridges, the lot. What do you think?'

'It's a great idea, apart from the fact that I can't afford to buy anything.'

'You can't literally have nothing. You must have an overdraft facility or something, surely? If it means that James can't eat for a week or two, well, he should have thought of that, shouldn't he?'

I can't help smiling, despite my pounding head. 'I guess I could try a few things on,' I tell her.

'That's the spirit. We'll get them to spray us with some lovely perfumes too. Who knows, we might even be able to wangle some make-up samples.'

Her coffee and carbs hangover cure doesn't exactly work, but I am feeling a little more human when we leave the house an hour or so later. We meander back into the centre of London on a series of buses, and I enjoy watching the world go by through the windows. Everything is busy, and people are hurrying from one place to the next with an urgency you just don't find in the country. There's such variety here too: restaurants featuring cuisines from all around the world, shops catering to every need, and even the occasional glimpse of a bustling outdoor market down a side street. I feel like a dormant part of me is waking up, and the energy of the capital city is working its magic on me.

Di is right; the retail therapy improves my mood no end. We spend the morning wandering happily around Selfridges, pulling clothes off the racks, matching them into combinations and trying them on. I'm very tempted by a gorgeous pair of Stella McCartney jeans that feel as soft as butter and do wonders for my figure, before coming to my senses and realising that, apart from the fact that there's no way I could afford them, they'd be covered in mud and dog hair within five minutes on the farm. It's still fun though and, by the time we emerge (empty-handed, thankfully), my hangover has gone and I'm actually quite hungry. We settle ourselves in a Vietnamese restaurant and order two bowls of pho.

'Is your phone still off?' Di asks, as we're making steady progress through the delicious spicy broth and trying not to slurp the noodles.

'Yup.' I feel a pang of sadness and wish she hadn't mentioned it. I've had such a nice morning pretending that everything is okay, but I suppose I can't hide from it for ever.

'Have you had any more thoughts since we talked last night?'

'I'm confused, more than anything,' I tell her, honestly. 'I hate James at the moment, and I can't tell you how much I want to hurt him. I want him to feel every bit of the pain that I'm feeling. I know you think I should divorce him, and I am tempted. But then I also still love him. I can't just turn that off, and lots of marriages survive infidelity, so maybe I should give him another chance. Oh God, it's all such a mess in my head.'

'I hear you,' she replies, 'but this isn't him forgetting an anniversary. This is him committing the ultimate betrayal. He's done the most intimate thing you can do, and something he vowed only to do with you, with another person. If Richard did that, his balls would be in the kitchen bin and I'd be taking him for everything he has. With me, it's one strike and you're out.'

'Don't get me wrong. I'm not saying I'm planning to waltz back down there, forgive him, and rely on blind faith that he won't do it again. Even I'm not that stupid. I'm just saying that I think I ought to hear him out, at least. There are two sides to every story, and maybe there are things I've done, or not done, that have contributed to his behaviour.'

'How do you manage it?' she asks.

'What?'

'Even when everything around you is falling apart, you still manage to be so... *nice*. That's not a bad thing – it's one of the things I love about you – but just once I'd like to see you lose your shit. It would help us mere mortals feel a bit better about ourselves.'

'I've lost my shit plenty of times, trust me!' I laugh. 'The problem is that, while it's very cathartic at the time, it usually makes everything much worse in the long run. So I'm trying to be rational, but there's still a considerable risk of me taking to James' wardrobe with the scissors and hiding raw prawns in the curtain poles before getting the hell out of there. It's a fine line, and I'm not yet sure which side of it I'm going to come down on. Does that help?'

She smiles. 'A little. Okay, tell me exactly how you think you could have contributed to your current situation. I'm curious.'

There's a pause while I think, and we concentrate on our food. I can feel the heat from the chillies in the back of my nose and it's a pleasant, warming sensation. James doesn't like spicy food, so this is a welcome treat for me.

'I think we've probably got ourselves into a bit of a rut,' I observe, after I've spooned the last of the broth into my mouth.

'In what way?'

'Well, since his dad died, James has really had to step up on the farm. He worked pretty hard before, but now it's relentless. There's always something to do, or something that needs fixing, or some animal issue. Summer is the worst, because the days are long and he often doesn't get home until nearly midnight, by which time I'm generally asleep. He's usually up and out before I wake, so we can literally go for days at a time without seeing each other. And, when we do get time together, he's always knackered. If he stays awake long enough for us to manage a conversation, all he wants to talk about is farming, which I don't know anything about. It's a little bit better in winter, but not much, because he still works late into the evening poring over the books or checking the weather forecast. Farmers are completely obsessed with the weather; did you know that? Sometimes I've resented him, because it's felt like I'm his housekeeper more than his wife, and then I've felt guilty for feeling like that. It's not his fault his father dropped dead and left him with all this to deal with.'

'But none of this is your fault either, is it?'

'No, but maybe I could have made more of an effort with him, learned a bit about farming and stayed up to ask him about his day, or something.'

Di snorts. 'If he's anything like Richard when he comes in late, you'd just get monosyllabic answers while he emptied a bottle of wine and then he'd fall into bed and snore the place down.'

'Mm. James is more of a beer man.' A thought occurs to me. 'Maybe I could take up home brewing, so there was a fresh pint waiting for him when he got home!'

'If I can give you one piece of advice that you'll actually listen to – don't try to fix this by being even nicer to him. That's just rewarding his bad behaviour and encouraging it. If you decide to give him another chance, he needs to know that he's on probation, otherwise there's no incentive for him to change his ways. How's the sex?'

I'm glad I've finished my broth, otherwise I'd be choking on it. I can feel the heat in my cheeks as a beetroot-red flush of embarrassment takes hold.

'Are we really doing this?' I ask.

'Not if you don't want to. But it's a bit of an elephant in the room, isn't it? Up to you. I'm pretty un-shockable, unless you're into some seriously weird shit.'

'No weird shit. We've always been pretty vanilla in that department, but I guess our sex life is in a bit of a rut too, if I'm honest,' I finally manage.

'A lot of that is marriage though, isn't it? Richard and I are hardly swinging from the chandeliers these days. These things settle down and find their own rhythm. You find what you like and stick to it.'

'Yes, but when we were trying to conceive, I think I probably got a bit obsessed. It wasn't romantic any more; it was more business-like.'

'What, like, "Quick, I'm fertile, get on with it"?'

'Yes, and then I'd have to lie there for ages with my hips raised when he finished so there wasn't much cuddling afterwards either.'

'I don't suppose he minded. He got what he wanted out of it, didn't he?'

'I guess so. But then, when nothing happened, and we went for the tests and found out that he was infertile, it's like he just gave up. We hardly ever have sex now. Do you think he's gone off me?' A single tear escapes and rolls down my cheek. I dab it away with the napkin.

'I doubt it. Look at you. You're just as gorgeous as the day he married you.'

'There must be something, though, mustn't there? Some way in which I'm not enough for him.'

'Or, more likely, he's just a selfish bastard who can't keep it in his pants.'

I laugh, despite myself. 'Yes, or that! There's only one way I'm going to find out though, and that's to hear him out.'

'Are you going to turn your phone back on?'

'God, no! Apart from the fact that this needs to be a face-to-face conversation, you're right. I'm not going to let him off the hook that easily. It won't do him any harm to stew until I go home.'

'I had a thought about that, actually. How do you fancy staying a bit longer? Richard will be home tomorrow night, but he'll be delighted to see you. We'll be at work from Monday, obviously, but

I'll give you the spare keys so you can come and go as you like. I just thought maybe a bit more time would help you get more perspective.'

'To come around to your way of thinking, you mean?'

She laughs. 'No. You know I'll support you, whatever you decide to do. Even if you decide to take the cheating scumbag back, I'll be cheering you on. I love you and I want you to be happy, however that looks.'

I consider it. 'Are you sure you wouldn't mind? I don't want to be in your way.'

'Hmm. Would I mind getting to spend more time with one of my best friends, who I haven't seen for six months? You're right, that's a hard one. Of course I don't mind! I'd love it.'

It is very tempting, but I wonder whether this is partly because it would be delaying the confrontation I need to have with James.

'It's a lovely idea,' I tell her. 'Can I think about it?'

'Absolutely. Just let me know when you've made up your mind. If you decide you'd rather get back and face the music, I'll completely understand. By the way, I've got a bit of a confession to make.'

'Oh yes?'

'It was going to be a surprise, but given the current circumstances I think that's probably not such a good idea. I've invited the girls over tonight. I thought it would be fun to get our little flat together again, and they were so excited about seeing you. Obviously, I didn't know about your situation and, if you'd rather not, I quite understand.'

I reach over and give her as big a hug as I can without toppling out of my chair or knocking the table over. 'I think that's a lovely idea. Thank you.'

'Are you sure?'

'Yes, I'd love to see them, and they're bound to find out what's happened sooner or later. They might as well hear it from me. Promise me one thing, though?'

'Anything.'

'Don't let the whole evening be about me and my marriage, please. That's just going to make everyone miserable.'

'Done. Now, why don't I get the bill and we'll see whether Harvey Nichols has anything to tempt you.'

5

'Why do Americans always keep their bras on during sex?' I ask.

Di and I are slumped in front of the TV, nursing fresh hangovers and vaguely watching some American political intrigue show on one of her streaming platforms. It seems to involve everyone leaping into bed with everyone else, and the current scene is a woman having revenge sex with her husband's nemesis, after she caught said husband in bed with one of his interns. I did briefly wonder whether I should take a leaf out of her book, but James only really hates the bank, and you can't have sex with one of those.

Yesterday evening was much more fun than I could have hoped. Admittedly, it was a bit weepy to begin with when I filled Maudie and Kate in on what had happened. We hugged and cried, and at one point they seemed to be competing with each other to see who could come up with the most outrageous form of revenge. Di was as good as her word, though, and quickly steered the conversation on to other topics. It turned out to be the first time that Maudie had been out on her own since giving birth to her daughter, and she was determined to make the most of it. We had to manhandle her into the Uber at the end of the evening, and the driver left us in no doubt what would happen if she was sick in his car.

'I think it's probably just a TV thing, to protect the actors' modesty,' she replies, after thinking it through for a while.

'Not very realistic, is it? Why don't they just use clever camera angles? Maybe it's a cultural thing, and Americans just don't like boobs. I saw a programme once about this tribe in Africa, where the women never covered up their top halves, because boobs weren't considered to be anything to do with sex. Maybe it's the same with Americans, except they never uncover them.'

'I doubt that, somehow. Richard says that men basically fall into two camps: those who like boobs and those who like bottoms.'

I'm intrigued. 'Which one is he?'

She jiggles her impressive chest at me. 'What do you think?'

'I'm not sure what type James is,' I muse. 'He pats my bum a lot, or at least he used to, so I guess he must be a bottom man.'

Di suddenly reaches for the remote and clicks the TV off, just as one of the main protagonists is about to start seducing another intern in the hope of using her to dig up some dirt on one of his rivals.

'Can I ask you a question?' she says, earnestly. 'Do you like living in the country?'

I take my time before answering. It's a big question, and I'm not sure my head is in any fit state to do it justice at the moment.

'I did when I first moved down there. It's a different pace of life and you're instantly absorbed into the community, even though they still describe people who have lived there for over twenty years as 'incomers'. Everybody knows everybody and that's nice. It's the little things, like being greeted by your name when you go to the shop, or just exchanging hellos in the street. You can't pass anyone without at least saying hello to them; they'll think you're rude if you ignore them. I've even started going to church, did I tell you?'

'Really? I thought you were a dyed-in-the-wool atheist!'

'Oh, I haven't suddenly become a card-carrying Christian or anything like that, don't worry. I'd say I'm an agnostic at the moment.'

'So why are you going to church?'

'I don't know, really. It started off as something to do, I think. James is supposed to have Sundays off, but that never happens in reality. There's not much else happening on a Sunday, so I trundled along one week and I've kind of stayed. I'm on all sorts of rotas now: coffee, flower-arranging and so on, and it's another little community for me to belong to. Does that make sense?'

'Honestly? Not really.'

'I've joined the WI too and, as soon as the village fête organiser heard about my previous job, I was drafted on to that committee as well. The downside of living in the country is that there's so little for me to do that I'd go out of my mind with boredom if I didn't have these distractions. I can't work because there isn't much call for event organisers in the middle of nowhere, and James is usually out all day. Of course, I was supposed to have children to keep me busy, but that obviously hasn't happened.'

'Poor you,' Di empathises. 'It sounds like you're lonely, if you don't mind me saying so.'

'I think I probably am,' I reply, after I've considered for a few moments. 'Everything and everyone on the farm has a purpose, except me. I didn't notice it to begin with. I was in love, and the country is a lovely place to be in the summer. In summer I can go for long walks and just enjoy the smells, the sense of space, and the fresh air. But then winter sets in, everything turns to mud – and mud gets everywhere, let me tell you. I can't remember the last time I wore a pair of heels; I seem to live my life in wellies these days.'

'What about your mother-in-law?'

'Also busy, even though she doesn't have any purpose on the

farm either. Even if she wasn't, I wouldn't want to spend time with her. I've always been civil to her, but I've never felt close to her or that I completely trusted her.'

'Well, your instincts were right on that one, weren't they? What does she do all day?'

'She plays a lot of golf, and I think she's a member of a bridge club as well as the WI. She has lived there for much longer than me, so she's got quite a wide circle of friends.'

'I thought you said there wasn't any money?' Di looks puzzled.

'There isn't.'

'So how can she afford to play golf? It's ruinously expensive. I've forbidden Richard from discussing green fees with me because, every time he does, I start thinking of all the things I could have spent the money on instead.'

'Welcome to one of the great mysteries of my life. There's no money to fix my Aga, but she can afford golf, a weekly cleaner, and Ocado deliveries.'

'Hmm. I think I'd want to know a bit more about that, if it were me,' she observes.

'You're right,' I agree. 'I haven't said anything before, because I know James is under a lot of pressure and I've been trying to be supportive, but I think there are a lot of questions I need answers to before I can decide what I'm going to do next.'

'I have to say, you've rather put me off the idea of moving to the country,' Di laughs. 'I've always quite fancied the idea of getting away from the city and living somewhere where I could look out of my window and see the sheep gambolling in the fields.' She sighs wistfully.

'Don't start me on bloody sheep!' I exclaim. 'I used to think they were lovely, until I realised that they just exist to piss you off. They appear completely unable to give birth without help, and they always seem to do it in the middle of the night rather than any kind of civilised hour, so nobody gets any sleep during lambing. Then, from the moment they're born, it's like they're trying to find ways to die. If there's a ditch they can fall into and get stuck, they'll fall into it. Or they'll get flystrike or some other revolting disease. And, my god, they're thick. If you think pheasants are dim, they're bloody Einsteins compared to sheep. And then...'

'Okay, I can see I've hit a nerve,' she jokes. 'I'll scrap the sheep from my rural idyll. How about cows, can I have those in the field?'

'Yes, I'll let you have cows. Much better.'

'Changing the subject,' she continues, 'have you decided whether you'd like to stay a bit longer or not?'

'I'd love to, Di, I really would. But I think I would just be putting off the inevitable, don't you? I've got to go back and deal with him at some point, and it might as well be now. Also, my train ticket isn't flexible, so I'd have to buy another one.'

'If it's just a question of the train fare, I can help with that.'

'You're very kind, but I'd feel guilty taking your money, particularly when you've already paid for everything this weekend. No, I think I'm ready to face him.'

'Have you decided what you're going to do?'

'No. I think a lot of it will depend on how he is. Whatever happens, we can't just brush this under the carpet and carry on. Things will have to change.'

'Okay, as long as you're sure you're ready.'

'I'm not, but I don't think staying here longer will make me any more ready, so I might as well go and lance the boil. Thank you, though, it was a lovely idea.'

'Have you checked your phone yet?'

'No.'

'You probably should.'

I feel nauseous as I head upstairs to collect the phone from the bedside table in my room, and it's nothing to do with the hangover. Although we've talked a lot about James this weekend, I've been able to keep my distance from it all, almost as if it happened to someone else. The prospect of turning my phone on and seeing the messages is going to bring it all back into sharp focus. I pick it up gingerly, as if it's going to bite me, and carry it downstairs to Di.

'Are you going to actually turn it on, or are you trying to communicate with it by telepathy?' she asks, after I've been sitting staring at it for nearly five minutes.

'Shut up. I am going to turn it on, I just need to psych myself up first.'

'Would it be easier if we did it the same way as before?' she asks, holding out her hand.

'Please,' I reply and hand it over. She powers it up and, after a minute or so, the pings begin.

'Okay,' she says. 'He's obviously realised you're not going to answer as he's stopped calling. It's mainly texts now. Do you want me to read them out?'

'No. I'll look at them later.'

'Okay, here you go.' She hands it back.

* * *

After a delicious lunch which thankfully takes the edge off my headache, we set off for the station. Having talked incessantly for most of the weekend, we've now lapsed into a comfortable silence. Di is watching me, and I can feel her trying to send me positive energy for the journey and confrontation ahead. When we get to Paddington, she envelops me in a massive hug that seems to go on for ever.

'Ring me,' she says into my hair. 'Whatever happens, ring me and let me know how you are.'

'Don't worry about me, I'm a big girl,' I try to reassure her. 'This is going to be horrible, I know, but I'll find a way through it.'

'Just ring me. I love you, and I will worry about you constantly until I hear. Do you understand?'

'Yes, Mum,' I sigh.

When we eventually break apart and she heads back towards the Tube station, I realise that I still have half an hour before my train departs, so I head for the nearest coffee shop, hoping that a cappuccino and a pastry will finish the job and kill the last vestiges of my headache. As I'm giving my order to the barista, I hear a very familiar voice coming from one of the nearby tables.

'For fuck's sake Emily, how did this happen?'

I glance in the direction of the voice and I'm right. It's my old boss, Annabel McManus, and she doesn't look happy.

'I don't care that it's a Sunday,' she continues. 'This can't wait. You need to find someone else, now! Put down that useless boyfriend of yours and sort it out. Call me as soon as it's done.'

My curiosity gets the better of me, and I take my coffee and pastry over to her table.

'Is this seat free?' I ask.

'There are God knows how many empty tables in here, so why don't you leave me alone, piss off, and sit at one of them?' she begins, before glancing up and exclaiming, 'Sophie! What are you doing here? Are you back in London? Please, sit down.'

I smile at her and take the seat opposite her. 'I couldn't help overhearing your conversation. Is everything okay?'

She sighs dramatically. 'No, it bloody isn't. The caterers that Emily booked for a corporate party tomorrow night have pulled out at the last minute, and she's whining that I'm expecting her to work on a Sunday to fix it. It's her mess, though, she needs to sort it out.'

'Emily's running events now?' I ask, slightly incredulously.

Emily was the office junior when I left, and she wasn't a huge success at that.

'Desperate times, all right? Good events planners don't just grow on trees, and at least she knows a little bit about it. You don't need a job, do you?'

'Sorry. I'm only here for the weekend, I'm just about to get my train back home.'

'Bugger. I could really do with you,' she sighs.

'What's the event?'

'The customer has just signed a big new client in Italy, so they're doing an Italian-themed evening to celebrate. Emily booked Cucina Italia to do the catering, but now they say they have a clash and they can't do it. One day before, would you believe it?'

The ups and downs of my old life prove to be a powerful distraction, and I can't help feeling drawn in.

'Cucina Italia are useless, why on earth did she choose them? Mondays are generally pretty quiet. Do you want me to see if I can get Giovanni to do it if he's available?'

She looks at me like she's drowning and I'm the lifeguard. 'Would you?'

'Of course,' I say, switching into professional mode. I feel useful suddenly, and it's a powerful sensation. 'Tell me the venue and the number of people.'

Ten minutes later, I've secured Giovanni and Annabel is practically crying with relief. I hear the announcement that my train is starting to board and make my way towards the platform. My brief feeling of euphoria pops like a balloon as I take my seat.

Fixing my marriage is going to be much harder than sorting out Annabel's catering woes, and I still have no idea what I'm going to do.

6

I'm unpleasantly surprised to find James waiting for me at the station instead of Dave. He's standing on the platform, holding an enormous bouquet of flowers. I was hoping to enjoy a little more peace before dealing with him, but he's obviously had other ideas. I did listen to the voicemails and read the texts on the train. He started off mortified, went on through stumbling apologies, one of which was obviously after quite a few drinks, before getting frustrated and ultimately sounding resigned. I'm no closer to deciding how I want to play this, and him forcing my hand by meeting me at the station irritates me.

'Nice flowers. Who are they for?' I ask sarcastically, as I push past him towards the exit.

'Sophie, please,' he replies, hurrying after me. 'Look, I know I've screwed up, okay? Can we not just talk about all of this?'

'We'll talk when I'm ready. Where's Dave?'

'I called him and told him I wanted to meet you. He wasn't very pleased about it and wouldn't tell me what train you were booked on until I agreed to pay him for the lost fare. He really is a miserable bugger.'

'He's always been fine with me. Perhaps he just doesn't like you. He's a pretty good judge of character,' I observe, as I pull open the passenger door of the farm truck and shove my bag inside. James is hurrying round to the driver's side, still awkwardly clutching the bouquet. I'm sure we look like something out of a sitcom to the casual observer, but there's nothing funny about the way I'm feeling. This is the first time I've seen him face to face since... well, it wasn't his face I saw last time, I suppose. I'm both shocked and energised by the murderous rage I feel towards him. As he manoeuvres the flowers into the back seat, breaking a couple of the stems in the process, I wonder what it would feel like to stab him, over and over again. I think I'd quite enjoy it. He obviously picks up on my mood, because he wisely says nothing as he fastens his seatbelt and starts the engine.

As the journey progresses and I watch all the familiar landmarks drift past the windows, my fury begins to dissipate. By the time we reach the end of the farm track, I'm just feeling exhausted and desperately sad. Although Di has been amazing, I realise that I've been carrying some tension for the whole weekend, wondering how I'd feel when I saw James again, and what I was going to say. Now that I've seen him, it's like an invisible tight rubber band around my chest has snapped, and I just want to get into bed and sleep for ever. Two late nights with far too much to drink probably haven't helped.

The dogs are delighted to see me, wriggling with excitement as their tails wag madly, and I set down my bag and take time to make a fuss of them. After all, it's not their fault that their master is the man he is.

'Would you like me to take your bag up for you?' James asks, solicitously. He's still holding the flowers, which look considerably the worse for wear after their journey in the back of the truck.

'No. I can manage,' I tell him.

'What about these?' He points at the bouquet.

'I don't know. Shove them up your arse? Give them to Becky? Look, I'm exhausted. I'm going to go upstairs, have a bath, and probably go to bed. We'll talk tomorrow.'

'Can't we talk now? I've been in such a state all weekend, wanting to tell you how sorry I am but not being able to get hold of you. I don't think I can wait any more.'

'YOU'VE been in a state?' I roar, catching us both by surprise. 'Did you bother to spend even five minutes wondering how I'VE been feeling, you selfish prick?' The rage is back with a vengeance, and I'm suddenly energised again. 'FINE!' I continue. 'You want to talk, let's talk. Let's start with you telling me how many times you've fucked Becky.'

He looks like I've slapped him. It's fair to say that I'm not normally one for swearing, but this is hardly a normal conversation and I need the catharsis. The dogs have obviously picked up on the mood and are watching us warily.

'It was just the once, I...'

'Bullshit! How many times?'

His eyes are on the floor; he hasn't even got the guts to look at me when he lies. I despise him for his lack of courage. He's shuffling his feet awkwardly, but I have no sympathy. He wanted this conversation, so he's going to get it. He's still holding the ridiculous bouquet, as if he doesn't know what to do with it.

'For God's sake, put those bloody flowers down somewhere,' I tell him, angrily. 'You look like a total idiot.'

He grabs his opportunity to escape and practically runs into the kitchen. He's filling a vase and haphazardly plonking the battered flowers into it when I follow him a few moments later.

'How many times?'

Even though he's facing away from me, I can see his frame crumple as he realises I'm not going to let him off the hook.

'I'm not exactly sure,' he mumbles, eventually.

'How can you not be sure? Is she that unmemorable? It all looked pretty bloody memorable to me. Okay, I'll ask a different question. How long have you been fucking her?'

'Do you have to use that word?'

'I'll use whatever language I like. Stop trying to duck the issue. How long?'

He carefully places the vase on the kitchen table before answering. 'Around six months, I suppose.'

'SIX MONTHS?' I bellow. 'YOU ABSOLUTE BASTARD!' Without thinking, I grab the vase and hurl it at him. He dodges and it hits the wall behind him, smashing into pieces and covering the floor with water and bits of flower. It feels good and I start casting around for other things to throw. My eye lands on the fruit bowl, but he's too quick for me and, before I'm able to pick it up, he's crossed the floor and wrapped his arms around me, pinning my own arms at my sides.

'GET OFF!' I wriggle furiously, simultaneously trying to escape his grasp and punch him somewhere that will hurt, but he's too strong for me and maintains his grip until the fight goes out of me. He releases me carefully, making sure he's positioned between me and the fruit bowl, in case it's a ploy. I pull out a chair and slump down at the kitchen table and, after a few moments, he does the same.

'Why?' I ask, and my voice is now barely more than a whisper.

'I'm sorry, I really am. I never wanted to hurt you.'

'But you have, James. You've hurt me in the cruellest way. Am I not enough for you? Have you gone off me?' The tears start to flow now, but I don't have the energy to get a piece of kitchen towel to mop them up with, so they just roll down my cheeks and drip off my chin.

'Of course I haven't gone off you! It's just that, well...' He stops, evidently unsure about whether to continue down the path he'd started on.

'Go on. You were the one who wanted to talk about this, remember?'

'It was just all the trying-to-get-pregnant stuff, you know? Sex kind of stopped being fun, because it became all about fertility windows and wearing the right underpants to ensure healthy sperm production. I felt like you didn't see me as a lover any more; I was just your sperm factory, expected to perform on demand.'

'So this is my fault? Is that what you're saying?'

'No! Not at all. But it did kind of take the shine off things a bit, and then when I found out that I was infertile, I felt like less of a man in your eyes because I couldn't get you pregnant naturally. Sex seemed somehow pointless, because a baby had become its only purpose and I couldn't provide that.'

'Does Becky know you're infertile?' I'm reminded of the conversation with Rosalind, who obviously hadn't known until I'd filled her in.

He looks down at the tablecloth. 'No.'

'I see. So she makes you feel all manly because she doesn't know your secret, while your baby-obsessed wife emasculates you for failing to give her what she wants. Is that it?'

'No! Well, not exactly. Look, you're twisting this all around.'

'Why didn't you talk to me and tell me how you were feeling, instead of just buggering off and shagging the stable girl?'

'I didn't know how. I wanted to, but I was scared of upsetting you.'

'Jesus, James. You make me sound like some fragile wallflower. I'm your wife, for goodness' sake. You're supposed to be able to talk to me about anything. If you can't talk to me, what's the point of our marriage?'

'I'm sorry,' he says again.

'Why Becky? Was it just that she was available? What does she get out of all of this? Were you planning to leave me for her?'

'No, I was never planning to leave you!' he cries suddenly. 'You're my wife and I love you.'

'You've got a bloody funny way of showing it, if you don't mind me saying. So, what was in it for her? I can't believe she doesn't have some sort of feelings for you. Women generally need a bit of an emotional connection before they can be persuaded to rip off their knickers. So what was it?'

'Okay, fine,' he sighs. 'If you really want to know, I'll tell you. But don't blame me if you don't like it.'

'I haven't liked anything you've said since I got home, but I need to know everything. If you can't be honest with me now, then we really don't stand a chance.'

'Becky and I have known each other since she was tiny. I was best friends at school with her older brother, Martin. She was always there when I went round to his house, and Martin told me once that she had the biggest crush on me. It was funny, because she was only about five and I was way older than her. She used to send me cards on Valentine's Day, and I would always send one back so as not to hurt her feelings. It all stopped when I went away to university, and then of course I met you and fell in love. When her job application landed on my desk, I honestly hadn't thought about her for years.'

'But you were curious.'

'Of course I was. I decided to interview her, just so I could see how she'd turned out. I never meant to hire her, but it turned out that she was better qualified for the job than any of the other applicants.'

'What happened then?'

'Nothing. She started work, she was very good, and I was pleased. But, as things got more strained between you and me, I found myself looking for reasons to be out of the house, and she's good company. I started to feel attracted to her, but I knew she was off limits, so I reckoned I could handle it.'

'Delusional. What tipped you over the edge?'

'We were reminiscing and talking about the cards we used to send. She admitted she still had a crush on me and then, before I knew it, we were kissing.'

'And you didn't feel any guilt about that?'

'God, yes! I was consumed with guilt, and I was convinced you would somehow see it in my face and know. But then, when I realised that you didn't see, it just became easier somehow.'

'When did it become more than kissing?'

He sighs. 'Straight away, if I'm honest. It sounds stupid, but we just got carried away the first time. I felt dreadful afterwards, and I told Becky it could never happen again. She agreed, and we decided to avoid being alone with each other going forwards.'

'What changed?'

'I couldn't stop thinking about it. When it became obvious that we'd got away with it and you didn't suspect anything, the temptation to do it again just got stronger and stronger. In the end, I couldn't resist. To begin with, we'd each promise that every time was the last time and we'd stop, but we never did, and I started to justify it in my head by saying that we weren't really doing any harm, as long as you didn't know. I never wanted to hurt you, I promise.'

I don't think I can hear any more. The exhaustion I felt earlier has returned and even the tears have stopped; I just don't have the energy to generate them.

'Enough.' I say to him. 'I'm going to bed now. We'll talk more tomorrow.'

'I understand,' he replies. 'Just one question?'

I raise my eyes to him, giving consent.

'Do you think we can fix this?' he asks.

'I honestly have no idea. Do you want to fix it?'

'I'll do anything I can. I love you and I feel terrible for hurting you.'

'I guess that's a start. I'd prefer it if you slept in the spare room for now, though.' I tell him, and drag myself up the stairs, shutting the bedroom door behind me.

7

'If we're going to stand a chance of fixing this, there are going to have to be some fundamental changes,' I say to James the next evening. He was up and out before I was awake this morning, as usual, so this is the first time I've seen him since last night. I woke to several WhatsApp messages from Di, wanting to know how I was and whether I'd come to any conclusions about what I was going to do. After replying to her, I've tried to use the time to make some decisions, and I also had a really long chat with my mum. Unsurprisingly, she took a very dim view of James' behaviour, but was very careful not to try to influence me towards one course of action or another. Instead, she just acted as a sounding board to let me pour out my anger and hurt, but also work out what I wanted to do. When I finally decided that I ought to give James the chance to save our marriage, she helped me come up with the list I'm about to present to him. I'm still not completely sure that I'm doing the right thing, but there's only one way to find out.

'What did you have in mind?' He looks wary but receptive, as he ought to. He's got a hell of a lot of ground to make up.

'Becky has to go, for starters.'

'I thought you'd say that. In fact, I've already spoken to her about it.'

'When?' I feel a sudden pang of jealousy.

'Today. I went to the stables and told her it was over, that I wanted to try to make a go of things with you. We agreed that, under the circumstances, it would be best if I started looking for a new groom. She's going to stay until I find one, and then she'll go.'

'Okay, thank you. How do you propose to deal with her in the meantime? I'm not comfortable with you being alone with her, for obvious reasons.'

'I'm not sure yet, but I take your point. I'll figure something out and let you know. What else?'

'You're going to book a doctor's appointment and get tested for STDs.'

He looks horrified. 'Is that really necessary?'

'Did you and Becky use condoms?'

There is an awkward pause before he answers. 'No.'

'I thought not. I don't know Becky's sexual history so, for my peace of mind, I'd like you to be tested please.'

'But what if word gets out, or I see someone I know at the surgery? It'll be so embarrassing.'

In spite of the seriousness of our conversation, I can't help smiling at his naivety. 'Come on, James. This is a village, so the likelihood is that everyone knows already. I expect they've been whispering behind my back in the shop for months.'

He smiles ruefully. 'Oh, God. I'm so sorry. I never even thought of that... I'll call the surgery first thing.'

'I've also called an engineer to come and look at the Aga.'

'I don't know about that one, Soph,' he starts. 'Things are really tight at the moment, and we can't afford any...'

'Sorry, but that's bollocks,' I cut him off. 'Tell me something. How is it that we can't afford to get a vital household appliance fixed, but your mother can afford weekly Ocado deliveries, a cleaner, and all the rest of it?'

He pauses again, obviously trying to work out how much to tell me. 'Dad left a letter of wishes with his will, stating that he expected me to make sure Mum was able to live comfortably until she either died or remarried. He specified a monthly allowance that should keep pace with inflation.'

'How much does she get?'

'At the moment, she gets fifteen hundred pounds a month.'

'Bloody hell, James! That's a fortune. How does the farm afford it?'

'We can't, really, but I feel like I owe it to her. It's not her fault he died and left her on her own, is it?'

'So you think it's okay that she can order in the best of everything, while I'm chasing the guy with the markdown stickers round the Co-op to try to save a few pennies?'

'No, of course I don't, but what am I supposed to do?'

'Be honest with her! Tell her that the farm can't afford to keep paying her that much, and that you need the money for other things.'

He looks unconvinced, and I know he doesn't want to address it with Rosalind, so I continue.

'Look, it's up to you. She's your mother. All I'm saying is that it's not fair to expect me to count every penny and put up with Tony's bodges on the Aga while she's raking it in. I'm not saying I'm suddenly going to take up golf or want a cleaner, but I should be able to get stuff fixed without having to beg.'

'Fine. I'll see what I can do. Is that it?'

I've saved the one I know he'll hate the most till last.

'Only one more. I think we should get counselling.'

His face falls. 'Anything but that, please. You know how I feel about navel-gazing.'

'I do, but we have to face the fact that something has gone badly wrong here. Think of it like the Aga: we could try to fix it ourselves, but we don't really know what we're doing. Doesn't it make sense to get help from a professional? I rang various places, but the only one that didn't have a long waiting list was a group session in Okehampton, so I've signed us up. They meet on Tuesday evenings.'

'A group session?' James looks absolutely horrified. 'You mean, we have to talk about this stuff in front of *other people*?'

'I know. I felt just the same as you, but the counsellor sounded really nice on the phone. She said it's actually a really good way to do it, because you feel like you're all on a journey together, and you support each other along the way.'

'If it was that good, there would be a waiting list, wouldn't there? How come she had space for us?'

'A couple dropped out.'

He studies me for a minute. 'Because?'

I sigh. 'Fine. It didn't work out and they're getting divorced, okay? That doesn't mean the therapy doesn't work. I tell you what. Let's do five sessions, and if you completely hate it and we're not getting anything from it, we won't do any more after that. Deal?'

'Two sessions.'

'Four.'

'Three.'

'Four. We need to give it a decent chance.'

'Fine,' he concedes. 'You have a deal.'

'Thank you,' I tell him. I know how much he really doesn't want to do this, so it's a good sign that he's prepared to give it a go.

'Actually, there is one more thing we need to talk about,' I say to him.

'What's that?'

'I had the most awful conversation with your mother.'

He buries his face in his hands. 'I know. She told me about it. I'm mortified. If it's any consolation, after she'd finished having a go at me for what I'd done, I gave her both barrels about what she said to you.'

'It was horrible. She basically told me that you'd only married me for the money, and I wasn't good enough for you. I've never had anyone make me feel like that before.'

'It's not true. You know that, don't you?'

I sigh. 'I don't know what's true and what isn't any more, James.'

He grabs my hands fervently. 'If you believe nothing else, you have to believe that what she said isn't true. I never married you for your money. When we got married, I didn't know that the farm was in a bad way. I married you because I loved you, pure and simple. All that stuff she spouted never even crossed my mind, I promise. You could have been penniless, and it wouldn't have made any difference to the way I felt about you.'

'It would have made a difference to how she felt about me, though. That's the point. She made it very clear that she and your father only accepted me because of my father's wealth.'

'All I can do is apologise. I was just as shocked as you when she told me what she'd said.'

'Did she tell you about her plan to produce an heir for the farm?'

'No. What did she say?'

'Basically, that you ought to be having sex with both Becky and me. If I'm not able to produce an heir, maybe Becky can.'

His head goes back into his hands. 'Please tell me you're joking.'

'Nope. It does beg a question, though. I thought we weren't going to tell her about the fertility thing. Why did you tell her, and why did you lead her to believe that it was me who was infertile?'

'It just came up. She was banging on about wanting a grandchild, and I kind of lost patience slightly and said she might have to wait a while longer because we were having a bit of trouble. I was deliberately careful about how I phrased it, so her putting it down to you is just her jumping to conclusions.'

I eye him suspiciously. 'Are you sure?'

'Yes! Look, I didn't want to tell her that I was infertile. It's not the sort of thing you like to boast about, is it? But I was very careful not to make it seem like it was your issue either. I deliberately chose 'we' in every sentence.'

'Well, I can tell you that your mum isn't going to be on my BFF list any time soon. It was like being in the ring with a heavyweight boxer. You and Becky were the first punch and, before I'd even had a chance to register it, in she came with the second.'

'I really am sorry. I don't know what got into her. The weird thing was that she didn't even think she'd said anything wrong. I had to spell it out to her, and I could tell she was still a bit confused even when I'd explained how she would have sounded to you.'

'What did she say?'

'She kept telling me that I was being silly, that she was only telling you things you already knew to show you why you were better off with me. I think she genuinely thought she was being helpful.'

'Dear God, if that's her being helpful, I'd hate to come across her when she's being unkind!'

We both laugh, and it's a good sound. I realise that there hasn't been much laughter in our little cottage for a while. When did we stop laughing?

The rest of the evening passes surprisingly well. James is very attentive, and the Aga manages to produce a meal that is perfectly cooked, for once. Even though it's a Monday night, we decide to open a bottle of wine and, after we've eaten and cleared up, we slump on the sofa together. As we sit and chat about nothing in particular, James' eyes sparkle with the reflections from the wall lights.

As we talk, I veer from wanting to lean in and kiss him to wanting to throw things at him again. On the one hand he's the husband I love, back to his old self, and it's wonderful to see. But he's also the cheating bastard who I caught shagging the groom. I wish I could just choose for him to be one of those things and forget the other, but I can't. Not yet, at least.

The wine does its work, and it's only just after nine thirty when we both realise we're exhausted and head upstairs to bed.

'I do want us to be able to fix this.' I tell him as he heads for the spare room. 'But it's going to take time, and I'm not making any promises, okay?'

'Okay.'

'Do you?'

'Do I what?'

'Want to fix this.'

'More than anything.'

'You'll need to prove that you're serious. If I sense you're just going through the motions, it's not going to work. Do you understand?'

'I do.'

'One last thing, James.'

'Yes?'

'If you ever do this again, I'm not going to stick around like your mother did, okay? I'll be out of here so fast you won't see me for dust. Get it?'

'Understood.'

8

'Tom and Audrey were on form tonight, weren't they?' I say to James, as we make our way back to the car from the church hall where the marriage counselling sessions are held. This is our third week, and James is holding up surprisingly well. I hesitate to say it, but I think he may even be enjoying them, at least when the focus isn't on us.

'Mm. I can't understand why they don't just give up. She patently hates him with a passion. Also, he is the most boring man I think I've ever encountered. How on earth did she not spot that before she married him?'

'They've been together for thirty years. Maybe he wasn't that boring to begin with?'

'Even so, it doesn't sound like either of them are having any fun now, does it? She's just bombarding him with thirty years' worth of built-up resentment and he's pretty much ignoring her. If I were Tess, I'd tell them to get a divorce. It would be the kindest thing, both for them and for the rest of us who have to listen to them.'

I link my arm through his as we walk. 'I'm not sure she's allowed to do that and, who knows, maybe Audrey will get to the end of her list of things she hates about Tom at some point, and then she'll start thinking that maybe he's not so bad. Although, having said that, I would have smothered him with a pillow by now if he were my husband.'

'Jane and Andrew are nice, though. I hope they make it,' he remarks, as we reach his truck and he unlocks it.

'You just like him because he's a dirty philanderer like you. He's a kindred spirit, hence the bromance,' I reply, as I climb in and fasten my seat belt.

'Unfair!' he retorts. 'Anyway, what do you think about what Tess said to us?'

I knew he was going to have locked on to this. Although we've been getting on well and James has continued to be attentive, I don't feel that I trust him enough yet to restart physical intimacy. The STD tests came back clear, but I still get occasional flashbacks to him and Becky in the hay store and, each time it happens, any physical desire I might feel for him goes out like a light. He's been very understanding, but I can tell he's keen to re-start that aspect of our marriage. Tess, the counsellor, told me in no uncertain terms tonight that I need to balance my current aversion to sex with him against the fact that, if I leave it for too long, sex might never restart or James might get so pent up he'll seek refuge back in Becky's arms.

'I know what she said is right,' I tell him. 'I just need a little more time, okay? We will get there, I promise.'

'Hey, no pressure from me. I can wait a bit longer, don't worry.'

I lean across as he drives and plant a kiss on his cheek. 'Thank you. I tell you what, why don't you come back into our room tonight? Just to sleep, for now, but at least you'll be there when I'm ready.'

'Are you sure?'

'I think so. It's a step we need to take at some point, and it might as well be tonight.'

'Okay thank you.'

The cottage is warm when we arrive home; since Terry from 'Aga Saga' came, the Aga has been on its best behaviour. His bill made James' mouth drop open, but he did have to replace quite a lot of the internals and delivered a lengthy lecture to me about how much cheaper it would have been if we'd had it serviced regularly instead of waiting until it was pretty much on its last legs. I was sufficiently embarrassed to book him to come back next year, much to James' consternation.

I open the warming oven and check the cottage pie I'd stuck in there before we went out. It looks perfect, so I set about boiling some peas to go with it. Although the Aga is now fully cured, it's still a juggling act to get anything to simmer on the hotplates, so I perform my now customary dance of moving the pan around, trying to find a sweet spot where the water is bubbling but not boiling over.

'What's up with Tony?' I ask, as we settle down to eat. 'I went out wearing a fitted shirt earlier when he was in the yard, and I swear he only spoke to my face.'

'He's in love,' James replies.

'Really? When did this happen?'

'The dairy sent a different driver a couple of weeks ago. A woman by the name of Monica. You know Tony's obsession with what he calls 'capable women', and a woman driving an articulated lorry probably ticks all his fantasy boxes. His eyes were certainly out on stalks the first time she reversed up. Anyway, she's our new regular driver, and he always makes sure he's doing something in the yard when she arrives.'

'I bet she's loving his special brand of attention!' I laugh.

'She seems to like him too. It's funny, because he's weirdly polite and attentive around her, like she's some exotic goddess that he can't quite believe is real. He's managed to find out that she only lives an hour or so from here, so he's psyching himself up to ask her out for a drink.'

'Well, here's hoping she keeps him distracted. He's much easier to get along with when he's not ogling me all the time.'

'I saw Mum earlier,' he tells me. 'She asked after you.'

'Did she? What did you say?'

'I said you were fine, and that the counselling sessions were really helping. I think she was quite impressed actually. She said that Dad would never have gone to anything like that, and she admired you for making me go.'

Rosalind and I seem to be pretending that the extraordinary conversation between us never took place. She obviously finished off my cakes for me, as Pauline thanked me for them at WI a couple of weeks ago. I'm still avoiding her as much as possible though and, when we do see each other, I would describe us as warily polite. She knows I was upset but, according to James, she's firmly holding on to the opinion that this is because I'm being over-sensitive rather than anything to do with her being incredibly offensive. I have to say that I don't really care what she thinks of me. I'm never going to be good enough in her eyes, so why bother trying?

It's rather liberating, in a funny kind of way.

9

Tonight's the night! It's supposed to be our fourth marriage-counselling session, but I'm planning to skip it. I have something much more important in mind, namely that I'm going to welcome James back into the bed again, and not just to sleep. I'm still not completely sure I trust him, but I've been pondering what the counsellor said to us last time, and I think she's right. I've planned the whole evening meticulously. Since our conversation about Rosalind's allowance, James has done some jiggling of the finances and we now seem to have a bit more money available. Not enough to go wild, but enough to swap the local Co-op for something a bit more exciting every once in a while. James' favourite dish is steak and chips, so I've bought two rib-eye steaks from the butcher and I'm going to serve them with some upmarket oven chips I found in Waitrose, grilled tomato, mushrooms, and a green salad. I've even bought a bottle of red wine that the assistant in Waitrose assured me would be a good match for the steak. Finally, I also swallowed my pride and phoned Rosalind to get her recipe for James' favourite treacle pudding and custard. It wasn't an easy conversation, but we were both on our best behaviour. The Aga continues to behave impeccably, so I'm confident that the food will all come out as I want it to.

Naturally, the food and wine are just the first stage of the seduction. I'm also going to be wearing my wedding lingerie underneath my normal clothes. It came from a boutique in Paris that my mum raved about, and we flew over there before the wedding just to get it. It seems ridiculously extravagant now, taking Dad's private jet, spending two nights at the Hotel George V and blowing nearly a thousand pounds on underwear that I've only worn once but, at the time, it was exciting choosing something special to wear under my wedding dress. It was definitely a different world back then. Even though James had seen me undressed loads of times before we got married, this underwear did something special, and I remember him being particularly eager to remove it on our wedding night. So, it seems only right that it should take a central role in our sexual 'reset'.

There's just one small issue. James won't be able to see the lingerie under my normal jeans and jumper, so I need something to give a little clue, to help him get the message. I've given this a lot of thought, and I reckon I've come up with the perfect solution. Initially, I was going to greet him wearing the lingerie and nothing else, but I quickly dismissed that idea as impractical. For one thing, what if I opened the door and it wasn't him? Even in his new loved-up, no longer leering at me state, I don't want to give Tony the accidental benefit of my wedding lingerie. Also, if the steaks spit at all while I'm cooking them, I'm going to be very vulnerable in just knickers and a bra – and that's assuming I get as far as cooking. James might take one look at me and haul me upstairs straight away, and that doesn't fit with my plans at all.

I have a beautiful Tiffany Victoria necklace that Mum bought for me to go with my wedding dress. Like the lingerie, I've only ever worn it once, but I'm sure James will notice it around my neck. I'm going to light lots of candles to set the mood as well, so hopefully he'll guess that something is up. I'm pretty sure he will, but men can be surprisingly dense about these things sometimes. In my favour, he's so pent up that I could just say 'hi' suggestively and he'd probably get the message, but I want to do something a bit more meaningful than just giving him the go-ahead. I want him to remember our wedding day and how we felt about each other then. Hopefully, all these little links and clues will do that.

I've got some prosecco in the fridge for afterwards. I know it should be Champagne, but even my improved budget doesn't run that far, and James can't tell the difference between the two anyway. It's symbolic more than anything else, so prosecco will do fine. I hum along to the radio as I beat together the golden syrup, butter, eggs, and flour to make the pudding. Once it's in the steamer, I head upstairs to get ready.

The lingerie is in a cardboard box in the top of our wardrobe, and I bring it down carefully. I open the lid and peel back the tissue paper to reveal the matching satin knickers and bra. They really are exquisite, and I feel a bit of the excitement of my wedding day as I wriggle out of my everyday pants and slip them on. Thankfully, I'm still the same size as when I got married, so they fit perfectly. The bra gently enhances my cleavage and gives me a lovely shape. I have to confess that I waste a certain amount of time twirling in front of the mirror before I get a grip and put my jeans and jumper back on. Even under the jumper, the enhancing effect of the bra is obvious to me, but I sincerely doubt that James will notice. It takes me several goes to get my make-up right. The first attempt is not over the top exactly, but too different from my everyday look. Eventually I settle for a natural shade of lipstick, a touch of foundation and just a hint of eyeliner and mascara. It's normal me, but with the volume turned up a little.

Satisfied, I retrieve the over-sized cash box that serves as our safe from the back of the wardrobe, enter the combination and open it up. It only takes me a couple of seconds to realise that something is very wrong. James' grandfather's medals are in here, as is his father's signet ring and a few other bits and pieces. But my Tiffany necklace and the Patek Philippe watch my parents gave him as a wedding present are both missing. My heart is in my mouth as I open the bedside drawer where we keep the boxes for them, and my mounting suspicions are confirmed when I see that the boxes are also gone. Suddenly, I don't feel sexy at all. If he's done what I think he's done, I am going to kill him.

In the hour I have to wait before James comes home, I try to think of alternative scenarios. Maybe he's taken them up to put them in the proper safe in the main house but, if he's done that, why hasn't he told me? My heart is banging away in my chest; I really don't want us to have a fight now, but if he's sold my wedding necklace without consulting me, we are definitely going to have a difficult conversation. I'm trying hard to be optimistic, and I continue preparing the meal, just in case I'm wrong. God, I hope I'm wrong.

'Something smells amazing, are we eating before marriage counselling tonight?' James asks, as he breezes through the front door and gives me a quick kiss on the lips. 'Give me ten minutes to shower and change, and I'll be with you, okay?'

He bounds up the stairs before I have a chance to say anything, so I carry on with what I'm doing. In a funny way, the delay is welcome, because I'm feeling increasingly uncertain about confronting him and ruining what was supposed to be a special evening. Equally, I know I can't just pretend nothing has happened and go through with my original plan; I've got to ask him, at least.

I'm still dithering when James reappears. The table is laid and the bottle of wine stands unopened on it. The pudding looks perfect, the chips, tomatoes, and mushrooms are in the oven, and all I have to do is cook the steaks.

'This is a bit posh for a Tuesday night,' James observes. 'We might have to leave the wine until we get back though.'

'I thought we'd have a night off from counselling,' I tell him, and I can hear my voice trembling slightly. 'I thought I'd cook you all your favourites instead. We've got steak and I've made you a treacle sponge to your mother's recipe.'

'A night off from counselling? Are you telling me that I don't have to listen to more of Audrey's moaning, and that I get to stay in with you and have this feast? What have I done to deserve such a treat?' He wraps his arms around me and kisses the top of my forehead. I feel sick with nerves, but press on regardless.

'Well, we've been doing pretty well, haven't we?' I tell him, as I ease myself out of his grasp. 'I thought we'd earned a night off, and I wanted to do something special for you. In fact,' I steel myself, 'I was going to put on the necklace that I wore on our wedding day, but I couldn't find it. Do you know where it is?'

He looks shifty. I can see him trying to think what to say, and my suspicions are confirmed.

Eventually, he speaks. 'I'm sorry, Sophie, but something had to give. I tried to talk to Mum about reducing her allowance, but she just got all emotional and said that I was going against what Dad specifically requested. Then there was the massive bill for the Aga, and you wanting more. I didn't want to let you down either.'

'You sold my necklace to pay the Aga bill?' I'm flabbergasted.

'Not just the Aga bill. I'm sorry. I know I should have talked to you first, but I didn't think you'd mind. It's not as if you ever wear it.'

'That's not the bloody point, James!', I snap. 'It wasn't yours to sell. I take it you sold the watch my parents gave you too?'

He nods.

'And how much did you get for them?'

He brightens considerably, 'Twenty grand. That's enough to keep us going for a good while, I reckon. Look, I know it probably had sentimental value to you, but you've got to admit that it's just been sitting in the cash box gathering dust. At least this way it's doing something useful.'

I can't believe my ears. This is so much worse than I'd suspected, and I'm furious.

'You absolute fucking imbecile,' I spit at him, catching him completely by surprise. 'To think that I was actually contemplating having sex with you tonight. Dear God, what a fool I was. Not only have you sold my wedding necklace without even having the decency to ask me first, but you've also let yourself be taken for the biggest bloody ride in town!'

I can see him trying to process what I've said. 'You were going to...wait, what do you mean, "taken for a ride"? I got twenty thousand pounds. That's a hill of money!'

'Listen, idiot,' I tell him. 'If you'd have bothered to speak to me first, you know, as your wife and the owner of the bloody necklace, before you skipped off down to the pawn shop or wherever you went, you'd have had an idea of its true value. So, let me get this straight. You got twenty thousand for the necklace *and* the watch?'

He's looking decidedly wary now. 'Yes. The guy said that was a fair price, and it seemed like a massive amount of money to me. I practically bit his hand off.'

'Unbe-fucking-lievable,' I sigh.

'What?'

'The necklace alone was worth over thirty grand, you moron. The two together, even second hand, would sell for around sixty to seventy thousand. And you came away with twenty and thought you'd done well.'

His face falls. 'Are you serious?'

'Do I look like I'm joking?'

'Shit.'

'Exactly. So let's just recap, in case you're still in any doubt as to why I'm massively pissed off with you and I'm probably going to give this steak to the dogs. You took something incredibly precious of mine without asking and sold it for a fraction of its true value, to get yourself out of the hole you'd created by being too much of a coward to stand up to your mother.'

'She was really upset, Sophie.'

'Horseshit. Have you never heard of crocodile tears? She knows she just has to turn on the waterworks and you'll fold. You're completely spineless where she's concerned. It's pathetic.'

'I really am sorry. I didn't know...'

'It's not good enough, James! Can't you see? You can't keep shitting on me, saying sorry, and expecting me to keep sucking it up. If you had any respect for me at all, you wouldn't be sneaking around doing all this stuff behind my back. I really thought we were making progress, but if we're going to have a chance of success here, I need to feel safe with you. You doing stuff like this doesn't make me feel safe, do you understand?'

The cottage feels stuffy and oppressive, and I suddenly need to be out of here. I head for the front door, slipping my feet into my wellies and pulling on a thick coat.

'Where are you going?' James asks.

'Out. I need some fresh air.'

'But what about dinner?'

'Fix it yourself. Or take some of your twenty grand and go to the pub. I don't care.'

I grab my keys and dash out, closing the door firmly behind me.

10

I cross the yard, heading for the cow shed. I don't know what it is about cows, but I find their presence incredibly soothing. They raise their heads with curiosity as I approach, taking me in with their big, soft brown eyes. Their mouths make slow, chewing motions and they twitch their tails occasionally, as if swatting invisible flies. Once they've satisfied themselves that I'm not particularly interesting, they lower their heads and resume eating the silage that's been spread out in the troughs in front of them. Every so often, one of them nudges another out of the way to get to a particularly tasty bit, but they paint a pretty harmonious picture on the whole.

I'm so angry with James. To be fair, I would have said no if he'd asked me, but to go behind my back like that, and then get such a pitiful price, that's unforgiveable. It's pretty ungrateful of him to have sold the watch my parents gave him too, but at least that was his.

'What am I supposed to do?' I ask the cows. A couple of them look up at the noise, but of course they have no answer. After what feels like an age, but is probably only around ten minutes, I start to shiver from the cold and reluctantly head back towards the cottage. James' truck has gone; I guess he's taken my suggestion and gone to the pub.

I go upstairs to the bedroom, where I take off the wedding lingerie, return it carefully to its box, and slip back into my everyday underwear. I carefully remove my make-up and then head back downstairs. I no longer have any appetite, so I remove the burned chips from the oven, along with the mushrooms and tomatoes, and put them in the bin. The dogs are instantly alert when I grab their bowls and hover expectantly as I chop up the raw steak. As soon as I put it down, they fall on it as if they've never been fed, and it's all gone in just a few mouthfuls.

I open the bottle and pour myself a generous glass of wine, taking the odd sip as I clear everything away. Part of me acknowledges that James may have a point, however stupid he's been. If I hadn't decided to wear it tonight, that necklace might have just sat in the box doing nothing for ever. At least this way it's done some good. Oh, I don't know. He's done the wrong thing and he definitely knows that but, unlike the Becky saga, at least his intentions were good this time. We need to have a proper chat and talk this through now that I've calmed down a bit.

This last thought energises me and, leaving my half-drunk glass of wine on the side, I put my coat back on, grab the keys to the Land Rover and head back out, locking the door behind me. The Land Rover is another ancient and temperamental piece of equipment that has been foisted on me. When I moved down here, it quickly became apparent that my Mazda MX-5 was totally unsuited to life on a farm. I used to scrape the bottom of it regularly on the way up and down the track and it was permanently filthy, so James sold it and got me this Land Rover instead. I can see that it's more practical, but it is a horrible thing to drive. It's heavy, stinks of diesel and, on the rare occasions that I've managed to get it to go faster than forty miles an hour, it's sounded like the world was ending. It's also prone to breaking down, and Tony has spent a lot of time showing me how to fix basic problems. It's amazing how many of his little tutorials required him to stand behind me while I was leaning into the engine bay, and I had to tell him off once when he put his hands on my hips to 'move me into a better position'. The engine starts with its customary death rattle, and I ram it into gear and set off down the track. The headlights are little better than candles, so I creep along carefully in low gear in case anything comes darting out of the hedge. James accidentally impaled a deer on one of the tractor implements once, and I can still hear the pitiful noise it made until he dispatched it with his rifle. Once I reach the road, I turn left towards the village.

It's around a five-minute drive from the farm into the village, which is pretty much in darkness apart from the blaze of lights coming from the pub. The car park is nearly full, but I manage to find one of the last spaces and squeeze the Land Rover into it. I can't see James' truck, but he may have parked it out on the road; I wasn't really looking for it. I climb down and wrap my coat tighter around me; it's really starting to get cold now.

I'm hit with a blast of heat and noise as I pull open the pub door. The bar is crowded with people enjoying a drink, and a few of them are watching the football match that's showing on the giant screen against one wall. I can't see James, so I head for the steps that lead down to the dining area.

'Hello, Sophie,' one of the waitresses says as I approach. 'Are you eating with us tonight? I didn't see your name in the book.'

'Hi, Libby. I'm just looking for James. Is he here?'

'I haven't seen him, I'm afraid. He might be in the bar – did you check?'

'Okay, thanks,' I tell her. 'I'll go and have another look up there.'

My scan of the bar comes up with nothing either, so I approach the counter where Chris, the landlord, is unloading glasses from the dishwasher.

'Hi, Sophie, what can I get you?' he asks.

'Nothing, thank you. Tell me, has James been in this evening?'

'I don't think so. Have you checked the dining room?'

'Yes. They haven't seen him either.'

'He's definitely not been up to the bar, sorry.'

'Okay, thank you. If you see him, can you tell him I'm looking for him?'

'Will do.'

I thank him and head back out to the car park. Maybe James has gone back home. I try to think if I passed anyone on the way here, but I honestly can't remember. I think there were a couple of cars coming the other way, so perhaps one of them was him. I clamber back into the Land Rover and start the engine. As I pull out of the car park, my headlights sweep across the cars parked over the road. One of them looks instantly familiar; James' truck is parked right opposite the pub. This stops me in my tracks. I must have made a mistake, or maybe he's just arrived. I carefully reverse back into the space and go back into the pub, checking everywhere carefully. He's definitely not in here, so where on earth is he?

I wrack my brains to think where else he could be, but this is the only pub in the village and everywhere else is shut. A niggle of doubt creeps into my head, but I push it out firmly. Even James wouldn't do that to me, would he?

The problem with niggles is that, without proof to convince you otherwise, they grow. There is a place he could be, but I can't believe he'd be that stupid. Nevertheless, now that I've had the thought, I won't have any peace until I'm sure. Wrapping my coat tightly around me, I set off down the street towards Becky's house.

When I get there, I'm consumed with doubt again. The downstairs lights are off – maybe she's in bed? It's not even eight o'clock, but everyone who works on the farm starts really early in the morning, so they're not exactly night owls. I'm not sure whether to go through with this; I haven't spoken to her since the hay store incident, so I doubt she'll be that pleased to see me. If I wake her up, that won't help at all.

I step back and look at the upstairs windows. There is a dim light in one of them so, if she is in bed, she's not asleep yet. I summon all my courage and ring the doorbell. After a few seconds, I see a light come on behind the downstairs curtain, and then the front door swings open and there stands Becky, wrapped in a dressing gown.

'I'm so sorry for disturbing you,' I begin. 'I know it sounds stupid, but I'm looking for James and I thought for a moment he might be here.'

'Why would he be here?' she replies, and her tone is hostile. She's got a nerve, really. If anyone has the right to be annoyed, it's me.

'Like I said, it was a silly idea, and I'm really sorry... hang on a minute, what are they doing here?'

As I'm talking to her, my eyes have landed on something familiar in the room behind her. James' boots. Before she has a chance to stop me, I'm barging past her and marching into her house.

'What the hell do you think you're doing?' she shouts angrily, as I head for the stairs.

'Finding out what my husband's bloody boots are doing in your house!' I call, equally angrily. I sprint up the stairs with Becky hard on my heels and throw open the door to her bedroom.

The room is empty.

'Have you lost your mind?' she demands. Both of us are breathing heavily.

'I... I don't understand.' I tell her. 'Those are definitely his boots, and his car is parked just up the road.'

She opens her mouth to reply, but just as she does, the door of her wardrobe pops open slightly and the movement draws both our eyes. I'm just about to shift my gaze back to Becky when something extremely odd happens.

Very slowly, as if trying not to draw attention to itself, the door closes again.

'Excuse me,' I say to Becky, and march over to the wardrobe, where I yank open both doors.

Inside, half hidden by Becky's clothes and naked as the day he was born, is James. He's clutching a bundle, which I guess is his clothes, and trying to cover himself up with it.

It's almost impossible to describe how I feel. I don't cry or start screaming the place down, which is what you might expect. Instead, I feel oddly triumphant, like Hercule Poirot when he gathers all the suspects together to unmask the murderer. Behind me, I'm aware of Becky's shoulders slumping as the fight goes out of her.

'There you are!' I say to him, as if this is nothing more sinister than a game of hide-and-seek. He looks absolutely terrified, as he should.

'Sophie, this isn't what it looks like...' he begins.

'I think it's exactly what it looks like,' I interrupt him, moving aside and indicating the crumpled sheets on the bed behind me. 'What other reason could there possibly be for you being in Becky's wardrobe with no clothes on? I know! Maybe you were playing an innocent game of strip poker, and you lost. But where are the cards? And why would you be hiding in a wardrobe?'

I turn to Becky. Her dressing gown must have come undone while she was chasing me up the stairs and she's in the middle of re-fastening it, but it's patently obvious she's not wearing anything underneath it either.

'It's a bit late for that, love!' I laugh, slightly manically. 'He's already seen it all, and I'm totally not into you. Have you got any theories about why my husband is stark bollock naked in your wardrobe, or shall we all stop pretending now?'

There's an awkward silence. James comes out of the wardrobe and starts pulling on his underpants.

'I wouldn't bother with that, if I were you. The horse has kind of bolted,' I tell him.

'Sophie, let's talk about this. Let me get some clothes on and—'

'There's nothing to talk about,' I cut in. 'I'm leaving you, James. I'm going to go back to the cottage now and start packing. You may as well stay here, because there's no way in the world I'm letting you in, do you understand?'

I turn back to Becky. 'He's all yours. Good luck,' I tell her.

Without giving either of them a chance to reply, I spin on my heel and sprint back down the stairs, banging the front door behind me.

11

As I drive back towards the farm, I feel oddly calm. There are no tears and I'm not feeling the hurt in the same way. I'm angry, absolutely, but mainly at myself for wasting four years of my life on James. Actually, let's make that seven, to include the time I should have been dating pretty much anyone else. At least this time there's no doubt about what I'm going to do.

The good thing is that, although there are lots of people in the village with whom I'm on friendly terms, I don't have any really close friends down here, so I don't feel that I'm leaving anything massively important behind, besides my marriage, of course. The dogs greet me enthusiastically when I get back in, and I realise that I will miss them, but you can't stick around with a useless husband just because you like his dogs, can you? I lock the front door behind me and insert the key, twisting it a quarter turn so James can't push it out to get his key in. I'm certain he won't be far behind me, and I meant what I said about not letting him in. He's very much made his bed, and it's not a bed I'll ever share with him again.

My half-drunk glass of wine is still on the side, so I retrieve it and take a good mouthful, enjoying the heat from the alcohol as I start to plan my escape. I top up my glass and head upstairs, bringing the bottle with me. It takes me a couple of attempts to work out how to operate the loft ladder, as I've never had to go into the loft before, but I manage it and am just bringing down the last of my suitcases when the pounding on the front door starts and I hear James shouting my name. I sit on the bed and take another mouthful of wine while I decide what to do. If I sit here and ignore him, he's bound to get the message eventually but, on the other hand, he's making a hell of a din and I'm not sure I want everyone on the farm knowing our business. After a while, I get up and open the window.

'Go away,' I tell him.

'Sophie, please. I can explain, just let me in, okay?'

'I told you. I'm not letting you in. Go back to Becky's and leave me alone.'

'Look, I'll do anything. Just give me one more chance. Please?'

'You had your chance, don't you remember?' I close the window and draw the curtain.

I'm not sure how long he stands out there, banging on the door and calling my name, because I pop my ear buds in, select an upbeat playlist on my phone, and turn the volume up while I start packing my clothes into the suitcases. The wardrobe is full of what I would describe as 'country clothes': sturdy, practical garments like jeans, shirts and jumpers. I also have storage bags with some of the clothes from my old life under the bed. They're the type that you fill up and then suck all the air out with a vacuum cleaner so, rather than unpacking them and reloading the contents into suitcases, I stack them by the front door as they are. I can sort out the contents when I get to the other end.

There's only one place I can go immediately, and that's back to my parents' house in East Sussex. I'm not sure if they'll be there, but they have a full-time housekeeper, so I know someone will be around to let me in. I don't plan to stay for long, but it will give me the breathing space I need while I make more permanent plans.

The suitcases are all full, and I haven't even started packing my shoes and boots yet. My wedding shoes and some of the other 'nice' pairs from before I was married are put away neatly in boxes with pictures on the front, so I know which pair is in which box. They don't need packing, so I stack them with the vacuum bags by the front door. The 'country shoes', low-heeled and once again focused on practicality, get lobbed into a bin bag.

I feel oddly detached as I pack; I'm calm and methodical, and the physical activity is distracting. I'm completely certain that I'm doing the right thing. I warned James that I'd leave if he was unfaithful again, so he's really left me with no option. I'm reminded of a mother I saw a few weeks ago in the Co-op. She'd only just started browsing the vegetables when her toddler son, sitting in the trolley, started kicking off about wanting sweeties. She had explained to him calmly that he would get sweeties at the end if he was a good boy. By aisle three, the sweeties were hanging by a knife edge and he was on his last warning. As I passed her by the washing powders, she was telling him that he would absolutely not get any sweeties if he kicked the trolley one more time and, by the time we got to the wines and spirits, he'd blown it and there would DEFINITELY not be any sweeties. My final glimpse of them was in the car park; she was loading her shopping into the car while he munched contentedly on some jelly sweets with a look of triumph on his face. I'd told James the story that evening, and we'd both agreed that a final warning would be a final warning if we were ever lucky enough to have children. The unintended outcome, for him, is that he's reaping the consequences of that discussion tonight.

I top up my glass and check the clock. It's half past ten already and I haven't started on any of the other areas of the house yet. I pull the curtain back a little way to check, and I'm relieved to see that James has gone. I was worried that he might decide to camp outside in his truck overnight, but there's nothing out there. I wonder briefly if he's gone back to Becky's. That would be an interesting conversation, rushing out of her house to chase me and then going back with his tail between his legs. If I were Becky, I think I'd be inclined to shut him out as well. I take a mouthful of wine and wander down to let the dogs out. While they're outside doing their business and sniffing around, I cast my eyes around the downstairs of our cottage. There are lots of pictures of James and me together, and I finally shed a few tears at memories of happier times, before my husband turned out to be such a massive dickhead. There are also items dotted about that we were given as wedding presents, including the KitchenAid mixer, which is one of my favourite items in the kitchen.

The dogs are still faffing about outside, so I lift the mixer and put it by the front door, along with its various attachments. I then stick my head in each of the cupboards and come to the conclusion that all this stuff belongs here, in my past. Once I start my new life, whatever that looks like, I'll get new stuff so I'm not constantly reminded of James. Part of me wonders whether I should leave the mixer too, but practicality wins out. It cost a fortune, James is never going to use it, and why should I lay out a hill of money on a new one when this one is perfectly good?

The dogs finally come back in, and I give them their bedtime treats before turning off the lights and heading up to bed. I change into my pyjamas and climb under the covers. Although it's late, I'm not quite ready for sleep yet, and I still have half a glass of wine, so I might as well finish that before brushing my teeth and trying to get some sleep. Tomorrow is going to be a long day.

* * *

When I wake, my head is groggy from the wine and my mouth feels all dry and scummy. I obviously fell asleep before I got around to brushing my teeth, a fact confirmed by the bedside light, which is still on. For a moment, I'm disorientated and start planning a normal day, before my brain kicks into some semblance of life and I remember what's going on. Carefully, I creep out of bed and peer out of the window. There's still no sign of James' truck, which is a relief, so I go down and let the dogs out. They're usually long gone with James by the time I wake in the morning, so it feels slightly unfamiliar to be fixing their breakfast on top of making my coffee. My suitcases, along with everything else, are stacked around the place; I'll make a final pass through the cottage before I start loading everything into the Land Rover.

Something about the Land Rover is bothering me as I sip my coffee and watch the dogs devouring their breakfast. My brain is still a little wine-fogged, so it takes longer than it should to get to the issue. Whenever I've made the journey between here and my parents' house in the past, we've taken a car capable of motorway speeds. The Land Rover wouldn't last five minutes on a motorway, which means I'll have to plot a route across country. I fish my phone out and fiddle with the settings on the navigation app. I know from past experience that the app will be useless until I get a decent mobile signal, but I can find my way as far as Exeter without it, and it should be fine from there. The cigarette lighter socket never worked, but Tony rigged up a USB charging point for me, so I can keep the phone topped up while I drive.

I decide to have a cooked breakfast, following Di's advice about carbs and caffeine being the best way to get rid of a hangover. I don't think I'm hungover as such, but I'm a long way from being at my best, and I have no idea whether I'll be able to stop and eat anywhere. James may decide to cancel my debit card as soon as I've left, which will make things difficult. When we first got married, I was determined that I would keep my own bank account, but it quickly emptied once I no longer had the income from my job coming in, so in the end I closed it and we've just shared the joint account. I decide to call into the Post Office in the village and withdraw two hundred pounds in cash, hopefully before he can get on to the bank and get the card voided, just in case.

By the time I've eaten my breakfast, showered, and dressed, I'm feeling much more human. My mind has been so busy with planning every detail of my escape (and it does feel like an escape, for some reason), that I almost fail to register the knock at the door. The dogs pick it up, though, and start barking. I run upstairs and peer through the curtain to see who it is.

Oh, great. James is standing outside again, and this time he has Rosalind with him.

'What do you want?' I ask him as I open the door. I'd really hoped he would have the decency to let me go without another confrontation, but it seems not.

'Why are there suitcases in the hall? You're not actually planning to go through with this, are you?' he asks, looking around me into the cottage. The dogs have bounded out of the house to greet him and seem confused about why he's not making a fuss of them.

'Did you think I was joking?'

'Look, I understand why you're upset, and I'm sorry—'

'I'm not upset, James. Don't talk to me like I'm some emotional basket-case. Was I or was I not very clear with you? I distinctly remember telling you that I'd leave you if you were ever unfaithful again. Do you remember that?'

'Yes, but—'

'Yes, but nothing. I told you I would leave if you cheated again. You cheated again, so I'm leaving. What part of that don't you get?'

'Sophie, darling, I'm not sure you've thought this through,' Rosalind pipes up.

'I'm sorry? What exactly is there to think through, Rosalind?' I snap at her.

She flinches, but holds her ground. 'For a start, where will you go?'

'Back to my parents to begin with, and then we'll see. What's it got to do with you?'

'Well, nothing, obviously, but I'm just trying to stop you making a serious mistake in the heat of the moment.'

'My mistake was marrying your son in the first place!'

'I admit that James has behaved appallingly, and I told him so in no uncertain terms when he pitched up at my door last night and told me you'd thrown him out.'

So that's where he went. Maybe Becky didn't let him in either. I feel a sense of grim satisfaction at the thought.

'I can see that leaving him seems like an attractive prospect right now,' Rosalind is continuing, 'but have you considered what you're *really* going back to? You won't be able to just pick up your old life as if nothing has changed; the world has moved on and you're not the same person. Your friends will be busy with their own lives, their husbands, and children. Your job will have been filled. The world is a cruel place for a thirty-something divorcee. Yes, James has been an idiot, but he loves you. You have a home and a life here.'

'And that's enough, is it? I'm supposed to turn a blind eye, like you did, while he merrily sleeps with whomever he likes?'

'Oh, for goodness' sake, stop being so bloody naïve! This is a temper tantrum, nothing more. When you calm down, you'll realise that your best chance of happiness is here with James. Go into your kitchen and throw a few pots and pans if it makes you feel better. But, once you've got it out of your system, I want you to have a good hard think about what you've got here.'

'And what do I have here? You've already made it perfectly clear that you don't think I'm good enough for him, but you're wrong. I'm way too good for him. Hell, even bloody Becky is too good for him! And as for you? I couldn't care less what you think any more. So do me a favour and get the hell out of my face. If I never have to see you again, it will be too soon. Do you understand?'

The expression on Rosalind's face is almost comical. She's opening and closing her mouth like a goldfish, but no sound is coming out. Beside her, James just looks dejected.

Eventually, she finds her voice.

'You ungrateful little bitch,' she hisses. 'I have never, ever been spoken to like that before. How dare you—'

I've heard enough.

'Rosalind, do me a favour and just fuck off, would you?' I tell her, and shut the door.

12

Once I've closed the door and locked it again, I lean against it for a while, waiting for my heart rate and breathing to settle. I think I can safely assume I won't be getting a Christmas card from Rosalind, and the thought makes me giggle slightly hysterically. I'm not a particularly confrontational person, but she just pushed me over the edge. It's a shame Di wasn't here; she'd have loved it. Once my breathing is back to some sort of normality, I go back upstairs to check, and I'm delighted to see they've gone. The dogs obviously went off with James as they usually do, so the cottage is deathly quiet. I do my final pass through but there's nothing else I want to take so I carefully open the front door and start loading the car. I'm hyper-alert, like a rabbit on the lookout for danger, but there's no sign of either James or Rosalind. Even Tony is nowhere to be seen.

It takes several trips to get everything out of the house, but eventually it's done. I leave my keys on the table in the hall, but then I'm paralysed with indecision. I can't work out whether to leave my wedding ring or not. In the end I decide to take it with me; James will only sell it if I leave it behind, and I don't want him to benefit in any way from my departure. I climb into the cab and start the engine. As I set off down the track, an awful thought occurs to me: what if James is lying in wait and he's going to try to cut me off, or he's blocked the track with his truck? The Land Rover is pretty sturdy, but his truck is too, and I don't think I'll have the nerve to try to ram him out of the way. My heart is in my mouth as I bump down the track, and it's only when I'm on the road and the farm sign is receding from view that I realise I've been holding my breath.

I have no trouble withdrawing the cash at the Post Office, and I offer a prayer of thanks to the God I'm still not entirely sure I believe in. Any guilt I might feel about taking money out of our account after I've left is assuaged by the realisation that my necklace is probably paying for it. The Land Rover needs diesel, but I reckon I have enough to get me to an anonymous station near Exeter, rather than filling up at the petrol station a short distance from the village where they know everyone and will want to chew the fat about where I'm going and how long for. I once had a conversation with Gary, who owns the site, about the best way to get to Barnstaple and I never want to repeat the experience.

For once, I'm not cursing the Land Rover for how horrible it is to drive. Just keeping it pointing in the right direction is a full-time job because the steering is so vague, and it takes a special technique to change gear without crunching the gearbox, so I don't have a lot of mental space to contemplate the collapse of my marriage. I narrowly avoid sideswiping something very shiny and new looking on the outskirts of Exeter, and I'm already wondering if I'm being over-optimistic about getting all the way to East Sussex when I pull into a petrol station to fill up. The reality is that the Land Rover really isn't up to the journey, but it's not as if I had a selection of comfortable cars to choose from, is it? I chance my luck and attempt to pay for the fuel with my debit card, and I'm slightly dizzy with excitement when the payment goes through with no issues. Assuming nothing goes wrong with the car, I'm in a good state to make it. I don't have any breakdown cover (too expensive), so I will be in serious trouble if anything falls off or stops working.

As I pick up the A30 to leave Exeter behind, I glance at the navigation app on my phone. It's confidently predicting that it will take me another five hours to reach my parents' house. I also notice that there's a message from James. That will have to wait until my next stop; there's no way I can deal with keeping the Land Rover on the road and his text message at the same time and, if I'm honest, I'm not that interested in what he has to say anyway. It's a beautiful crisp winter's day and, as the distance builds between me and the farm, my mood becomes ever more optimistic. Although I'm not on the motorway, this is a busy A road and queues quickly form behind me, so I pull over whenever I can to let the faster moving traffic pass. Despite that, I'm making reasonable time, and the navigation app is predicting that I will arrive at my parents at around half past three, which means it will still be light.

Somewhere between Sherborne and Shaftesbury, I become aware that something isn't quite right with the Land Rover. The handling has become even more wayward than usual and there's a weird rumbling coming from the back. I slow down, doubtless frustrating the queue behind me even more, and pull into the first lay-by I see. It doesn't take me long to find the problem; one of the rear tyres has obviously had a puncture because it's almost completely flat. With a sigh, I set about retrieving the jack and the tools from the boot. Tony's tuition is about to be put to the test. I slip into the overalls that he insisted I keep in the car for just such an occasion, and which he'd made me wear during every car maintenance session that we had. He always said it was to protect my clothes, but

I think he just liked the sight of a woman in overalls. I lay the tools on the ground in order, to make sure I've got what I need, and then I undo the bolts holding the spare wheel on to the back door and try to lift it off the holder.

Bloody hell, who knew a wheel could be so heavy? It takes me a couple of goes to grip it in such a way that I can actually lift it. I'm puffing my cheeks out like a weightlifter as I hug the wheel into my chest to stop it toppling me over, bending my knees to lower it to the ground. I just hope I'll be able to pick it up again when the time comes. Remembering what Tony told me, the next step is to loosen the nuts on the wheel I want to change. He made sure I had a special extending wheel brace so that I could undo even the tightest nuts, but it's still a struggle. By the time they're all loose, I can feel the sweat running down my back, even though it's pretty cold out here.

Thankfully, things start to get a bit easier from this point. I chock the wheels and jack up the car before undoing the nuts completely and pulling off the wheel. I use the same cuddling technique to wrestle the new one into place, doing up the bolts as fast as I can before it falls off the hub. By the time I've lowered the car, tightened the nuts, and fought the old wheel on to the carrier at the back, I can feel my hair clinging to my scalp and I'm sweating profusely. My overalls are also filthy, so maybe Tony had a point after all. I do, however, feel a massive sense of achievement, although my arms feel shaky from the exertion. Tony may be a lecherous old pervert, but I'm immensely grateful to him for showing me what to do and making sure I had the right tools. I can't be bothered to take off the overalls, so I climb back behind the wheel and set off once more. The navigation app has updated my time of arrival to four o'clock, so I've amazingly only lost half an hour.

By the time I reach Salisbury, it's after lunchtime and I'm starving. This presents a dilemma. I could stop somewhere for a hot meal, or I could just grab a sandwich from a petrol station and keep going. I really fancy something hot, especially after my unexpected workout, but stopping will only delay me more, and I don't want to drive this thing in the dark any further than I have to. In the end, practicality wins out and I stop at a petrol station with an M&S store, walk in, and grab a sandwich, a packet of crisps, and a diet Coke. The cashier looks at me curiously while I pay, but I imagine that's just because of my filthy overalls. Back at the car, I wolf them down as fast as I can before hitting the road again. Before long I'm past Winchester and Petersfield, and then the app is telling me I have less than an hour to go. The light is starting to fade, but I've only got another twenty miles. I start fantasising about a hot bath and maybe a glass or two of wine.

At last, the gates of my parents' house come into view. Darkness has pretty much fallen as I enter the access code on the keypad. Nothing happens. I should have thought of this; they change the code regularly and I don't have the latest one. I press the intercom button instead and, after a pause, a man's voice answers. It's Gerald, the groundsman.

'Beresford-Smith residence, how can I help you?' he asks.

'Gerald, it's Sophie. Can you let me in?'

'We aren't expecting you, are we?' He sounds confused, as if I might be an impostor simply because I've turned up unannounced.

'No, it's...erm... it's a surprise!' I tell him.

There's a long pause while he obviously digests this information. I love Gerald; he's a very gentle human being, but he's not one for doing anything unless he's thought it through completely. Eventually, he speaks again.

'Well, you'd better come in then, I suppose,' he says, and the gates silently swing open.

This is the first time I've been home since a brief trip here in the summer with James. Back then, everything was in full bloom and looking amazing. Even in winter, though, the approach to my parents' home is impressive. You drive for what feels like miles through the dappled light of the woods, and then the trees fall away and you get your first glimpse of the house. There was some grotty run-down old manor here when Dad bought it, but he persuaded the council to let him knock it down and build the house that stands here now. It's Georgian in style, even though it's modern. It's also enormous; although I spent most of my later childhood and adolescence here, I never quite got used to the size of it.

As I pull on to the gravel in front of the house, the front door swings open and our housekeeper, Margot, comes running out waving her arms and shouting. I have to wind down the window to hear what she's saying over the noise from the engine.

'Trade round the back please!' she's calling. 'You should have seen the sign to direct you. The front of the house is family only, I'm afraid.'

I stop the engine, open the door and climb down. She stops in her tracks.

'Sophie, is that you?'

'Hello, Margot.'

'What on earth happened to you? You look, well...' She runs out of words and resorts to flapping her arms at me again.

I glance down at my filthy overalls. 'I had a puncture on the way,' I explain to her. 'I had to change the wheel.'

She looks absolutely horrified for a moment but, to give her credit, she recovers quickly.

'Goodness!' She exclaims. 'I expect you'd like a hot bath. Come in and let me run you one. What a lovely surprise to see you. Don't worry about your luggage, I'll get Gerald to deal with that.'

She doesn't quite drag me into the house, she's much too polite for that, but she makes it very clear through her body language that she's expecting me to follow her.

'Mrs Beresford-Smith is currently in the studio with her Pilates instructor,' she tells me as we hurry into the hallway and up the stairs. 'They should be finished in another half-hour or so, and then I'll tell her you're home. She'll be delighted to see you. I'm afraid Mr Beresford-Smith is staying in town tonight, but we expect him home tomorrow. I noticed quite a lot of luggage in your car – are you planning to stay for a while?'

'I don't know,' I tell her. 'It's a long story.'

'One which your mother will hear in due course, I'm sure.' Margot always makes a point of 'not intruding on our privacy' as she puts it. It makes me laugh, because she's as inquisitive as anything and always seems to know exactly what's going on.

'As soon as I've run your bath, I'll pop down and let Donald know that you're here, so he can adjust supper accordingly,' she continues. Donald is the chef; like Margot and Gerald, he's been here for as long as we've lived here. My father may be financially cautious, but he knows the value of good staff, and ensures that his are paid significantly more than they'd get anywhere else to ensure their loyalty.

'Here we are!' she exclaims as we reach the door of my childhood bedroom. 'I trust you'll be comfortable in here? The bed is all made up and there are fresh towels.' She switches on the light and follows me into the room. Although the posters that adorned the walls when I was a teenager are long gone, it's still instantly familiar. The queen-sized bed that I used to get lost in as a child has the same soft pink bedclothes, and most of the other furniture is also unchanged. James always said sleeping in my childhood bed made him feel weird, like some sort of paedophile, so we never stayed in here when we visited my parents together. However, Margot has obviously picked up that something's not right with me and selected the room that's going to make me feel most at home. She bustles into the en-suite bathroom and busies herself with running the bath.

'If you want to get undressed, I'll take your dirty clothes down to the laundry with me when I go. There's a dressing gown in the wardrobe,' she calls. I smile as I start to wriggle out of the overalls; it suddenly feels just like I'm twelve again. I remember having to beg my mother to let me bathe on my own, as I was hitting puberty and it suddenly felt uncomfortable being supervised by Margot. I wrap the dressing gown around me and pick up my phone from the bedside table. I've just remembered James' message. I unlock the phone and read it. It's short and to the point:

Sophie, I get that you're upset and it was stupid of me. Please don't do this though. I'm sure we can work it out. Give me a call when you've calmed down and we'll talk, OK?

I need time to work out how to respond, so I set the phone back down on the bedside table. I'll deal with it later.

As soon as the bath is ready, Margot calls me through. She's put some bubble bath in it and the whole room smells amazing. I catch sight of myself in the mirror and suddenly I understand why she and the assistant in M&S looked at me oddly to begin with. My face has a huge black smudge running across it, and my left ear and the surrounding hair are completely black. I look a bit like one of those camouflaged army commandos that you see on the TV adverts.

I wait until she's left the room before carefully closing and locking the door behind me. I slip off the dressing gown and sink gratefully into the bath. I try to keep my mind empty and focus on the blissful sensation of the warm water lapping against my body as I wash off the grime of the journey, but it's not as easy as that, and I find myself mulling on James' message. I try out various responses in my mind as I wash and dry myself and, by the time I emerge, wrapped in the dressing gown with my clean hair in a ponytail, I've decided on the best one.

I open the app on my phone and delete his message without replying.

13

Gerald has brought all my stuff in from the car and stacked it neatly outside the bedroom while I was in the bath but, beyond carrying it in and selecting a clean pair of jeans and jumper to wear, I haven't unpacked any of it. I have no idea how long I'm going to be staying, and I don't want to give the impression of having moved back in without talking to my parents first. To be honest, my initial plan didn't extend much beyond getting away from my philandering husband and his awful mother. Now that I've dealt with the immediate problem, hopefully I'll be able to free up some mental space and decide what I'm going to do next. There is one thing I ought to do sooner rather than later, though. I pick up my phone and navigate to our housemates' group in WhatsApp.

Sophie: James did it again, so I've left him. Currently at Mum and Dad's.

I wait, and it's not long before the replies start coming in:

Maudie: Oh no! What a bastard. Are you OK?

Kate: Did you hurt him? Please tell me you did.

Di: Group call?

The phone is buzzing before I have a chance to reply and it's so good to talk to my best friends. I fill them in on everything that's happened, and Di laughs uproariously when I replay my conversation with Rosalind this morning. They're all completely supportive, reassuring me that I've done the right thing and berating me for not doing James any permanent injury. We do explore a number of possibilities, most of which seem to feature some form of genital mutilation and a great deal of hilarity, which I definitely need after the last twenty-four hours. They also promise that we'll all get together soon, once I'm sorted, which gives me something to look forward to.

I'm in reasonable spirits as I wander downstairs, although my stomach is growling with hunger. A long time has passed since my M&S sandwich, and James and I normally eat fairly early. Supper here isn't served until eight o'clock, so I have another hour to wait.

'Hello darling, Margot told me you'd come. What a lovely surprise! Are you staying for long?' My mother gets up from the armchair where she was sitting reading one of the crime thriller novels that she loves and wraps her arms around me.

'I don't know,' I tell her. 'James cheated again. I've left him.'

Something about the finality of saying this to my mother hits a nerve, and I realise I'm crying. I'm not really sure why, I think it's probably the release of tension and pent-up hurt, along with grief that the marriage I'd poured myself into wholeheartedly four years ago has come to this. My mother takes a very practical, matter-of-fact approach to things, so her response to my sudden weeping is simply to hand me a tissue.

'Fix yourself a drink, darling. When you're ready, you can tell me all about it.' She settles herself back in her chair and picks up her book. I wander over to the drinks trolley and decide on a stiff gin and tonic. It's been quite a day and I reckon I've earned it. I can feel Mum's eyes on me as I slosh a generous measure of Tanqueray into the glass, but she doesn't say anything.

'You know you're welcome to stay here as long as you like, don't you?' she tells me, once I've had a couple of mouthfuls and the tears have stopped.

'Thank you. I hoped you'd say that. Obviously, I need to decide what I'm going to do, but it all feels a bit overwhelming at the moment.'

'Are you ready to tell me what happened?'

I nod and take her through the series of events from deciding to re-start our sex lives (my mother is pretty unshockable, so I've always been able to talk to her about things like that), through discovering that he'd sold my wedding necklace, to finding him naked in Becky's wardrobe. I gloss over the worst bits of my confrontation with him and Rosalind this morning, as she does have strong views on bad language. She'll listen to streams of invective from my father without batting an eyelid but, ever since she read some article in *Tatler* about it, she's held a firm opinion that swearing is unladylike and picks me up on every profanity. She listens intently, but doesn't offer any opinions until I've finished.

'Is this definitely it?' she asks, when I've finished.

'I can't carry on, Mum. The first time, I was prepared to accept that maybe I'd played a part and it was worth trying to put things right. But for him to do it again just four weeks later, when he's supposed to be trying to save his marriage? I think that tells me everything I need to know about how much I mean to him, don't you?'

'Mm. Wait until your father hears how much he got for the necklace and watch. If you hadn't already left, I think he would have driven over to the West Country and dragged you away! If it's any consolation, I don't think you could have done any more than you did. I'm proud of you for trying to make it work, and I'm sorry that you married such an idiot. Your father and I were never completely convinced by him, you know. I'm afraid your father had a rather nasty nickname for him.'

I'm not surprised. Dad has nicknames for most of the people he doesn't like. I just never knew James was on that list.

'Go on.'

'He calls him "Tim nice but dim", after the Harry Enfield character.'

'Why didn't you tell me that you had reservations?'

'Because you were in love with him!' she exclaims. 'It didn't matter what we thought, as long as he was making you happy. If we'd said anything, it just would have escalated into a row. Anyway, besides coming across as a bit lacking in oomph, he was nice enough. And, stupidly, we thought he would take good care of you.'

My hackles rise, probably helped by the gin, which is making me feel a little light-headed. 'Do I need taking care of, then? I seem to remember I was doing a pretty good job of taking care of myself before I got married,' I reply, more harshly than I intended to.

'Don't be so touchy, you know I didn't mean it like that. Of course you can take care of yourself, but you were also moving a long way from your friends and family to a place where you didn't know anyone. In that circumstance, anyone who professes to love you would look out for you, wouldn't they?'

I see her point and adopt a gentler tone. 'He did, to begin with. He was always trying to get me to hang out with his mother, though, and I just never clicked with her.'

'I never liked her either,' Mum replies. 'She always gave me the impression she was looking down her nose at me.'

'Yeah, well that's probably because she was,' I tell her, and proceed to fill her in on some of Rosalind's opinions. Now that I've left, I don't feel any need to protect either of them. I'm expecting Mum to share my outrage, but her response surprises me.

'What a very unhappy woman she must be,' she muses. 'She had no right to talk to you like that, and her views are at least a century out of date, but I suspect that she was jealous of you, deep down.'

'Really? Why?'

Before Mum has a chance to answer, we're called through for dinner. Our conversation is paused until we've been served our starters and Donald and Margot have retreated.

'You were saying?' I prompt her.

'I beg your pardon?'

'About Rosalind being jealous of me?'

'Oh yes. Sometimes I wonder whether I'm starting to lose my marbles. Think about it. She's lost her husband and the only other man in her life has left her behind for you. I don't know, obviously, but I've heard that there is a very strong bond between mothers and sons, just as strong as between fathers and daughters. So, at a time when she needs her son for emotional support, she can't have him because you do. That might make her pretty resentful. Are you popular in the village?'

'Yes, I think so. People seem to like me, and they're always very friendly.'

'Is she?'

'I don't know. She's much more stand-offish than me when I've seen her talking to people. She likes them to use her proper title and know their place. A few of them did start calling me 'your ladyship' after James succeeded to the baronetcy but I don't really have time for all that nonsense; plus, as a newcomer, I needed them to like me so I stuck with "Sophie". I don't think she cares whether people like her or not, particularly.'

'She'll have noticed how much happier people are to see you, though. Another nail in your coffin, if you ask me. It's sad when people are like that, but there's nothing you could have done about it without suppressing your personality, which would have made you miserable and probably done no end of harm to your mental health. What happens to your title if you divorce him?'

'I have no idea, and I don't care. I'll be happy to be shot of it if it reminds me of him.'

Our conversation moves on to safer ground as Donald and Margot clear away the starters and bring in the main course of monkfish with steamed vegetables. I'd forgotten that Mum likes to eat fairly lightly when Dad isn't around. The fish is delicious, but I'm still hungry when I've finished.

'I'm just going to have some fruit,' Mum tells Donald as he clears away. 'Sophie might need something more substantial after her adventures. What have we got?'

Donald reels off a list of sumptuous-sounding puddings and I opt for a chocolate mousse with a glass of Sauternes to wash it down. By the time I've finished, the alcohol and food are doing their work and I'm starting to feel drowsy. Mum and I retreat to the television room to watch the news, which is full of the latest refugee crisis. I try to stay awake, but obviously fail because the next thing I'm aware of is Mum shaking me gently and suggesting that I might like to go to bed.

The events of the day have definitely caught up with me as I haul myself up the stairs and along the corridors to my room. The house has two wings at either side. Mum and Dad's bedroom, bathroom and dressing rooms are in one, and my room and the guest bedrooms are in the other, with extra guest rooms in the centre section. Even when I lived here, I pretty much never went into their wing except for once a year at Christmas, when I'd take my laden stocking down to their bedroom and sit between them on the bed to open the presents. I'm not sure why they have so many guest bedrooms; I can't think of a time when more than a couple of them were in use. I think some of it is just to keep my mother occupied, as she likes to change the décor in them regularly.

Margot has obviously been in at some point, as my suitcases have disappeared and everything has been carefully unpacked. I have to suppress a giggle when I open my underwear drawer and see my knickers and bras all neatly folded and arranged by colour. The bed has been turned down and the room is gently illuminated by a single bedside lamp. A glass of water stands on the bedside table next to my Kindle. In the bathroom, all my toiletries and make-up have been laid out or put away in the cupboards. I brush my teeth and wash my face before getting undressed, folding my clothes neatly as I go, and slipping into the satin pyjamas that have appeared from nowhere.

Already, my life on the farm seems to belong to a different era. Promising myself that I'll start to make some proper plans tomorrow, I turn off the light and fall asleep within minutes.

14

It's been a productive day. I opened a new bank account, a process which was nearly derailed when I realised that I didn't have any money to put in it. Thankfully, Mum came to the rescue and transferred a couple of thousand pounds from their account as a loan while I get myself back on my feet. She also made it clear that, charming as the Land Rover is (her words), it's not really suitable for life off the farm. Apparently, Gerald has already had to deal with an oil stain that it left on the gravel. I'm idly looking at cars on the internet and trying to work out what the various finance options mean when a commotion in the hallway lets me know that my father is home and, a moment or two later, he marches into the drawing room.

'Sophie! Your mum told me you were home. How are you?'

'Hi, Dad.' I step forward and give him a brief hug and kiss on the cheek. My father is not one for lavish displays of affection. When I was in my teens, I went through a phase of rushing up to him shouting 'Daddy!' and wrapping my arms and legs around him, just to embarrass him. He particularly hated it when I did it in public, and he refused to come to my school unless I promised not to do it. I know he loves me though, because he'll let something slip every so often, like the time I asked him, aged around ten, why I didn't have any brothers or sisters.

'Sophie,' he'd told me, looking deadly serious, 'when I held you for the first time, I couldn't believe how perfect you were. I knew straight away that I'd hit the jackpot with you and, as any wise gambler will tell you, when you hit the jackpot it's time to leave the table.'

It wasn't until several years later that I got the real story out of my mum, which was that he was so traumatised by the process of her giving birth, seeing her in pain and being unable to do anything about it, as well as all the blood and gore that goes with a birth, that he vowed never to put her through it again and promptly got a vasectomy. Needless to say, I prefer his version of events.

I settle myself back in the drawing room while he goes upstairs to get changed. Mum goes up with him, asking about his day and being every inch the loving wife. It's nice that they're still so close after all these years. It was something I'd hoped for in my own marriage, and I can't help feeling a little envious tonight. Dad always wears a dark suit with a crisp white shirt and a tie when he goes to the office. Once he's home, however, he's more of an open-necked shirt and jeans kind of person. He's a slightly odd shape, so clothes don't hang very well on him unless they're bespoke. To look at, he most resembles a boxer. His nose is squashed and bent to one side, apparently a result of a car accident years ago, and he's squat and barrel-chested. Both my parents worked hard to lose their London accents when he made his first million, but his is still very evident, especially when he gets worked up about something. Physically, I'm nothing like either of them; I'm blonde with blue eyes, where they're both dark-haired with brown eyes. I did wonder if I was adopted for a while, but they put me straight pretty sharply on that one when I asked.

'So,' he says, when he's poured himself a drink and settled on the sofa next to Mum, 'give me the summary.'

I give him the broad outlines of the collapse of my marriage, including the multiple infidelities and James selling my necklace. Telling the story like this, in a matter-of-fact way, keeps my emotions at bay. He listens intently and waits for me to finish.

'What's the plan now?' he asks. 'Divorce or reconciliation?'

'I think reconciliation's out,' I tell him. 'I made it clear that I would leave him if he did it again, and he went right ahead and did it anyway. I don't respect him any more, and I can't be with someone I don't respect, so I think divorce is the only option, don't you? I also had a very revealing conversation with Rosalind, where she made it quite clear that the only reason they accepted me as their daughter-in-law in the first place was because I stood to inherit a fortune one day, otherwise they'd never have let me marry James. Pity, in a way. She could have saved me a lot of heartache. Anyway, the point is that she did a lot of damage too.'

'What a bloody cheek! What does she think is wrong with you, exactly? He was lucky that we let him marry you, from where I see it. Don't get me wrong sweetheart, I know you were smitten with him, but he's not exactly the sharpest tool in the box, is he?'

'She thinks we lack class.'

'Does she, indeed? Well, let me tell you something. Being a baron, or whatever he is, ain't no bloody use when you don't have the money to stop your house falling down, is it? Who the hell does she think she is?'

Apart from telling him about the necklace just now, I've always been very careful not to share James' financial situation with Dad, so I'm a little surprised by his latest remark. Mum's obviously concerned that he's working himself up and lays a hand on his arm.

'What do you mean "don't have the money"?' I ask.

'Didn't he tell you? He was quite candid with me about his financial problems. He even asked me for a loan.'

'What? When?'

'When you came over in the summer. You and your mum went off after supper and he stayed behind. We had quite the chat, him and me.'

I'm burning up with embarrassment. How dare James go behind my back and brazenly ask my father for money?

'Dad, I'm so sorry. I didn't know anything, I promise. If I'd have had even the faintest inkling, I would have stopped him.'

'Don't worry about it. He wasn't the first, and he certainly won't be the last.'

I'm still mortified. James was generally never that keen on coming here; he said that he found the opulence oppressive. I'd have to drag him down every year after Christmas, and he always gave me the impression that he was counting the hours until we could leave. Now that I come to think about it, he was uncharacteristically keen on visiting in the summer. I think it may even have been his suggestion that we came. I remember that I'd been really pleased that he seemed to be softening towards my parents, but now I know the real reason I'd quite like to drive back to Devon and hit him repeatedly over the head with a frying pan.

'Obviously you didn't give him any,' I say to him. I'm pretty sure he wouldn't have, but I wouldn't put it past James to wheedle some money out of him and not tell me about it.

'No. I had my guys look into the farm to see if there was any investment opportunity there, but they came back and advised me to steer well clear. I felt bad, because I wanted to support you if nothing else, but there was no way I could put money into it. He had no business plan; he just wanted to do the same stuff, but on a bigger scale. I told him straight: "Son, if you're making fuck all on ten thousand litres of milk, you're going to make equal amounts of fuck all on twenty or fifty." The really stupid thing is that he's sitting on a hundred acres of land that he'd get planning permission for in a heartbeat, and there are developers lined up to buy it, but he won't sell it.'

'Really? I didn't know about this.'

'It sounds like there's quite a lot you didn't know. Your husband was a bit of a secretive bugger, wasn't he? Yes, my guys found that the council down there are way behind on the amount of new development that they're supposed to be allowing because of a lack of suitable brownfield sites. Although it's greenfield, the piece of land that James is sitting on is ideally located, apparently. They could build a whole community there, with schools and everything, but he turned them down when they approached him.'

'Why?'

'Pride, I think. His type sees selling off land as breaking up the farm and failing the ancestors. Complete nonsense, if you ask me. Keep a thousand acres and go bankrupt or keep nine hundred and stand a chance. I know what I'd do in his shoes. Reminds me of that Bible story.'

'I'm sorry?' My father is widely read, but I wasn't aware the Bible had made it on to his radar.

'They must have taught it to you at school. You know, the guy with the sheep who loses one, so he leaves the other ninety-nine on the hill and goes to look for it. Much rejoicing when he finds it and so on. What a stupid thing to do! If one sheep wanders off, you protect the ninety-nine that you still have; you don't leave the rest of your investment to be eaten by wolves while you traipse around looking for a single sheep. That's financial suicide. Jesus might have been the Son of God and all that, but he was a lousy economist. The story about the woman and the coin is just as bad. She searches high and low for the thing and, when she finds it, she throws a party which probably cost more than the value of the coin, so she's worse off than when she started. Anyway, your James falls into the same category. He's holding on to a hundred acres out of pride, and risking losing a thousand in the process. So no, I didn't give him any money.'

'I still can't believe he asked. I'm so embarrassed. How dare he, without at least talking to me about it first? Is there anything he wasn't getting up to behind my back? The sooner I'm divorced from him, the better.'

'Well, let's get that in motion and then we can move on to happier topics over supper. What do you say?'

He takes my silence as agreement, pulls out his phone, and calls one of his assistants.

'George, what's the name of that swanky firm of divorce lawyers? Yes, that's them. Call them tomorrow, would you, and get an appointment for Sophie. Yes, in their offices, there's no need for them to send anyone here. Thanks.'

He ends the call and turns to me. 'George will get you an appointment as soon as he can. I take it you're okay going up to London? They'll charge me full whack for travelling time if I bring them here, and I'm not paying their rates for some guy just to sit on a train and stare out of the window.'

Dad obviously considers the topic closed, and we move on to other subjects for the rest of the evening. He has his fingers in a number of pies, both commercial and philanthropic, and he regales us with tales of various meetings and events over supper.

'Andy came up with a company he thought I should look at,' he tells us. 'Some game that people play on their phone where they have to guide this squirrel around, first to bury nuts, and then to dig them up again. Apparently, it's gone viral with over twenty million downloads, but it turns out the whole company is just one bloke who wrote it in his bedroom!'

'Are you going to buy it?' Mum asks.

'Unlikely. These apps are too unpredictable. Is it going to grow and grow like Angry Birds, or has it already peaked? If we get the app but not the guy, is that going to be a problem? I've told Andy to come back with a detailed proposal and some reliable forecasts. At the moment I think it's too big a risk for me, but if he comes up with the right numbers, I'll certainly look at it. Talking of work, have you had any thoughts in that direction, Sophie? Knowing you, I expect you'll want to be back on your feet as soon as you can.'

'I thought I'd call my old boss, Annabel. I helped her out of a hole a few weeks back, and she sounded like she'd be receptive if I wanted my job back.'

'That sounds promising. Tell her you'll only come back if she gives you a promotion, though. You were good at what you did, so don't undersell yourself.'

'I was, but I'm also four years out of the industry, Dad. If I go back, I'm going to have to prove myself again and things may have moved on. I think I'd rather get my feet back under a desk and check I've still got it before I start getting bolshy.'

'Fair enough,' he replies. 'Just don't let her ride roughshod over you. It sounds to me like you've had enough of that with your lame-duck husband and his idiotic mother.'

15

The offices of the divorce lawyers, Watson & Fletcher, are tastefully luxurious in a way that lets you know that you're going to get great service, but that you'll also be paying through the nose for it. I'm no connoisseur, but I'm pretty certain the artwork on the walls is all original and probably worth a fortune. This is not a cheap, framed-print sort of place. I'm a few minutes early for my appointment, so the receptionist has supplied me with coffee in a china cup so delicate that I'm worried it will disintegrate if I sneeze.

Although I feel slightly out of place, having been a farmer's wife for the last four years, it was nice to get up and put on some more formal clothes and a pair of heels for a change. It took me a while to pick out an outfit, but in the end I went for a pink blouse and a dark blue trouser suit.

'Lady Huntingdon-Barfoot?' a female voice asks. I look up to see a pleasant-faced woman, probably a little older than me. She's dressed exactly as I would expect a top London lawyer to look: a beautifully cut, white blouse over a knee-length, black pencil skirt, with dark tights and patent leather shoes.

'That's me,' I reply, placing my coffee cup carefully on the table in front of me and standing up.

'I'm Rosie, Mr Wells' personal assistant. Mr Wells is ready for you now. Would you like to follow me?'

Bloody hell, if the PAs dress like that, I dread to think what the bill is going to be. Dad has told me not to worry about it, that it's worth paying for the best in situations like this, but even so.

Rosie leads me past the reception desk and into a corridor with doors on either side. She stops outside one of them, opens it, and stands aside, indicating that I should walk through. She follows me in, carefully shutting the door behind her.

We're in a kind of anteroom. There's an empty desk in front of me, which I assume is hers, and then a glass partition behind, revealing a large office where a man who I'd guess is in his mid-forties is sitting behind another, much bigger desk, typing on a laptop. There's an area in front of the desk with a sofa and some chairs and, at the far end, a large picture window gives an impressive view over the city. The man obviously notices our arrival, as he shuts the laptop and strides across the office, opening the door into the anteroom where we are.

'Lady Huntingdon-Barfoot,' he exclaims, as if we're old friends who haven't seen each other in a while, 'Ed Wells. I'm delighted to meet you.'

'Pleased to meet you too,' I reply, shaking his extended hand.

'Before we go in and get down to business, is there anything you need? Tea? Coffee? Something stronger?'

'I'm fine, thank you. The receptionist made me a coffee while I was waiting, and it's a little early in the day for anything else.'

'I'm sorry to have kept you waiting,' he sounds genuinely contrite.

'Not at all, I was early. Thank you for seeing me at such short notice.' Dad told me delightedly on Friday that Watson & Fletcher have quite a waiting list, but George had managed to get an appointment for the following Tuesday – today. I know well enough not to ask for details, but I do wonder sometimes how he pulls these things off.

'No problem at all. Your father's assistant made it clear that he'd like this matter resolved swiftly,' Ed tells me. 'Before we go in, let me just explain a little bit about how we work, so that you can be assured of our discretion. The area we're in is soundproofed, so there's no chance of anything you say being overheard by anyone else in the building besides Rosie, who is sworn to silence. We take great care to protect the anonymity of our clients. If you're uncomfortable using the main entrance, we have a dedicated entrance from the underground car park, which will give you greater privacy.'

'Thank you, but I don't think anyone is going to be particularly interested in me.'

'Trust me, they'll be interested because you're nobility. Also, the press are a peculiar bunch and your father has clashed with them in the past, so they'll be gunning for anyone connected to him. Now, Rosie will generally be out here at her desk during our meetings, but I may ask her to join us from time to time. This will be if we need to discuss any of the intimacies of your marriage, or anything else that either you or I consider to be intensely personal. Her presence will be to reassure you that my questions do have a professional purpose, and she will also act as an independent witness to the discussions, in the unlikely event that you feel dissatisfied with our services for any reason and wish to make a complaint. Does that make sense?'

'Yes. I don't think I have anything salacious to share, though.'

'It's always wise to tread cautiously. If you wish to bring someone with you to any of our sessions for the same reason, that's absolutely fine. All we ask is that you let Rosie know in advance. Do you have any questions before we begin?'

'No, I don't think so.'

'Great, just one more from me then. Do you prefer Lady Huntingdon-Barfoot or Sophie?'

'Sophie, please. I'm hoping not to be Lady Huntingdon-Barfoot for too much longer.'

He leads me into his office and invites me to take a seat in the area in front of his desk. He joins me, resting a notepad on his knee. We go through all the questions I'm expecting, including how long we've been married, whether there are any children, and the reason for the divorce petition. When we get to the finances, I can't help noticing that Ed looks a little puzzled.

'Is something wrong?' I ask him.

'No, not at all. It's just that, I'm not sure how to say this, the sums involved are rather smaller than we usually deal with. Please don't be offended, the only reason for me raising it is that, should your husband contest the divorce and we end up in court, I need to warn you that our fees will easily eclipse the settlement you're seeking.'

We've talked about what I might be entitled to, but I've told him that all I want is to get out what I've put in, namely the two hundred thousand pounds that my father gave me and the thirty thousand pounds that the necklace was worth. Even this small amount is going to cause James a world of pain, but I don't see why he should get to keep it.

'I understand that,' I tell him, 'and, under normal circumstances, I would completely agree with you. However, I think my father is particularly keen to make sure that James can't make a claim on any inheritance I might receive in the future, which will be a considerably larger sum.'

'Ah, okay. That makes sense now, although I can reassure you on that one straight away. Your husband can't claim against an inheritance that you haven't yet received. Even if you had received it, it would be put to one side and only considered if the court felt that his basic financial needs could not be met without allocating some of it to him. Your inheritance can't be taken into account at all at this stage, because it's not a certainty. Your father could decide to leave it all to charity, or he might lose it all before he dies.'

'I think he'd be unlikely to lose it all.'

'I would hope so but I have seen it happen. Anyway, your inheritance is safe, don't worry. May I make a proposal?'

'Of course.'

'Given that this seems to be a fairly straightforward case, I would like to bring one of my associates in to perform the bulk of the work. Please be assured that you will still get the quality of service for which Watson & Fletcher is renowned, and I will oversee the process at every stage, but it will considerably reduce the fees. Are you comfortable with that?'

I nod, and he gets up and sticks his head out of the door. 'Rosie, would you ask Alison to join us please?'

She makes a brief phone call and, a minute or so later, a young woman who looks to be barely out of college comes into the office. I'm starting to wonder if I've made a mistake, and Ed obviously notices because he's quick to reassure me.

'Don't be fooled by Alison's apparent youth,' he tells me with a smile. 'She's one of the most tenacious lawyers I've had the pleasure of working with. She won't leave a stone unturned and, as I mentioned earlier, I'll still be involved at every stage.'

The meeting concludes fairly swiftly after that. Ed promises that he'll brief Alison fully, and that they'll be in touch in due course. It's just after midday when I leave their offices and I've got time to kill before my next appointment, so I go in search of some lunch. I called Annabel yesterday, and it would be an understatement to say that she was delighted when I asked whether she'd been serious about offering me a job. We're meeting this afternoon, ostensibly for an interview, but she pretty much bit my hand off during the phone call, so I'm hoping it will be a formality.

* * *

'How did you get on?' my mother asks me, when I get back to the house sometime after five.

'Good. I've got a job and I'm getting divorced,' I tell her.

'The interview went well, then?'

'It wasn't much of an interview. It was pretty much just a massive hug, a brief discussion of salary, and working out when I could start. After that, it was mainly just catching up on gossip.'

'Excellent, well done. How was the lawyer?'

'Nice, but he didn't think much of my finances. He very politely hinted that I was too small fry for him and palmed me off on a junior. I'm okay with it, though. As long as the job gets done, that's all I care about.'

'Mm. They're probably used to dealing with Russian oligarchs and the like. I think your father was primarily worried about your inheritance. I can't tell you what he said exactly, because a lot of the words are unrepeatable, but the gist is that he didn't want James to get his hands on a single penny of it. Anyway, it sounds like it's all in hand. When do you start your job?'

'In a couple of weeks, at the beginning of next month. Annabel says she's already got stuff lined up for me, so it sounds like I'm going to be busy from the start. She told me she's going to be relying on "my experience of the country" to try to expand our reach beyond London. I'm not sure what she thinks happens out here, but she made it sound like an alien planet. It was quite funny, actually. I've just got to work out what I'm going to do about the commute until I find somewhere permanent to live. I'd forgotten how long the train from Uckfield to London Bridge takes.'

'It's a shame we don't still have the London house. It would have been a perfect base for you.'

Up until a couple of years ago, my parents had a house in Eaton Square that my father used to use when he stayed over, or if he was entertaining business contacts. He likes to keep what he refers to as 'the country house' for family and friends. However, when he was offered a membership of one of London's most prestigious clubs, he decided that was a much better place to stay and promptly offloaded the London house.

'It's okay,' I say to her. 'I think the commute will keep me focused on finding somewhere to live. You don't want me under your feet for ever, do you!'

'Don't feel you have to rush at everything, will you? I know you like being independent, but you're going through a lot and you don't have to deal with it all at once. Would you like to hear something interesting?'

'Go on.'

'Margot tells me that Gerald is quite smitten with that Land Rover of yours, despite having to clean up after it when you arrived. She caught him admiring it yesterday, and he gave her quite the lecture on its qualities. She said she's rarely seen him so animated.'

I smile. 'It does have a lot of qualities, but I'm not sure any of them are particularly desirable.'

'According to Margot, he's been looking for one just like it for a while. So, if you're thinking of selling it, you might want to have a chat with him.'

This puts me in a dilemma. I am oddly fond of the Land Rover after our marathon journey together, but I need a reliable way of getting to the station and I will be driving a lot if I'm going to be organising events away from the convenience of London public transport. I also need to present a professional image, which the Land Rover definitely won't do with its plumes of exhaust smoke, dented panels, and death rattle. The problem is that I can't sell it without all the documentation, which is back at the farm. If I want it, I'll have to contact James, and that's not a conversation I'm looking forward to.

16

'I'm sorry to bother you,' Margot says to me, as Mum and I are chatting before dinner a week or so later, 'but your husband is at the gate, asking to be let in. Gerald wants to know what he should do.'

'What do you mean, "at the gate"?' I ask, stupidly. Although there is no doubting what Margot has just said, I can't get my head around James being here, or why on earth he would have come.

'He rang the bell just now,' Margot explains. 'According to Gerald, he said he needed to talk to you. We don't have him in the visitors' book and, given your situation, neither of us were sure what to do. Would you like Gerald to let him in?'

I consider the question. On the one hand, I really don't want to see James again, but if he's driven all the way from Devon, I suppose I ought to at least do him the courtesy of hearing what he has to say. So far, our only exchange has been about the Land Rover, which evidently enraged him. When I sent the message asking for the documents so I could sell it, he replied with lots of capitals explaining that it belonged to the farm, wasn't mine to sell, and I was lucky he hadn't reported it stolen. I replied to his torrent of invective with the word 'Necklace' and the documents arrived a few days later.

The registration certificate was interesting; I'd always assumed that James had bought the Land Rover with the proceeds from selling my MX-5, but he can't have done, because the farm has owned it since it was bought new in 1992. I scanned the document and emailed it to Alison to investigate. If he didn't buy it for me, then where did the money from the sale of my sports car go? Ed was right; Alison is very tenacious, so I'm sure she'll get to the bottom of it. Anyway, I've sold the Land Rover to Gerald, who appears every bit as delighted with it as Mum said he would be, and put some of the money towards a second-hand VW Golf, which is much more suitable.

'I suppose I could ask Donald whether he could stretch dinner to accommodate an extra person,' Mum offers unenthusiastically.

'No,' I tell her firmly. 'I don't want him staying for dinner. I don't really want to see him at all and, if we let him in, we'll feel obliged to put him up for the night. I'd better go and see what he wants. Margot, can you apologise to Donald on my behalf and ask him very kindly if there's anything he can do to put dinner back by half an hour or so?'

'Certainly, and what would you like me to tell Gerald?'

'Ask him not to let James in, but instead tell him that I'll meet him at the gate shortly. Also let him know that I'll be taking the quad bike if that's okay.'

'Very well. Excuse me.'

'Are you sure we shouldn't let him in?' Mum asks, as soon as Margot has bustled off.

'Absolutely,' I reply. 'He's got a bloody nerve showing up here uninvited, and I intend to make sure he knows that.'

* * *

It's a beautiful evening, but I'm so irritated by James' unwanted arrival that the joy I normally feel at the sensation of the wind rushing through my hair as I hurtle up the drive on the quad bike is completely absent. When I was younger, I used to hare about all over the place on it, often earning lectures from Mum, Dad, and even occasionally Gerald about treating it with respect and how badly it could hurt me if things went wrong. As the gates come into view and I see James standing there with the farm truck behind him, my irritation turns to anger.

'Why are you here?' I demand, as soon as I've shut off the engine.

'What the hell is this?' he replies, holding out an envelope. I approach warily and take it off him, through the gate. The Watson & Fletcher logo on the envelope is enough to tell me exactly what 'this' is, but I draw out the contents and read them, before sliding them back into the envelope and returning it to him.

'It would appear to be a letter from my solicitors, informing you that I'm petitioning for divorce.' I say, mildly.

'I know that!' he shouts.

'Why did you ask then? It seems a lot of faff to drive all the way here just to have me tell you what you already appear to know.' I'm fully aware that I'm goading him, but I can't help it.

'Come on, Sophie,' he says, obviously trying to rein in his temper, 'I've said I'm sorry, and I meant it. I understand how much I hurt you, and I understand why you felt you needed a bit of a break—'

'A bit of a break?' I interrupt. 'Is that what you think this is?'

'Yes. Look: what happened with Becky and me, it didn't mean anything, you must see that. I was just confused and pissed off because I got home and you were all dressed up, cooking steak and stuff, and I thought we'd been making really good progress so I was hopeful, you know? And then you kicked off about that bloody necklace and stormed out, and I just didn't know what to do with myself. I couldn't understand why you were so upset about something you never wore. I was going to go to the pub, but then I saw Becky and, well... it was a mistake, okay? Am I not allowed to make any mistakes? Can you honestly say you've never made a mistake? So, yeah. I get it. You were really angry and you needed some time away. But this?' He waves the envelope at me. 'This is totally out of proportion.'

'Are you for real?' I ask incredulously. 'Let me quickly recap here, you know, just to make sure I've understood what you're saying. When I caught you and Becky the first time, did I leave then, or did I come back and try to fix the marriage?'

'You came back, but I don't see—'

'Shut up. It's my turn to talk now. As part of the deal, did I not tell you that I would leave you if you ever did something like that again?'

'You did, but—'

'But nothing. I was very clear. Did you sleep with Becky again?'

'You're twisting this all around!'

'I'm not. It's a simple question. Did you sleep with her again? You're obviously struggling with your memory, so I'll help you out. You did. I caught you. Again.'

'Technically, you didn't actually catch us having sex.'

'Are you denying it? What were you doing then? Come on, I'm listening.'

'I was... umm, we were...'

'You were both naked, and you were hiding in her bedroom. Let's stop trying to rewrite history, shall we? So, let's go over it one more time to make sure you understand completely. You were unfaithful; I told you I would leave if you did it again; you did it again and I left. What on earth did you think was going to happen next?'

'I thought you'd have some time away, you'd calm down and then we'd talk and sort things out. Mum said—'

'Stop. I have no interest in hearing any of your mother's opinions ever again, do you understand me?'

'Okay, but you'll lose your title if you divorce me, have you thought of that?'

'Dear God, you're right!' I exclaim in mock-alarm. 'I'm such a fool. How could I even contemplate going back to being plain old Sophie Beresford-Smith having experienced the incredible social elevation that came with being Lady Huntingdon-Barfoot? I tell you what, give me ten minutes to grab my stuff, and we can be on our way back to Devon.'

'Really?' He looks delighted to have finally got through to me.

'No, you total imbecile. When are you going to get it? I want a divorce. I don't want your surname, your title, or anything to do with you. You have treated me exactly like the trash your mother is clearly convinced I am, and nothing on earth could persuade me to take you back.'

'So that's it, then? That's all you have to say to me after four years of marriage?' He's sounding bitter now.

'That's it. I'd like you to leave now.'

'What? Where am I supposed to go? I've just driven for hours to get here. Aren't you going to let me in?'

'Of course I'm not!'

'But what am I supposed to do? I can't drive back to Devon now.'

'I don't know. Check yourself into a hotel or something. I don't care.'

'I can't afford that!'

'That really isn't my problem. I didn't ask you to come, did I?

You're not welcome here and, if you're thinking of sleeping in your car overnight, let me tell you that Gerald has CCTV and will call the police if you're not gone by the time I get back to the house. Goodbye, James.'

Before he has a chance to object any more, I fire up the quad bike and set off at top speed back down the drive.

17

I've been back at work for a month and, for the most part, I'm loving it. The only fly in the ointment is that I don't seem to be as sharp as I used to be. Although I've set up all the same spreadsheets and checklists that I'd used for years, I somehow seem to miss something every time. Luckily, I've managed to either correct my mistakes or work around them so far, but I'm starting to wonder if I'm not up to it any more. Annabel is delighted that I'm back, and we're incredibly busy, but the mistakes are definitely starting to dent my confidence a bit.

Thankfully, even with the monthly payments for the car, I've still got a decent amount left for rent and living expenses. I've also got enough left from the sale of the Land Rover to put down a deposit on a flat, when I find one. I definitely need to find something, and soon. The commute is horrible, but the only accommodation I seem to be able to afford in London are rooms in grotty run-down flats like the one I lived in before I was married. Flat sharing is fun in your twenties, but I need my own space now. I've registered with lots of agents, but so far nothing has come up that's even close to my budget. Thankfully, our expenses policy allows for me to stay overnight in a hotel when we have an evening function, as I did yesterday. The last train from London to Uckfield leaves just after eleven at night and, even if that wasn't way earlier than the function end time, I wouldn't have felt safe on my own on a train that late at night. Di always says I'm welcome to stay with her and even offered to give me a key, but I don't like the idea of barging into their house in the early hours of the morning, especially as I'm terrified of accidentally setting off the alarm.

I'm engaged on another fruitless scan of all the property websites I've bookmarked while sitting on the train heading for Kent. Toby Roberts, the photographer who did my wedding, is having a charity gala evening at his studio in Sevenoaks, and he's engaged us to organise the hospitality element for him. He's auctioning off signed copies of some of his most famous photographs and some other donated items, with the aim of raising several thousand pounds for a cancer charity. Given my recent record, I'm leaving nothing to chance and I'm getting there early to double-check everything. This is a high-profile event with a celebrity guest list, and it could be very good for us as long as it goes smoothly. I've already been here a couple of times to meet with the various contractors I've brought in, so, even though this is the first time I've come by train rather than driving, I know the route to his studio well, arriving there just after ten. Toby is already there, arranging artworks and removing his studio equipment, and he smiles warmly as he lets me in.

'Hi, Sophie. All set for tonight?'

'I hope so. Have the fridges, Champagne, and glasses arrived?'

'Yes, the fridges are all plugged in and the glasses and Champagne are in the kitchen, I think. I've been busy with the art, so I haven't really done anything except let people in and leave them to get on with it.'

'Okay, brilliant. I'll go and take a look.'

Toby goes back into the main studio area, which is surprisingly large. I've been in a few photographic studios in my time, and most of them are pretty poky, with barely room to move without banging into a light or some other piece of paraphernalia. Toby's studio is like a barn, and he's making the most of the space, with displays around the walls and on carefully arranged stands. It looks beautiful, so let's just hope that the stuff I've organised will do it justice.

The three industrial fridges I've ordered are in place and humming quietly, which is a good start. One of them is purely for drinks. It's impossible to tell how much people will drink at these occasions, so I've ordered seventy-two bottles of Champagne, with the option to return any that are unused. That's a bottle per person, which should be more than enough. I've spent a long time working with the caterers to select the perfect range of canapés to cover every dietary restriction we could think of without compromising on taste and presentation, and Annabel happily gave her blessing for me to use the shirts and blouses with our company logo tastefully embroidered on them that we ask the waiting staff to wear at high profile events like this.

I set my laptop down on the counter and start working through my checklist. I put on my rubber gloves and go through the boxes of glasses to make sure that they're all pristine without any fingerprints or lipstick marks on them, and that they all match. So far, so good. The trays for the canapés, napkins, and plates also pass muster. I'm particularly pleased with the plates, which have a little cut-out in them so the guests have somewhere to put their Champagne glass when they're eating. In my opinion, it's this kind of attention to detail that makes us stand out.

Humming quietly to myself, I open the wine fridge. I count the bottles of still and sparkling water, checking them off against my spreadsheet. The freshly squeezed orange juice is also present and correct, but I can only see twelve bottles of Champagne. That's not right. I count them twice, in case my eyes are deceiving me, and then scout round the kitchen to see if I can find the others, but there's no sign of them anywhere. I pull out my phone and call the wine merchant.

'Hi Ian, it's Sophie from Rushmore Events here. I'm just going through the inventory, and I can only find twelve bottles of Champagne. Are you able to contact your driver to find out where he put the rest?'

'Let me have a look.' I can hear him shuffling pieces of paper and tapping on a keyboard.

'Umm. Sophie, you only ordered twelve bottles.'

'I ordered twelve *cases*, Ian, I remember distinctly. Twelve bottles wouldn't even come close to what we need for an event like this!'

'I was a bit surprised, but Sharon said she'd double-checked it with you, and you'd said very clearly that it was twelve bottles.'

'I haven't spoken to Sharon about it, Ian. I promise you.'

'Hang on, let me check.' He obviously puts his hand over the mouthpiece, as I can hear muffled sounds of conversation but I can't make out any of the words.

'Hi Sophie, I've just checked with Sharon, and she said she spoke with one of your colleagues – Emily someone. Does that sound right?'

Somewhere in the dim recesses at the back of my head, a penny is starting to drop and a murderous thought is forming, but I can't deal with that yet. I need to solve the immediate problem that I'm sixty bottles of Champagne short.

'Okay. I'll follow up at this end. I really need those other sixty bottles though, Ian. What can you do?'

'I'll have to check the schedules. Can I call you back in five minutes?'

I can't concentrate on the rest of my checklist while I'm waiting.

The questions that are racing round my head are, 'What if I'm not losing my touch at all? What if I've been sabotaged every time? But why would Emily want to do something like that? What on earth could I have done to upset her?'

I'm no closer to answering any of them when Ian calls back.

'Sorry, Sophie,' he tells me. 'I've got the stock, but I don't have any drivers that can get out there again today. If you can pick it up, you're welcome to it.'

'Put them aside. I don't care what happens, or who calls you, or anything. Those bottles are mine, okay?'

He laughs. 'No worries. Understood.'

Now all I have to do is work out how to get from Sevenoaks to Lewisham and back with sixty bottles of Champagne when I don't have any transport. I search for car hire places and I'm relieved to find a couple nearby. However, neither of them has any cars on site unless they're pre-booked, so that proves to be a dead end. I check to see whether I can get back to Uckfield and pick up my car, but that will take way too long. I really don't want to involve Toby in this mess, as it looks unprofessional and he's got other stuff to worry about, but I'm running out of options.

'Toby, I'm really sorry to bother you,' I call to him, 'but there's a slight issue with the Champagne, and I need to go to Lewisham to sort it out. I've tried both the car hire places I've found on the internet without any joy. Do you know of anywhere else round here I might be able to rent a car?'

He considers for a while. 'To be honest, I didn't know there were any car hire places around here at all. I'd lend you mine, but I need it myself and I'm not even going in that direction, otherwise I'd give you a lift.'

'Okay. Don't worry. It's my problem to solve, not yours.'

Shit. What am I going to do? In desperation I load up a site featuring cars and vans for sale, put in Toby's postcode and a one-mile radius and wait for the results. There are only three. A Range Rover and a Lexus that are both way too expensive, and a battered Transit van that would make my old Land Rover look smart. At least it's not much more than the car hire would have been, and I only need it to get me to Lewisham and back. I have no idea what I'll do with it afterwards, but I'll cross that bridge later. Maybe I'll be able to flog it to Gerald. He seems to have a penchant for beaten-up old vehicles. The thought makes me smile.

I call the number and a man answers. After introductions and a brief conversation, he tells me that the van is still available. He's a little surprised when I ask if I can see it immediately, but agrees and gives me the name and address of the café he works at. I'm in luck; it's literally next door, so I arrange to meet him in the car park behind, where he says the van is parked.

Toby has obviously been listening to my conversation and lets me out of the back door of his studio without a word. To be fair, he doesn't need to say anything, as the crinkle of amusement in his eyes tells me exactly what he's thinking. I scan the parking area behind the building and the van is not hard to spot. It looks even more ropey in the flesh than it did in the pictures, but as long as it's roadworthy and will get me out of the hole I'm in, I don't care. As I'm walking towards it, the back door of the café opens and a man in a chef's uniform comes out. He has close-cropped hair and a scar across one of his cheeks, and is definitely not the sort of person I'd even consider buying a used vehicle from if I wasn't desperate.

'Are you Sophie?' he asks.

'That's me,' I reply. 'You must be Matt.'

'Pleased to meet you. This is the van. Can I ask why you're so interested? If you don't mind me saying, you don't look like the sort of buyer I would have expected.'

He's got a point. I'm wearing my work uniform of tailored blouse with matching jacket and skirt, with kitten heels underneath. I'd match the van better if I was wearing my overalls.

'It's an emergency.' I tell him, honestly. 'I'm doing an event for Toby Roberts, and sixty bottles of Champagne that are supposed to be here are in Lewisham. I tried renting a car, but no joy. So, your van is the only option. I assume it will make it to Lewisham and back?'

'Oh, it'll make it, all right. I know it looks shabby, but the mechanicals and structural parts are all good. I'm only selling it because my fiancée doesn't like it, so we go everywhere in her van and I never use it.' He indicates a shiny modern van with 'Daisy's Diner' written on it alongside a logo of two interlocking Ds.

'Are you saying', he continues, 'that you only need it for one journey? What are you going to do with it afterwards?'

'I don't know. I haven't got that far.'

'Look, Toby's my neighbour, and this thing he's doing is for charity, isn't it?'

'Yes.'

'Take the van. Do what you need to do, replace the fuel you've used, and then bring it back, okay? It seems silly to buy it just for one journey.'

'But what if I have an accident or something? I'd only be covered third party on my insurance.'

He laughs loudly. 'If you crash it, you've bought it. Okay?'

'Are you sure?' I can't believe this man I've never met before is just lending me his van, however shabby it is.

'Absolutely. Here's the key. Give me a call when you're done and I'll come out and get it from you.'

I don't need to be told twice. Thanking him profusely, I take the key from him and hop into the cab. Unlike the Land Rover, I can't see out of the back, but Tony went through a phase when he was certain I'd need to be pulling trailers, so we spent much more time than I wanted to reversing trailers around the yard while watching in the wing mirrors. This is going to be much easier than that. The engine starts with a clatter, I reverse it swiftly out of its space, and I'm soon on the motorway heading for Lewisham.

18

I'm in the office early, as I want to try to catch Emily before either Annabel or Lucy, the other main event organiser, come in. I've been thinking long and hard about how to play this. I could have just gone to Annabel, but I don't really have anything concrete to prove that Emily has been sabotaging me. I'm hoping that confronting Emily directly will get a better result. The story I tell Annabel will depend entirely on what she says.

Thankfully, the event at Toby's studio went off without a hitch once I returned from Lewisham with the Champagne. Matt's van was exactly as he described; it may have looked like it was on its last legs, but it was actually much nicer to drive than the Land Rover. I replaced the fuel as asked and also gave him a couple of extra bottles of Champagne that I picked up, which delighted him. I'm going to have to find a way of squaring them through the expenses but, once she hears the story, I'm reasonably sure Annabel will sign them off.

While we were chatting before the event, Toby gave me some interesting advice about my property problem. He had remembered me from the wedding and asked, very delicately, after James. I didn't go into the details, but explained that we were divorcing. I mentioned the problems I was having finding somewhere to rent in London and he suggested I might want to widen my search, particularly as I could be in central London within half an hour of getting on a train in Sevenoaks, and Orpington and Bromley were even closer. Coincidentally, one of the flats above his studio happens to be vacant, and he gave me the details of the agent. I rang them over the weekend and I'm viewing the flat on Saturday. I'm pretty sure I won't take it; I don't know anyone in Sevenoaks, and I don't fancy being stuck on my own in the middle of nowhere every evening and weekend. However, it will at least give me an idea of what I might be able to afford outside London, so it's worth a look just for that.

The door opens and Emily strides in, humming to herself.

'Good morning, Emily. Nice weekend?'

She starts briefly, before regaining her composure. I'm pretty sure I saw something flicker across her face before the shutters came back down.

'Oh, hello, Sophie. You're in early!'

'I am. I was hoping to have a chat with you before Annabel comes in. When you're settled, shall we pop into the meeting room?'

I've rattled her, I can see that. There's no more humming as she hangs up her coat and powers up her computer.

'I'll just get a cup of tea,' she tells me. 'Would you like one?'

'No thank you. If it's all right with you, I'd prefer it if we went straight in. Can your cup of tea wait?'

She's definitely looking rattled now. 'Okay.'

We make our way into the meeting room, which is a rather grand name for a table and chairs behind a glass partition wall, but at least it's not called the boardroom or anything sillier. I bring a notepad, not because I have any notes or plan to take any, but simply out of habit. I notice Emily does the same.

'What's up?' she asks, after we've taken our seats.

I decide to go straight for the jugular. 'Tell me about the Champagne for the Toby Roberts event,' I begin.

She tries to look baffled, but I can see disquiet in her eyes.

'What do you mean?' she replies.

'I ordered twelve cases, but only twelve bottles turned up. I nearly had to buy some complete stranger's van and drive to Lewisham to collect the rest, otherwise the event would have been a disaster. Do you have any idea how that could have happened?'

'No. Should I?' I think she knows I'm on to her; she's looking increasingly shifty and starting to fidget.

'I don't know. You tell me.' I'm not letting her off the hook by telling her what I know just yet. I want to see if she has the grace to come clean.

'I've no idea. I guess the wine merchant must have written down bottles instead of cases. Didn't you double-check?'

Okay, she's had her chance.

'The merchant is one I've dealt with for a long time, Emily, and they told me they did ring to confirm. According to them, they spoke to someone with the same name as you, who told them that the order was definitely twelve bottles and not twelve cases.'

'Really? I don't remember.'

She bloody does. She's trying to sound nonchalant, but she's fidgeting so much that she's either guilty as hell or I need to call pest control.

'Cut the act, Emily.' I say, firmly. 'You were trying to sabotage the event, and this isn't the first time, is it? The thing that I don't understand is why.'

There's a long silence. I can see her wrestling with her thoughts, trying to decide whether to tell the truth or not, before she starts to speak.

'Look,' she says, 'you and Lucy have always been Annabel's golden girls. Nobody ever noticed me; I was just the office junior. Every day, I'd get you all coffee just how you liked it, and sandwiches and whatever, but it felt like I was invisible. Even after you left, it took years before Annabel really noticed me. She started letting me organise small events last year and I thought I was on the way at last. But then I cocked up and she was really pissed off with me.'

'The Cucina Italia thing?'

'The Cucina Italia thing. Anyway, it was fine and I was all set to sort it out, only you bloody popped up again, didn't you? Waving your magic wand and being the golden girl, even though you didn't even sodding work here any more. Do you have any idea how that made me feel?'

I'm shocked. It never occurred to me that this was how she saw me.

'I was just trying to help,' I say.

'Of course you were, but you ended up with all the glory – "Aren't you lucky, Emily, that Sophie was passing by." I could have fixed it, you know, but you never gave me the chance.' She's starting to cry now.

'So, when I came back...' I prompt her, a little more gently.

'I couldn't believe it. There you were, as if nothing had ever changed. I might as well have gone straight back to being an office junior, while you and Lucy and Annabel swanned around exactly like you always used to. It was so *unfair*.'

'So, you decided to try to make me look bad, in order to make yourself look better. Is that it?'

'Well, it sounds horrible when you say it like that, but basically yes. I thought if you screwed up an event, maybe I'd be the one to fix it, and then Annabel would be telling you how lucky you were that I'd ridden to your rescue. I never did anything serious, just little things that would take the shine off. Only you always spotted them or managed to work round them somehow.'

'Okay. I understand what you're saying, and I'm really sorry I made you feel like that. It was certainly never my intention. But can't you see that what you were doing wasn't just damaging me? If something had gone seriously wrong, it would have damaged the company, which means it would have affected you too. We're not in competition, you know, we're supposed to be on the same team.'

'That's easy for you to say. You're not the one running in circles just trying to keep up.'

'Did it never occur to you that you might not be running in circles so much if you put as much effort into your own work as you obviously have done trying to subvert mine? What am I supposed to say to Annabel about this?'

Her face is a mask of horror. 'You wouldn't, would you? Please don't say anything to her, she'll fire me on the spot and I really need this job!' The tears are falling fast now.

'I won't say anything, but I have two conditions.'

'What?'

'One, this stops. Now. If I even suspect you're trying to undermine me again, I'll go straight to Annabel. Do you understand?'

'Yes.'

'Two. Let us help you. It doesn't make you look bad if we help. It makes you look like you want to learn. Annabel, Lucy and I might look as if we're on top of everything, but you've had a taste of it now, and you know how much hard work it is. We've all been doing this job for years and we've got a feel for what works. So, rather than trying to bring us down, let us bring you up. Let me give you an example.'

'Go on.' She's looking incredibly relieved, if a little snotty from the tears, and I really hope I'm going to be able to trust her from now on.

'Cucina Italia,' I say to her.

'What about them?'

'Okay, here's how it works, or at least how I do it. I choose the companies I work with very carefully. If they're too big we won't be an important enough client to them, and they'll muck us around when someone bigger than us comes along. Then, when you try to get hold of someone to complain, you just get passed from pillar to post until you lose the will to live. Does that sound familiar from your experience with them?'

She looks interested. 'Yes, that's exactly what happened.'

'So, I steer clear of the really big firms. However, if they're very small, like a one-man band, then they will love you for ever, but you're absolutely stuffed if someone gets sick, because they're too small to have any backup. You're at risk again, but for a different reason. Okay?'

'Yes.'

'I learned to pick very carefully, and I always ensure I choose companies that are small enough that our business matters to them, but not so small that they can't adapt if circumstances change.'

'Cucina Italia is one of the best-known firms in London for Italian food, so I thought I'd chosen well.'

'Exactly, but they're massive. So, as soon as something more interesting than your little corporate event came along, they dropped you like a hot brick and left you in the lurch.'

'Are you saying you'll share your contacts with me?' she asks.

'Not exactly. My contact book is like my book of spells, but I'll certainly help you build up a good list of contacts of your own. Also, if the nonsense stops, I'll see if I can persuade Annabel to let you help me with some of the big events, with a view to stepping up yourself when you're ready.'

'And you'd do that, even after what I've done?'

'What's the alternative? Let you stew in your own juices making the same mistakes we've all made but without anyone to guide you and pull you out of the mud, getting more and more resentful until you do something that makes Annabel fire you? Who wins there? If we do it my way, everybody wins.'

'Thank you, I think.' She looks wary, but I'm hopeful that I've got through to her.

'No problem. Now, why don't you go to the loo, sort yourself out, and then make that cup of tea. When you're sorted, I'll tell you all about a massive cock-up I made about six weeks after I started.'

She doesn't need telling twice, bolting from the room and barely stopping to put her notepad on her desk. I follow her out and settle myself back in my chair. If I'm not going to dump Emily in it, which was only ever going to be a last resort anyway, I need to think of a different way to explain the Champagne problem and get Annabel to sign off my slightly bizarre expenses. On the plus side, I'm mightily relieved to have got to the bottom of the problem. I've still got what it takes to do this job after all.

'Is everything all right?' Annabel's voice comes from behind me. 'I just saw Emily in the corridor, and she looked like she'd been crying.'

'Did she? Maybe she had some bad news over the weekend or something,' I say, keeping my voice completely nonchalant.

'Perhaps I should have a word with her. What do you think?'

'I'd leave it, if I were you. I'm sure she'll tell you in her own time if there's anything you need to know. By the way, can I have a chat when you've got a moment? I had a couple of interesting moments during the Toby Roberts gig, and I need to talk you through the expenses.'

'Give me five minutes,' she tells me.

Perfect. Just enough time to send an email to Emily to tell her what I've said, so we can keep our stories straight.

19

As I'm waiting on the platform at Parsons Green Tube station, I automatically unlock my phone and start scrolling through the property websites. Di, Kate, Maudie and I had a night out last night which was enormous fun, even though I had to be careful how much I drank, knowing that I had to be up early to get to Sevenoaks. Opinions were divided about whether I was doing the right thing looking at flats that were 'so far away', but when I showed them the alternatives, they understood.

I'm still not convinced I'm doing the right thing myself; although I've widened my search to include towns within half an hour of London, and I now have lots of financially viable options, I don't know anything about any of these places, which makes me hesitant. Perhaps I should just wait until I've seen the flat in Sevenoaks and decide after that. I close the websites and, after a quick check of social media, log into the app store to see if there's anything interesting to distract me and pass the time while I'm travelling. I'm not normally one for playing games on my phone, as I'm not really into that sort of thing, but I could happily while away some time if they have Scrabble or Tetris. I looked up the journey from Sevenoaks to Uckfield, and it's going to take ages because I have to come back into London and get a different train back out, so I definitely need something to keep me occupied.

Most of the games don't look remotely suitable and I can't find Scrabble anywhere. I'm despondently scrolling through when something catches my eye. Nutsy the Squirrel is £2.99, has thousands of five-star reviews, and nearly thirty million downloads. This must be the game that Dad was talking about when I first got home. Thirty million people can't all be idiots, so I pay the money and download the game. I launch it as soon as I've boarded the Tube, and it's surprisingly entertaining. The first level is pretty simple; you have to guide Nutsy round his 'world', finding nuts on the ground. When you've gathered ten nuts, you have to find a suitable place to hide them. Once you've hidden a hundred nuts, the season changes to winter and you have to guide him around in the snow and find all the places where the nuts are hidden to stop him starving. It's harder than it sounds, because all the hiding places are covered over with snow, so you spend quite a lot of time digging in the wrong places, which uses precious energy. I'm afraid poor Nutsy has starved to death twice by the time I reach Charing Cross.

I'm surprised to find that the train to Sevenoaks is absolutely packed, and it takes me a while to find a vacant seat. A bit of eavesdropping on my fellow passengers reveals that there's some sort of festival in Hastings this weekend, so that's presumably where they're all going. I settle back into the game, but I'm not doing particularly well to begin with. I've sadly murdered another Nutsy by the time we reach Waterloo East, where another load of festival-goers board the train. However, by the time we reach London Bridge, I've hit the heady heights of level two. This is like level one, only you have fifteen sets of nuts to bury and then find, and there are other squirrels also looking for them, so you have to chase them away, which unsurprisingly uses energy and means you have to balance digging up the nuts with chasing away the competition very carefully. I'm so absorbed in the game that it takes me a while to notice that the man sitting next to me is watching me.

'Can I help you?' I ask, slightly more aggressively than I mean to. To be fair, I am a little frustrated as another Nutsy has just starved to death.

'Sorry. I didn't mean to intrude,' he replies, removing his earbuds. 'I was just watching the game. What's it called?'

I study him for a moment, trying to work out if this is some sort of chat-up line. He's a good-looking guy, but I'm in no mood to have some creep hitting on me. He doesn't look like a creep, though. I imagine him to be in his late thirties; he's dressed in a slightly crumpled, light-blue shirt with dark-blue trousers underneath and black shoes and his face is open and honest-looking. I decide to give him the benefit of the doubt, for now.

'Nutsy the Squirrel,' I tell him.

'I've heard of that. Is it any good?'

'You're asking the wrong person, I'm afraid. I'm not really into playing games on my phone. I just downloaded it because I'm going to be spending a lot of time on trains today, and I thought it would keep me entertained.'

'And is it?'

'Yes. It's just hard enough to make you think, but not so impossible that you give up.'

'Hm. Thank you. Maybe I'll give it a try.' He re-inserts his earbuds and settles back into his seat and, although we get off at the same station, he grabs what looks like an overnight bag from the rack and bounds off the train ahead of me. Not a chat-up line then, thank goodness.

Miranda, the agent, is waiting for me outside Toby's studio. She's brisk and to the point, explaining all the benefits of the flat as she walks me through a passageway that leads to the car park where I nearly bought the van last week. According to her, the flats above this parade of shops are in high demand because they're close to the station and the commuter trains to London. I don't dare point out that they can't be in that high demand because this one has been on the market for at least a week. Properly desirable properties in London sometimes go within minutes of being listed. People will commit to them without even seeing them because of the location.

'This flat is a little different from the others,' she explains as we approach the back door of Toby's studio. 'Most of them are accessed by walking up communal staircases, with two flats opposite each other at the top of each staircase. This flat was altered by a previous landlord, so it has an extra access point just inside the rear door of the unit here, which is currently a photographic studio. It's up to you to decide which entrance you prefer. I'll take you in via the studio entrance.'

She unlocks the rear door of Toby's studio and uses another key to open a door on the left that I'd never noticed before. It has a small sign on it that reads 'Private', presumably to prevent people from the studio from trying to open it.

'The landlord is the owner of the studio,' Miranda continues to explain. 'He has keys to the back door we've just come in through, but not the flat. The tenant also has a key to the back door and the flat, but can't access the studio. I'll show you the entrance via the communal staircase as well before we leave.'

She leads me up the stairs into the flat. Whatever I thought I was prepared for, it wasn't this. I'm trying not to let my mouth drop open as I wander around. There's a spacious living room, which is flooded with natural light. The kitchen is modern with sleek units, an electric fan oven and, joy of joys, an induction hob. The main bedroom is also bright and airy, and there's an en-suite with a power shower.

'The landlord used to live here himself,' Miranda tells me. 'So he spared no expense on the fit and finish. For example, the mirror in here is heated so that it doesn't mist up when you have a shower. It's attention to detail like that which really makes this property special.'

I can't get terribly excited about a heated mirror, but she does have a point. This flat is beautifully kitted out. All the windows have evidently been re-glazed fairly recently, and Miranda assures me that it won't cost much to heat as it's well-insulated. It's way better than most of the places I've seen advertised in London and, crucially, I can just afford it on my salary. I've done my research and checked the train ticket prices so I could factor those in, and it's doable. However, I'm nervous about taking the first flat I see in a town I know nothing about.

I continue wandering around. There's a decent-sized second bedroom; I don't imagine I'll be having many overnight guests, but it might make a good study, and a proper bathroom, which is also nicely fitted out. Miranda also shows me the other entrance via the communal stairwell. As she described, there's only one other flat in this stairwell, with the front door directly opposite mine.

'It's really lovely,' I say to Miranda after I've seen everything. 'Can I think about it and give you a call in the week?'

'Of course you can,' she replies. 'Although I have to warn you that I have three other viewings of this flat lined up today, and one of them is a second viewing, so I don't expect it to hang around for long.'

Why does that always happen? I'm paralysed with indecision as I take another walk around. It really is lovely, and I can see myself living here, but I hate being pressured into a major decision like this. What if the neighbours are all nightmarish, or it turns out that the car park is a major drug-dealing spot? Miranda obviously senses my unease.

'Is there anything else you need to know?' she asks. 'I forgot to mention that there is a dedicated car parking space, which is pretty much at the bottom of the communal stairwell, so you don't have far to walk from your car. There are security lights as well and, from what I understand, most of the people who live here are either professionals commuting to London, or they run the businesses on the ground floor.'

I'm still undecided as Miranda locks up and we walk down the communal staircase together. I think I'd feel happier if I knew anything at all about the neighbours. God (if he exists) is obviously listening and having a laugh, because the bottom door opens just as we reach it, and the man from the train steps back to let us out. He's obviously had time to get changed, as he's now dressed in blue jeans under a rugby top. It's clear that he recognises me as well, and I sense he's feeling the awkwardness of the situation just as much as I am.

'Excuse me,' I say to him. 'Is this where you live?'

'Umm, yes,' he replies, looking slightly embarrassed. 'I'm in the flat opposite the one I assume you've just been viewing.'

'I see. Do you like it here?' I continue.

'I do. The rear-facing flats like mine and the one you've just seen are the best ones, because they get better light and they're away from the main road. Plus you're only about five minutes' walk from the station, which is convenient if you need to get to London.' He stops himself. 'I'm sorry,' he continues. 'I guess you already know that part.'

'I do,' I smile.

'I'm not usually on the train on a Saturday, but I had a work thing last night.' He stops again and blushes, obviously realising this is way too much information. 'Is there anything else you'd like to know? There's a really nice café on the ground floor, if that's your thing. That's not an invitation, by the way. Sorry, I'm not very good at this stuff.' He's blushing furiously and the awkwardness hangs in the air like a cloud.

'That's really helpful, thank you,' I tell him, and he practically bolts upstairs, slamming the flat door behind him. Once he's gone, I turn back to Miranda. 'I'll take it,' I tell her.

'Excellent. You won't regret it, I'm sure,' she replies. She gives me a lift to her office, where we fill in the mountain of paperwork that goes with these things, I pay the deposit and she promises to get in touch with a moving date as soon as she's taken up my references. She offers to run me back to the station, but I decline. It's a nice day, and it will give me a chance to have a look at my new home town while I walk back down the hill. On the way up in the car, it seemed that there were just two main streets, but I discover a wealth of little alleys running between them, with interesting-looking shops and cafés. It's not London, but there's a surprising amount here. It'll do, I reckon, although I'm glad I bought the car. Apart from getting to the station and back, I've not had much need for the car as most of my work has been either in London or in places that are easy to reach by train. A bit of internet searching shows that, although there is a small supermarket around fifteen minutes' walk from the flat, the large superstores are both a couple of miles away, so the car is going to come in handy.

I fire up Nutsy the Squirrel again once I'm back on the platform, and I finally manage to complete level two as the train pulls into London Bridge. Level three, however, looks completely impossible. As well as having to chase away the other squirrels, there are now dogs that will chase you and eat you if they get close enough. I've lost several Nutsys to the dogs by the time I reach Uckfield, and I'm no closer to working out what the secret of this level is.

* * *

Once I get home, I start making a list of all the things I'm going to need, and I realise I'm going to have to ask to borrow some more money from Dad, as the costs soon start to mount up beyond my means. I've got a little bit left from the sale of the Land Rover and the money they lent me to begin with but, until my divorce settlement comes though, it's not even going to cover the basics such as furniture. I'm not going to actually order anything until Miranda has confirmed that everything is in place, but it's still fun to scan the websites and see what my limited budget might get me. Whenever I see something I like, I make a note of it so I can come back to it and order later. By the time I've finished, the list is a quirky mix of things from Argos and IKEA, and I've also decided to investigate some second-hand shops when I get time, to see if I can pick up things like sofas, chairs, and tables cheaply. The only thing I can't sort out are curtains, because I didn't measure the windows. I drop an email to Miranda to ask if she can get the measurements for me, but it's after closing time, so I doubt I'll hear back until Monday.

I'm definitely feeling optimistic though, and this is reinforced when Dad agrees to lend me another couple of thousand pounds, which is more than enough for the items I've selected. Even the loss of another four Nutsys and my abject failure to complete level three is not enough to dent my mood. I ring Di and fill her in on the events of the day and, although she's cautious to begin with and worried about how I'll cope 'so far from London', she's very intrigued when I tell her about the man on the train who is to be my new neighbour.

'Is he good-looking?' is her first question.

'I'm going to stop you there,' I reply. 'I'm not even divorced yet, and I'm certainly not in any hurry to get involved with anyone. Plus, he's super shy, I reckon.'

'Still, no harm in a bit of window-shopping so you know what you're looking for when you're ready to buy,' she laughs.

The final piece of good news is a letter from Alison, the lawyer. She tells me that James has agreed to a financial settlement of two hundred and forty thousand pounds. Despite the modest size of the financial settlement in Watson & Fletcher's eyes, the process of reaching agreement has been surprisingly torturous. After receiving the initial demand, James' solicitors deducted five thousand for the Land Rover, which turned out to have been sitting in a barn for years before he got Tony to fix whatever was wrong with it and gave it to me. Alison then promptly slapped on another fifteen thousand for the MX-5, as he'd obviously either pocketed the cash or given it to his father. He was predictably furious at first, apparently, but couldn't come up with a convincing story about where the money had gone, so it stayed in. Then he tried to plead poverty, but Alison told him she knew all about the hundred-acre plot, and that seems to have finally shut him up.

The most surprising thing of all, though, given the fact that I was dating him for three years and married to him for four, is how little of my head space he occupies these days.

20

After what has felt, at times, like the longest six weeks of my life, it's moving day tomorrow! To be fair, I've had the keys to the flat for a couple of weeks, but the furniture has been arriving in dribs and drabs and the curtains are finally supposed to be arriving in the morning. There was no way I could move in without curtains, but Gerald has been a star, going over regularly to receive deliveries or assemble flat-pack furniture while I've been at work. It's starting to look quite homely, from the pictures he's sent me, and I'm looking forward to getting in there and having my own space again. I loaded my clothes and things into the car as soon as I got home from work, so I'm all ready to set off in the morning. Gerald is going over first thing to be there when the curtains come and assemble the final pieces of furniture, and I'm going to do a food shop on the way and join him a bit later.

'Are you all set for your move tomorrow?' Dad asks.

'I think so. Gerald has been incredibly helpful, so everything is pretty much ready to go.'

'You're his favourite human being at the moment, from what

I've heard. He's absolutely thrilled with that Land Rover. Have you seen it?'

'No.'

'Let's sneak out and take a look before dinner. I have to admit that I'm a little curious myself.'

If Margot and Donald are surprised to see Dad and me marching through the kitchen and out of the back door, they're both tactful enough to conceal it. We cross the courtyard and make our way towards the barn where Gerald has been working on the Land Rover in his spare time. Neither of us are surprised to find him in there; what does surprise me is how little of the car is left. The bodywork is nowhere to be seen, the engine is on a bench in the corner, and the chassis is sitting on blocks.

'Evening, Gerald. How is it going?' Dad asks.

'Good evening, sir. It's a bit of a mess, but I'll get there. Like a lot of these cars, it's had a hard life and not been looked after properly. Did you ever try to use the low-range gearbox, Sophie?'

'The what?'

'I thought as much. It has a low-range gearbox, but the mechanism to engage it was completely seized. You only had two-wheel drive as well. They're tough as old boots, these things, but they do need a little bit of TLC from time to time.' He strokes the chassis affectionately as he speaks.

'Where's the rest of it?' I can't help asking.

'I've sent the body off to a mate of mine who is a panel beater. I don't want it immaculate, but I'd like it to be considerably more Land Rover-shaped than it was when you had it.'

'Just so you know, only one of those dents was caused by me,' I warn him, before he takes that line of conversation any further. 'I had a slight disagreement with a gatepost early on, before I'd got used to the size of it.'

'So what's the plan?' Dad asks Gerald. According to Mum, Dad was always tinkering with his cars in the old days, trying to make them faster or louder. It's obviously an interest he still has, because he and Gerald launch into a lengthy conversation about complete strip-downs, nut and bolt restorations, and a load of other stuff that I don't understand. I think the gist of it is that he's taking it apart completely, and then he's going to fix everything that's wrong with it before putting it back together. I'm pleased that someone's showing it some love, but I'm also starting to get a little bored and fidgety.

'We'll leave you to it, Gerald,' Dad says eventually. 'I look forward to seeing it when you've finished.'

'I'll be over at your place first thing to put the curtains up, Sophie,' Gerald tells me as we make our way towards the door.

'Thanks, Gerald. I really appreciate everything you've done,' I reply.

'I'd like to get him a gift, to say thank you,' I mention to Dad, as we're crossing the courtyard back to the house. 'I don't know what he likes, though.'

'Your mother will know. She organises Christmas presents for all the staff. We'll ask her. Now, I've got a bottle of Champagne on ice. It seems only fair to toast your new start.'

* * *

I'm delighted to see that the sun is shining and it looks like it's going to be a glorious day when I open the curtains the next morning. After breakfast, I throw my overnight bag in the car, kiss Mum and Dad goodbye, and set off. I open the sunroof and sing along to my favourite playlist as I follow the satnav through Crowborough and Tunbridge Wells, before picking up the dual carriageway to take me to my new home. When I get there, Gerald has already hung the curtains and he's in the middle of assembling the desk in the second bedroom, now my study. I dump my clothes in the main bedroom, put the KitchenAid mixer on the worktop in the kitchen, and head straight back out to the supermarket.

I'm still feeling upbeat and humming to myself quietly as I wander around, picking up the items on my list. I haven't had to cook for myself since leaving James, so I spent some time deciding exactly what I was going to eat for each meal over the first week and writing down the ingredients. I reckon I'll be back in the swing of it after a few days and next week's shop will be much easier. The trolley is surprisingly full by the time I get to the checkout and I wonder whether I've overestimated the amount of food I need, but I'm committed now, so I smile brightly at the assistant and start loading my bags as if I know exactly what I'm doing. I've included a bottle of whisky for Gerald, as Mum told me that's his guilty pleasure, plus a bottle of gin, some tonic, and a few bottles of wine for me, but I'm still surprised when the bill comes to just over two hundred pounds. James would have had a coronary if I'd spent that much on a weekly shop, but I keep reminding myself that I'm starting from scratch and a lot of the things I've bought will last much longer than a week.

Gerald is pretty much done when I get back, but he still insists on helping me to unload the car and is very pleased with his bottle of whisky. He helps me unpack the shopping, and then we walk round the flat together so he can check that everything is exactly how I wanted it. Suddenly, I feel a strange sensation in the pit of my stomach that I haven't felt since I was a child. It's nervousness mixed with a little bit of dread, knowing that he's going to go very soon and I'll be on my own for the first time in years. I used to have it at the beginning of every term and the end of every exeat when I was at prep school; there would always be crumpets for tea before Mum and I climbed into the car to take me back, and I'd struggle to eat them, even though I love them normally. I can still remember all the landmarks that I used to look out for on the journey. The first one was a house on the corner of one of the junctions where we turned. I have no idea why I chose that house and not any of the others we passed on the way. Every time we passed it, the feeling in my stomach would ramp up a notch because we were that bit closer to our destination. Then we would pass the sign indicating the village where the school was, followed by the turn into the driveway. The smell of polish and expensive perfume in the hallway and the noise created by a hundred or so parents dropping off their daughters was the final indicator of my impending abandonment, and I frequently had to fight back tears. It was ridiculous, really, as I quite enjoyed being at school and would throw myself into it quite happily once Mum was gone. It all comes back to me so clearly, despite the fact that I'm an adult and this situation is completely different.

Eventually, Gerald declares himself satisfied, hands me the key he's been using, and we walk down the stairs together. The parking spaces are very generous here, so I've tucked my car behind his pick-up, but I need to move it to let him out. Once he's gone, I park the car back in the space and let myself back into the flat. Suddenly, for no reason that I can fathom, I'm crying. The tears build into huge sobs, and I sit on the sofa and just let it all out. I'm not even really sure what I'm crying for; it's a mixture of facing the future alone, mourning the years wasted on a man who didn't love me as he should have done, and being in a strange place where I don't know anyone. I'm desperately homesick even though this is now my home, and the paradox of that just makes me cry harder. Maybe I've been holding it all in recently, putting on a brave face, but I don't think I have been. Now that I'm here, in the private space that I've craved for so long, everything just seems overwhelming.

I don't know how long I sit sobbing on the sofa, but eventually the tears start to slow, and I set about unpacking my suitcases. I still have the odd sniffle, but the activity gives me something else to focus on for a while. I'm conscious that I've got a whole weekend to get through before I'm back in the office and will have work to distract me, and that feels very daunting at the moment. The desire to jump back in the car and spend the weekend with Mum and Dad is pretty strong, but I remind myself that I'm never going to be able to start over properly if I keep rushing back to their house every time I'm a bit lonely.

Once I've unpacked, I treat myself to a chilled glass of wine, put on some soothing music, and decide to run myself a hot bath. The en-suite only has a shower, so I wrap myself in my dressing gown and pad across to the main bathroom. I try to empty my mind as I lie back in the bath, enjoying the warmth of the water and listening to the music, but another unwelcome thought has broken in and I can't get rid of it.

Eventually, I can't take any more. I climb out of the bath, dry myself, and stand naked in front of the mirror. I let my eyes wander up and down my reflection as I ask myself the question, 'Is this it? Will any man ever see or touch my body again?' James and I are patently over, but I still can't imagine being naked with anyone else. Despite Di's jokes about my neighbour, even the idea of going on a date fills me with horror. Maybe this is it, and I'm going to be single for the rest of my life, dying alone surrounded by angry cats. That thought is too depressing and I take a swig of wine to wash it away.

One day at a time, I tell myself. Concentrate on getting through the weekend and worry about the big things later.

21

I wake in a much more positive frame of mind, thankfully. My new bed is incredibly comfortable and, after a pretty successful supper of salmon with new potatoes and broccoli, washed down with some more wine, I slept like a baby. I quickly learn that the power shower has to be treated with respect, as the jets are almost strong enough to skin you alive if you turn it up all the way. I've decided to treat myself to breakfast at the café downstairs before heading out for a proper explore of the area. It's another bright day and the sunlight pours into the flat when I open the curtains. I let myself out through the original front door into the communal stairway. I haven't seen the man from the flat opposite again and, after the awkwardness of our last encounter, I'm not sure whether I should knock on his door and introduce myself properly or not. We never had anything to do with our neighbours in London, apart from the occasional row if someone played music too loud or too late at night, but maybe people are friendlier here? He certainly seemed like he was trying to be friendly, in his excruciating way.

The café is jam-packed, but the young woman behind the counter assures me that a table will come free soon if I'm prepared to wait. It's not as if I have anything else to do, so I tell her that's fine and, after five minutes or so, an elderly couple vacate their table and I take their place. The menu features every type of breakfast dish, from omelettes and eggs Benedict through to a full English breakfast. I think the full English is probably a bit much for me – I can see another customer attacking theirs with gusto and it is certainly generous – so I wander up to the counter and order eggs Benedict and a flat white coffee.

'Got any special plans for the day?' the assistant asks conversationally as she's writing down my order and ringing it up on the till.

'I don't know yet,' I reply. 'I just moved here, so I thought I might explore, try to get a feel for the place and learn where everything is.'

'That's nice. Whereabouts are you living?'

'Literally upstairs, in one of the flats above the photographic studio. I moved in yesterday.'

She looks up from her pad and beams. 'We're neighbours, then! Yours must be the flat that Steve used to live in. He moved up to London a month or two ago. My other half and I live in the rear flat above the café, next to you. Daisy, who owns this place, lives with her fiancé in the flat in front of ours, and then there's elusive Elliott the other side of you. The Singhs, who own the pharmacy next door, live the other side of us, but we don't see much of them, and I have no idea who lives in the flat in front of yours or Elliott's. Is your partner not with you this morning?'

'Umm, I don't have a partner,' I tell her, while trying to digest the information overload she's just delivered. 'I moved here on my own.'

'Oh! I'm so sorry,' she blushes. 'It's just that we've seen a man coming and going, bringing in furniture and stuff, so I'm afraid I assumed...'

'Don't worry,' I tell her, as understanding dawns. 'That was

Gerald. He works for my father and was just helping me out, doing all the flat-pack assembly and stuff.'

'That makes sense,' she replies, and her smile is back. 'If you don't mind me saying, he did look a bit old for you.'

I can't help laughing at her candour. 'I'm Sophie,' I tell her.

'Bronwyn,' she replies. 'Now, if you want to take a seat and relax, I'll bring everything over to you when it's ready.'

While I'm waiting, I take in my surroundings. The café is bright and cheery, with lots of pictures on the walls. Each one has a little label next to it with a price on it, so they're obviously for sale. If I thought I was getting special friendly treatment from Bronwyn, I'm soon proved wrong; she's exactly the same with everyone. Quite a few of the customers appear to be regulars; she greets them enthusiastically by name and seems to be able to predict their orders without them having to say anything. The whole place is buzzing with conversation, which is nice in one way, but also brings my isolation into sharp focus. Momentarily overwhelmed, I toy with the idea of getting up and leaving, but Bronwyn appears with my coffee just before I do, and I'm actually quite hungry. There's no sign of Matt, the guy who lent me the van. He probably wouldn't remember me anyway.

I sip my coffee, which is as delicious as it smells and, after a few minutes, Bronwyn brings my eggs Benedict. My stomach growls with anticipation as I spot the beautifully poached egg sitting on top of thickly sliced ham, with the muffin peeking out from underneath. The whole thing is covered with just the right amount of hollandaise sauce.

'I hope you don't mind,' Bronwyn tells me as she sets it down, 'but I was just chatting with Daisy in the kitchen, and I mentioned that you'd moved in. The four of us usually get together on a Saturday evening, for something to eat and a few glasses of wine. If you're free, we'd love you to join us tonight.'

'Are you sure?' I ask. 'I wouldn't want to impose.'

'Of course I'm sure!' she laughs. 'It's no big deal, honestly. Consider it a welcome thing.'

'In that case, I'd love to,' I tell her.

'Excellent. It's our turn to host, so if you ring the bell for Flat 2b at around seven, that would be perfect. Is there anything you don't eat?' She glances at my breakfast. 'I'm guessing you're not a vegetarian.'

'Unless you're planning on serving oysters, I'm pretty easy. Can I bring anything?'

'Just yourself. See you later!'

After my breakfast and my conversation with Bronwyn, I feel even more buoyed up. I'm just letting myself back into the flat when my neighbour comes out of his front door.

'You took it then,' he observes.

'How could I not have done after your wholehearted recommendation?' I smile, to indicate that I'm joking.

'Erm, yes. Sorry about that. You caught me a little bit by surprise, and I'm afraid I babbled a bit.' He blushes slightly.

'It's fine. It really was useful. I don't know anything about Sevenoaks, so it was handy to get the lowdown from a local.'

'I wouldn't exactly call myself that, but I'm pleased I could help. I'm Elliott, by the way.'

'Sophie.' I hold out my hand and we shake, but then another awkward silence descends as neither of us appear to know what to say or do next. Eventually, he breaks it.

'Well, I'm off to the supermarket. I'll see you around, yeah?'

With that, he bounds down the stairs and out of the door. I make a mental note to ask Bronwyn about him later. I remember her referring to him as 'elusive Elliott', so there's obviously a story there. I'm also curious to meet Bronwyn's partner; she seems such a free spirit that I find it hard to imagine what sort of man she would go for. I doubt there's ever a dull moment when Bronwyn's around.

* * *

I take my time exploring Sevenoaks and the surrounding area. I drive up into the centre of town and wander up and down the streets and alleys until I've got a pretty good idea of where everything is. As it's a Saturday, there is a market on the High Street, so I stop and buy myself some olives, cheese, and a loaf of artisan bread. I also pop into the Waitrose at the top of the High Street and buy a couple of bottles of wine to take with me tonight. I know Bronwyn said not to bring anything, but I can't turn up empty-handed; it would just feel wrong. On the other main street, I discover a home store that sells everything from nails to cookware, and I take the opportunity to buy a couple of items I forgot about in my planning, including salt and pepper mills. I'm happily loading my purchases into the car when my phone rings. I glance at the caller ID and my heart sinks. It's Rosalind.

'Hello?' I try to keep my voice as neutral as possible, but it probably still sounds hostile.

'Sophie, dear, it's Rosalind. I know our last conversation didn't end on the best of notes, but I realise you were probably upset and so I've decided to forgive you. I wanted to have a little chat, woman to woman.'

Evil old witch to woman, more like.

'It's not really a good time, Rosalind. Can I call you back later?' I ask her, in the hope she'll get the message and I can hang up on her. I make a mental note to block her number as soon as this call is over. There's no way I'll be calling her back.

'I'll be quick,' she continues, completely ignoring me. 'It's about this divorce settlement. You know as well as I do that James can't possibly pay the amount your solicitor is demanding. It would ruin him. I was hoping that I could appeal to your better nature and we could come up with something more, um, *reasonable* between us.'

I'm flabbergasted. She obviously doesn't know that James has already agreed the settlement, and thinks it's okay to stick her nose in.

'Rosalind, do you have any idea how inappropriate this conversation is?' I ask her, incredulously. 'Does James know you're ringing me?'

'No, but he's been very stressed lately and I'm worried that he's not coping. Look, I know he acted like a fool and I understand that you want to make a point, but bankrupting him isn't the way to go about it.'

I can hear Alison's voice in the back of my head telling me to back away, to refuse to discuss it and to leave it to her, but Rosalind has riled me and I can't help myself.

'Do you seriously think I'm doing this just to "make a point"?'

'Well, it's not as if you need the money, is it? Your father...'

'You are absolutely unbelievable,' I interrupt. 'None of this is any of your business, yet you still feel entitled to ring me up and have a go? Since you're so obsessed with how wealthy my father is, shall I let you into a little secret?'

'If you like.'

'Do you know one of the reasons why he's wealthy? It's because he doesn't let himself be taken for nearly a quarter of a million pounds by a low-rent con artist like your son, and I'm not going to let that happen either. Am I making myself clear?'

'Crystal,' she spits, and the tone of faux camaraderie with which she started the call has totally vanished. Her claws are definitely out now. 'But let me be just as clear in return. He *will* lose the farm that's been in our family for generations, and it *will* be your fault. How will you sleep at night, knowing what you've done?'

'I will sleep just fine because that's bullshit,' I reply. 'I know about the hundred-acre plot, Rosalind.'

'What plot?' She sounds truly blindsided.

'Ask James,' I reply, and hang up.

My hands are trembling with anger as I go into the call log and find the icon to block her number. My only consolation is that she genuinely didn't seem to know about the plot of land that James is refusing to sell; I wouldn't mind being a fly on the wall in that conversation. Unfortunately, her call has completely popped my good mood, and even the delicious bread-and-cheese lunch doesn't get rid of the dark cloud that talking to her has left. I send an email with the details of the conversation to Alison so that she knows what has happened, and I feel a new surge of anger as I replay Rosalind's words. I need to let off some steam, so I pull on my coat and go for a good stomp around the block, but all that does is defuse the anger and leave me feeling sad and empty. I'm certainly in no mood to be good company tonight and I decide to call into the café on my way back and make some excuse as to why I can't go. However, when I get back, it's closed for the day. I don't have a number for Bronwyn and I don't want to disturb her before the time she gave, so it looks like I'll just have to put a brave face on and make the best of it.

I'm not feeling much better when I ring the doorbell at the bottom of the next stairwell along from mine at seven o'clock, clutching the two bottles of wine I bought earlier. The buzzer goes to let me in, one of the doors at the top bursts open and Bronwyn appears, beaming from ear to ear. She's wearing a white T-shirt, dungaree shorts that show off her shapely legs, and Doc Martens on her feet. I never really noticed earlier, but she is incredibly beautiful. Her smile takes over her entire face, and her eyes are sparkling with delight.

'You came!' she exclaims, as she wraps me in a hug. 'I wasn't sure whether you would. Come in and meet everyone.'

She releases me and stands aside so that I can enter the flat. Straight away, I can see that the layout is a mirror of mine but, where my flat is modern and possibly a little sterile, hers is a riot of colour. The walls are covered with paintings, the sofas have throws and cushions that border on the psychedelic, and the theme is continued with the rugs on the floor. It's not my taste, and I think it might give me a headache if I lived here, but I can't help but admire the style. Despite the myriad colours and patterns, it all works.

I turn my attention to the other people in the room. I recognise Matt instantly; he's sitting on one of the sofas with his arm around a curvaceous, dark-haired woman that Bronwyn introduces as Daisy, the owner of the café. If I thought Matt would have forgotten me, I was mistaken.

'I remember you.' He beams and turns to Daisy. 'This is the woman who wanted to buy my van a few weeks ago.'

'Really? That's such a good story,' Bronwyn interjects. 'I love how you were prepared to buy Matt's clapped-out old van, just so Toby could have his Champagne reception. That's really going above and beyond, I reckon.'

I can't help but smile. 'I'm just so grateful to Matt for lending it to me and getting me out of a massive hole,' I tell her, before turning back to him. 'Have you managed to sell it yet?'

'Yup,' he replies. 'I sold it to a pigeon fancier who wanted something to transport his birds in. He was delighted with it.'

'Not as delighted as I was to see the back of it,' Daisy retorts.

At that moment, the door to the kitchen opens and another dark-haired young woman comes out, holding a glass of wine.

'Dinner should be another half-hour or so. It's lasagne,' she announces.

'Katie, this is Sophie, our new neighbour,' Bronwyn tells her, indicating me. 'Sophie, this is Katie, my other half.'

22

The evening with Bronwyn, Katie, Daisy, and Matt carries my mood through the rest of the weekend. I can't remember the last time I enjoyed myself so much – actually, it was probably the evening I spent with the girls at Di's house just after I'd caught James and Becky the first time. However, this one was even better for not having the spectre of James hanging over it. My surprise at Bronwyn's partner being another woman was nothing compared to finding out that Katie and Daisy were sisters. Yes, they both have dark hair, but the resemblance pretty much stops there. I learned that Katie is at Cambridge University studying for her law degree. She stays in her college in the week but comes back pretty much every weekend. It turns out that Bronwyn only works in the café on Saturdays; the rest of the time she's a successful artist. Katie told me proudly that the pictures for sale in the café are all hers, and they sell pretty well. She also exhibits in a local art gallery and gets quite a few commissions.

Daisy and Matt were lovely too, if a little quieter than Bronwyn. They recently got engaged and are just starting to plan their wedding, so we chatted about that for a little while. From the noises that Katie and Bronwyn were making, I don't imagine they will be far behind. What surprised me was that, although I should have felt like a massive gooseberry, they all just welcomed me and made me feel comfortable. I didn't learn any more about Elliott, although there was a lot of speculation. Apparently, he calls into the café every weekday morning and gets a latté with an extra shot to take away, but nobody ever sees him other than that. Penny, who does Bronwyn's job in the café on weekdays, tried to engage him in conversation to find out more about him once but, although he was perfectly polite, she got nowhere.

It's now Monday morning, and I've taken a leaf out of Elliott's book and grabbed a coffee from the café before heading for the station to catch my train to Charing Cross. I've got a busy week ahead, putting the finishing touches to a launch party for a new celebrity perfume on Thursday evening. All of the printed materials have already arrived, including very swanky-looking bags for the guests to take their samples home in. The caterers are also under control, as is the booze side of things. From here on in, I'm going to be poring over every detail, no matter how small, and double-checking it. Thankfully, Emily has been as good as her word and there haven't been any more sabotage attempts since I confronted her. In fact, she's actually started asking for help and, as I predicted, everyone is being very supportive. Annabel is starting to trust her more, although she still makes sure that one of us checks everything with her to make sure she hasn't missed anything. She's coming on well, though, and I don't think it will be long before she's flying solo.

The platform is busy as I work my way along. Most of the people here are obviously commuters, because there are little clumps of them at regular intervals, presumably where they know the train doors will be when it stops. I join a group near the front and sip my coffee. The train, when it comes, is already very crowded and I can't see any free seats. The doors open and our little group squashes its way inside. I try to secure a spot near the door so I've got something to lean on but I'm pushed towards the centre of the carriage by the people boarding behind me. In the end, I stick my legs out as far as I dare to give me something to brace against as the train rocks and shudders its way down the track. The last thing I want to do is bump into someone and spill coffee on them. My cup has a lid, but I've seen those fly off in the past. I make a note to buy myself a reusable cup like the man standing next to me.

I lift my eyes to his face, and I'm surprised to find out that the guy I'm practically pressed against is Elliott. He's holding a tablet computer which appears to have one of the daily newspapers on it. He seems engrossed, so I take the opportunity to study him. Facially, he's fairly unremarkable. He has light, sandy-coloured hair, even features, and round, wire-framed glasses. His light-blue, open-neck shirt is perfectly pressed today, he's wearing what look like the same dark trousers over well-polished black shoes, and I can detect a faint whiff of cologne. He obviously takes pride in his appearance. I glance at his face again; his skin is smooth without a hint of stubble. There's a tiny mark on his neck where he obviously nicked himself shaving, but other than that, his skin is flawless. I'd love to stroke it, to see if it feels as smooth as it looks.

'Hello again. How are you settling in?' he asks, snapping me back to reality and causing me to blush slightly. He obviously caught me staring at him.

'It's going well, thank you. I've already met some of the other neighbours.'

'Oh yes?' He seems genuinely curious.

'I tried out the café on Saturday morning, and ended up spending the evening with Daisy, who owns it, her sister Katie, and their partners. They were really nice.'

'Ah, okay. I don't really know them. The people in the café always seem pleasant enough, though. So, I take it you work in London?'

'Yes, I'm an events planner. How about you?'

'IT.'

Just then, the train gives an almighty lurch, and I accidentally squeeze my coffee cup as I try to keep my balance. It's not enough to dislodge the lid, thankfully, but a little bit of coffee spurts out of the drinking hole, catching Elliott on the cheek.

'Oh, God. I'm so sorry!' I exclaim. 'Let me see if I can find you a tissue.' I start rummaging in my bag.

'Don't worry about it. There's no harm done. You might want to think about getting a more robust coffee cup, though. Those single-use ones are a bit of a liability.' He wipes his cheek and turns back to his tablet, indicating that the conversation is over.

I don't want to be caught staring at him again, so I busy myself looking at emails on my phone. There's nothing on there that can't wait, so I decide to pass the rest of the journey playing Nutsy the Squirrel. At one point, I'm sure I can feel Elliott watching me, but his eyes are firmly on his tablet when I glance up, so it's probably me being irrational.

When we get to London Bridge, there's a bit of shuffling around while those getting off the train try to squeeze past those who are staying on. Elliott is one of those getting off, and he gives me a brief nod of acknowledgement as he goes. The good news is that there are now plenty of seats available and I sink gratefully into one of them. It's about twenty minutes' walk from Charing Cross to the office and I arrive at ten to nine, pleased that my new commute seems much more manageable than the flog from Uckfield. Yes, standing on the train wasn't ideal, but it's no different to standing on the Tube or the bus, and I do that a lot when I'm travelling around London. Emily is already at her desk when I arrive.

'Can I run something past you?' she asks, once I'm settled and have powered up my computer.

'Sure.'

This is normal behaviour from her lately. We have a weekly meeting every Monday where Lucy, Emily and I have to walk Annabel through each event that we're working on. After a couple of rebukes from Annabel, Emily has taken to getting me to check her stuff before she presents it. She leads me through the plan for a wedding she's working on and I have to admit that I'm impressed. Everything is neatly documented along with backup plans and schedules.

'This looks really good, Emily,' I tell her.

'Is there anything I've missed?'

'Nothing that I can see. How's the bride?'

'Hard work, but I think she's beginning to trust that I know what I'm doing.'

'The trick is to come across like a swan. You will probably be paddling like mad until it's over, but if she doesn't see that then she'll be more relaxed and stay off your back.'

Emily laughs. 'Here's hoping!'

Annabel is obviously pleased too, and Emily is positively beaming by the end of the meeting. She's like a different person these days, and I find it hard to find any evidence of the bitter woman who wanted to bring me down. Let's hope she stays that way.

The rest of the day passes in a flurry of emails and phone calls, along with a visit to the venue to check the preparations. It's well after eight o'clock by the time I get to Charing Cross to catch my train, and I'm delighted to find that there are plenty of seats available; it's been a long day and I don't really want to stand all the way home. Once I'm back at the flat, I pull out the tuna pasta salad that I made yesterday in anticipation that I'd be too tired to cook and flop in front of the TV. Now that I'm back at work and I've got a sense of what my 'normal' life is going to look like, I'm not at all unhappy. The commute is okay, the flat is very comfortable, and I have some lovely neighbours. Even Elliott was reasonably friendly this morning.

Thinking of Elliott makes me remember that I was going to look for a reusable coffee cup. Realistically, that will have to wait until the weekend at the earliest. I'm going to be flat out until Thursday now. Still, the launch is shaping up nicely, and I'm looking forward to a late start and working from home on Friday. Annabel is a stickler for us taking rest time the next day if we've had to work through an evening, as she's convinced tired planners are a liability.

* * *

The next couple of days follow a similar pattern. I see Elliott on the platform each morning but, despite being crammed together in the carriage, we don't have any more conversation. We do acknowledge each other, but only with a nod or raised eyebrow when we clock each other on the platform and when he gets off at London Bridge. I never see him on the evening train, but that's not surprising given that the earliest I leave work is half past seven.

By the time Thursday dawns, everything is in place for the launch. I've checked and double-checked every detail, and even run the whole plan past Emily, which absolutely delighted her. I took the evening gown I'm planning to wear, along with a reserve in case of disaster, to the dry cleaner near the office earlier this week, so they're both pressed and ready to go. Shoes and tights are also sorted, and I'll change at the office just before I leave to go to the venue. I'm staying over in London tonight so I don't have to worry about missing the last train, but I'll head home as soon as I can tomorrow.

The venue looks amazing when I get there and I breathe a sigh of relief. I stick my overnight bag in the cloakroom and check in on the caterers, who seem to have everything under control. The waiting staff also seem well briefed, but we walk through the timings on a whiteboard just to be certain. The main function room layout is exactly as I'd planned it, and every table has a large bottle of the new fragrance as the centrepiece. They're actually filled with coloured water to keep the costs down, but nobody will notice that, particularly once they've had a glass or two of fizz. The celebrity, an American pop star, is due to make her appearance at 9.30 p.m., when she will give a short speech written by a publicist at the perfume company followed by a meet-and-greet with selected guests. It's all choreographed to the second and, assuming nothing goes wrong, there shouldn't be much for me to do.

Of course, things do go wrong, but I'm able to keep on top of them and the client declares himself delighted when the evening finally wraps up a little after two in the morning. The guests have melted away, clutching their freebies, and the staff are packing everything up as I do my final checks before summoning a taxi to the hotel.

My mind is already contemplating the weekend as the taxi trundles through the deserted streets. I don't really know why; I've been invited to Daisy's on Saturday evening, which should be fun, but I don't have anything else planned. I'm looking forward to sharing what I've learned about Elliott. It's slim pickings, but it's more than Bronwyn has been able to find out. I do need to sort out the reusable coffee cup, though; I don't think I'm going to learn much more about him if I keep throwing coffee at him.

23

I am a free agent, at last. It's been just over six months since I left James, and the divorce has finally come through. I don't miss him at all, but I am weirdly going to miss Alison, the lawyer. Ed was completely right about her; she's been as tenacious as a Rottweiler all the way through. I know she was just doing her job, but it's felt like more than that. It's as if she's been fighting my corner for me, which I suppose she has, and I'm hugely grateful to her for it. The money landed in my account a few days ago, and I've not only repaid the various loans Mum and Dad have given me, but I've also arranged a bouquet of flowers as a thank-you gift to Alison. Dad won't tell me what the bill from the law firm was, but I know it must have been a lot.

The train is a bit quieter today and Elliott and I are sitting opposite each other at a table. We do have the occasional conversation now, but it's still pretty limited. On Mondays we enquire after each other's weekends, and on Fridays we wish each other a good weekend. Mostly, we only see each other on the train platform, but we have occasionally found ourselves leaving our flats at the same time, or we've met by chance in the café when getting our coffees.

When that happens, we walk to the station companionably enough, but our conversation is strictly surface level.

Now that I'm completely free of James and I have the money to start again, it feels like I need to make some decisions, so I'm staring out of the window and pondering things this morning rather than dealing with emails or fighting with Nutsy. Even after repaying Mum and Dad, I've got enough to put down a substantial deposit on a property if I want to, but I'm not sure I do. I'm quite happy in my flat for the time being. It has everything I need, and there's a real sense of community. Okay, so I still don't know Elliott that well, but I'm kind of used to him, and he seems to have accepted me in return. Bronwyn has firmly inducted me into their Saturday-night club, and we now rotate around the three flats. It does get out of sync occasionally if I'm working over a weekend, but the Saturday nights are definitely the highlight of my week. I'd lose all that if I moved. On the other hand, paying rent is 'dead' money, as my father puts it. I don't know. Maybe I'll keep a vague eye on the property market and see if anything tempting comes up.

'You seem preoccupied this morning, if you don't mind me saying. Is everything all right?' Elliott's voice makes me jump.

'Sorry?' I bring my focus back inside the carriage and look at him.

'I didn't mean to pry, it's just that you look like you've got the weight of the world on you this morning, and I wondered if you were okay.'

'I'm fine, just grappling with some decisions, that's all.'

'Work stuff?'

'No, personal. My divorce has just come through, so I'm thinking about what to do next.'

'I'm sorry. I didn't realise you were married.'

'I'm not. At least, not any more,' I smile. 'But now that it's all finalised, I'm trying to decide whether to stay in the flat, or whether I should look at buying something.'

He studies me for a minute. Just as I'm starting to feel slightly uncomfortable under his gaze, he speaks.

'Would you consider it very rude if I made a suggestion? One divorce veteran to another?'

That's an interesting nugget. I didn't know he'd been married either, and I file it away to report back to Bronwyn.

'Go ahead.'

'Don't feel you need to make any decisions right now. Divorce is traumatic, so take time to heal. Rediscover yourself and what you want out of life, and then make the changes you need.'

I know he's probably right, but I do feel a little patronised and annoyed. I did invite his comment, though, so I thank him as gracefully as I can, and he seems to take that as his cue to disengage. I resume staring out of the window. Annoyed as I am, he does have a point. Maybe I can invest the money from the divorce, and then it's there at a later date if I need it. That seems like a sensible idea, and I make a note to ask Dad to put me in touch with one of his financial advisers as the train begins to slow down on the approach to London Bridge. To Elliott's obvious surprise, I also get off the train.

'I've got an all-day meeting with a client near here today,' I explain to him as we make our way towards the escalators. 'I'm not stalking you, I promise.'

'I never thought for a moment that you were,' he replies with a smile. I find his smile slightly unnerving. I've only ever seen it a couple of times because he's normally very serious. But when he smiles, there's a brief glimpse of a different person to the intensely private man he normally is. I'd love to meet that one; he looks like he might be fun.

* * *

The engagement is one of the biggest we've ever pitched for. We've been shortlisted to organise a trade fair, and we're all involved with it. It's so important to her that Annabel has even hired a temp to answer the office phones for the day so that we can all be here. I hurry to the coffee shop where Annabel, Lucy, and Emily are already waiting. We've agreed to meet here beforehand for final checks before we go up in front of the prospective client. It's going to be a gruelling day and we've got to make sure our plans are watertight to have any hope of landing the job. If we get it, it will be a major boost for the company, but we're up against tough competition and Annabel is keen that we leave nothing to chance. We're the last to pitch, so we've really got to stand out. The fair itself is not for another twelve months, but we'll need to start work on it right away if we're successful. It's going to be a stretch handling this on top of our other work, but Annabel is muttering about recruiting another planner if we land this client, so that will help.

Annabel is going to be first up, presenting the company and its ethos. The aim here is to demonstrate 'synergy' between us and the client, according to her. Then we'll walk through our proposals, and she has warned us that the people on the panel are going to be forensic, diving deep into every detail. We've prepared a wealth of materials, from slide decks to 3D walkthroughs, as well as large-scale prints to go on the walls and packs covering every aspect of our proposal. Annabel has spared no expense on this one, so we're all really keen for it to pay off.

By the end of the day, we're exhausted but optimistic. The panel was initially hostile, but they definitely softened through the day and were making very positive noises by the end. Everyone on our side worked incredibly hard, and I was particularly impressed by Emily, who answered some challenging questions confidently and with just the right amount of detail. I really don't think we could have done any more, and now we just have to wait. We agree that we'll debrief in the office tomorrow and head our separate ways.

* * *

If I thought Charing Cross was busy during rush hour, it's nothing compared to London Bridge. It may be an enormous station, but it's teeming with people. I make my way over to the departure boards to try to figure out when the next train to Sevenoaks leaves, before heading towards the escalator to take me up to the right platform. It's even worse when I get up there. The whole platform is crammed with people and, every time a train comes in, there's a surge forwards as people rush to board. It's making me feel quite claustrophobic. A Sevenoaks train arrives, but it turns out I'm standing in the wrong place and, by the time I get to the nearest door, it's obvious that I'm never going to be able to squeeze myself in there even if I wanted to.

'There'll be another one along in fifteen minutes or so,' a familiar voice tells me. I turn and come face to face with Elliott.

'This is horrific!' I exclaim. 'Do you do this every day?'

'It's worse today, because there has been a load of cancellations due to a signal failure earlier, so people are just getting on any train that will get them out of London in the hope of changing trains later. It's always pretty busy, though. We'll get the next one with any luck.'

'I'm not sure I can face it,' I tell him. 'I might come back later when it's calmed down.'

'Really? What will you do?' He seems genuinely interested.

'I don't know. Maybe I'll find a pub somewhere and have a glass of wine, perhaps get something to eat. You don't fancy joining me, do you?'

I have no idea why I said that, a definite case of failing to engage my brain before opening my mouth. Elliott is obviously embarrassed, as I can see him trying to find a way to turn me down politely.

'Sorry, that was silly of me. Forget I said anything,' I tell him. 'I'll see you on the platform tomorrow, okay?'

I don't wait for his reply, but turn away and start fighting my way through the crowd to get back to the escalator. I really need to get out of here, as the sheer number of people pressing against each other and blocking my path is starting to make me feel a bit panicky. Eventually, I reach the escalator and make my way back down into the foyer, positioning myself out of the main flow of people while I catch my breath. Once the claustrophobia has subsided, I reach into my pocket and bring out my phone to search for somewhere suitable to go.

'How are you with Lebanese?' Elliott's voice asks. I look up from the screen to find him standing right in front of me. I'm so surprised that it takes me a moment to reply.

'Umm, fine, I guess,' I manage.

'There's a place about five minutes away. It's always pretty busy, which I reckon is a good sign, but there are usually a couple of free tables. I've never been in, but I'm happy to give it a try if you are? There are plenty of other places if not.'

'Lebanese it is,' I tell him.

The restaurant is obviously popular, but there are some free tables outside under the patio heaters as Elliott predicted, so we settle ourselves at one of them and start perusing the menu. It all looks delicious, but what I'd really like is a glass of wine, so we place our drinks order with the waitress and promise to order food shortly.

'Have you had any more thoughts about what you're going to do?' Elliott asks, as I take the first sip of Sauvignon Blanc. It's cold and crisp, and I almost sigh with pleasure.

'What do you mean?' I reply.

'The thing that we were talking about on the train this morning. Sorry, I'm not being nosy, I'm just trying to make conversation. It's been a while, so forgive me if I'm a little rusty.'

'You do seem very private,' I tell him. 'We're next-door neighbours, and we get on the same train pretty much every morning, but I feel like I hardly know you.'

'I'm sorry. The truth is that I seem to have lost the knack of chatting easily with people I don't know well. I've never been particularly outgoing, but I guess living on my own has made me even less sociable.' He smiles. 'Perhaps I'm a modern-day hermit.'

'Hmm. You don't look like a hermit. I'm pretty sure most of them don't commute, for a start. In fact, I'm fairly certain that a central part of the whole hermit gig is kind of staying where you are. I think you're also supposed to have a long beard with bits of twig and stuff in it.'

He laughs. I've never heard him laugh before, but it's deep and rich. Again, I get that tantalising glimpse of someone else. He's like a crab in some ways. On the outside there's this hard, protective shell, but there's something completely different inside. Thinking of crab meat puts my mind back on to food, and I pick up the menu again.

'What about you?' I ask him, once we've placed our orders.

'What about me what?'

'You said you were divorced. What happened?'

He looks deeply uncomfortable, and I realise I've overstepped the mark.

'I'm sorry. That was crass of me,' I tell him. 'I was just curious because it's something we have in common, that's all. Let's talk about something else.'

'It's fine. You just caught me unawares,' he replies. 'Her name was... is, Nikki. She was a friend of a friend, and we met at said friend's birthday party one year. I should have seen the warning signs at the start, but she was beautiful and I was smitten. We got engaged after six months and married a year later. I thought I'd hit the jackpot; this might come as a surprise to you, but IT isn't the kind of career that many people consider to be especially sexy, so I was definitely batting above my league.'

'What were the warning signs?'

'Her mother, mainly. She was completely overbearing. I think Nikki was looking to me as a way to escape from her mum, but they were so totally enmeshed, it was never going to happen. I was just so desperate for this beautiful girl to be my wife that I didn't pay it the attention I should have.'

'So, when you got married...?' I prompt him.

'Did you ever see that interview with Princess Diana where she said she felt there were three people in the marriage? It was like that. There was me, Nikki, and her mum. We just couldn't escape her. The other issue we discovered, which perhaps I also should have noticed before we got married, is that we had absolutely nothing in common. So things began to unravel very quickly.'

'Whose idea was it to split up?'

'Mine. She went berserk and, of course, so did her mother. Between them, they decided to make things as difficult for me as possible. We fought over every little thing, and when I got exasperated and said I didn't want anything and she could keep it all, she wanted to fight about that too.'

'I'm sorry. That sounds awful.'

'It was. Anyway, in the end I moved out into the flat opposite yours and left her to get on with it. I've been there for four years, and I reckon I'm healing slowly. What about you?'

I fill him in on James and his multiple infidelities as we eat our starters and, by the time we've eaten our puddings, I wouldn't say we were friends exactly, but we certainly know a lot more about each other. I'm used to the fact that he's easy on the eye but I've learned that, when he relaxes, he's also very good company. I'm surprised to see it's after nine o'clock by the time we brave the station again. It's a lot quieter now, and we manage to get on a train without having to jostle anyone. There are quite a few seats, and we pass the short journey to Sevenoaks in companionable silence. I've seen a different side to Elliott tonight and I've realised that the hard shell is there to protect the wounds his ex-wife has inflicted on him. I'm flattered that he chose to share some of his story with me, and I know I have to treat it with respect. Bronwyn, Katie, and Daisy will have to go without a full debrief this time.

24

'Sophie, can you come into my office for a moment?' Annabel has stuck her head out of her door and all eyes are on me as I grab my notepad and head for her glass-fronted cubicle.

'Have a seat.' She indicates the chair in front of her desk and I follow her instruction, nervously perching on the edge. Annabel generally only summons people into her office to tear them off a strip when they've cocked something up. When we didn't get the trade fair contract a few months ago, she went through a phase of picking us up on literally everything until Lucy got the hump and told her she wouldn't have a company at all if she pissed us off so much that we all upped and left. Since then, things have returned to normal.

I know Annabel was really disappointed not to have won the contract, but I think Lucy, Emily, and I were all secretly a little relieved in the end. There's no doubt that it would have raised our profile immensely, but the reality is that we're probably too small to cope with a job that large. It would have taken all of us working full-time to bring it to fruition, and we'd have lost a number of existing customers in the process. It's never a good idea to have all your eggs in one basket, in my opinion, and that contract would have put us firmly in that situation. The good news is that the client was really impressed by our pitch and has already engaged us for a few smaller events, so it wasn't a total loss.

'What's the matter?' I ask Annabel as she closes the door. I'm trying to think if I've messed anything up recently, but nothing is coming to mind.

'It's slightly delicate, so I wanted to chat with you in private. We've had a new enquiry, and the client specifically asked for you.'

'That's good, isn't it?' Annabel is normally delighted if a client asks for one of us by name because it makes the relationship more personal, which she believes increases their loyalty. She doesn't look delighted this morning, though.

'I'm not sure you'll see it that way. It's something very different from our normal line of work, but that doesn't bother me. You're pretty adaptable. It's the client that's the problem.'

'Tell me more.' I'm curious, if nothing else. I have a good relationship with all my clients, and I can't think why the new one would be any different.

'Okay. It's definitely up your street and fits in with the brief I gave you when you came back. It's a shooting weekend at a country estate.'

I suddenly have a suspicion I know where she's going.

'The client, and this is where the problem lies, is your ex-husband.'

'Ah, well that makes it easy. Simply write back to him and tell him that his budget is not sufficient for the type of event that we organise. I imagine this is some hare-brained money-spinner he's dreamt up, but he'll be expecting the whole thing to happen on a shoestring budget. It'll be a car crash and we probably won't get paid either.'

'Interesting. He hasn't mentioned budget in his email. He talks a lot about providing a top-quality experience for his guests and setting up something that can be repeated on a regular basis during the pheasant shooting season. Do you know when that is?'

'The beginning of October to the first of February,' I reply, without thinking.

'Which brings me back to my dilemma,' Annabel continues. 'You're patently the best qualified to put together an event like this. None of the rest of us would have a clue. He's specifically asked for you as well, and it's exactly the kind of market I'd like us to break into. But I don't want to put you in a difficult position.'

She's good, I'll give her that, but I can see through her. She really wants this, and I'll have to put up a hell of a fight to stand a chance of getting out of it. What the hell is James playing at now? The fact that he chose us, and me specifically, when there are probably companies closer to him that have more experience and would charge less, tells me a lot. I'm being manipulated here, and I don't like it at all.

'Can I think about it?' I ask Annabel.

'Of course. I'll send you the details. Have a look and let me know tomorrow morning, okay?'

* * *

'What did Annabel want? She didn't seem to be having a go at you,' Emily asks, as we head out to grab a sandwich at lunchtime.

'She wanted to talk to me about a new client who wants our help to organise a shooting weekend.'

'What, like paintball and stuff? Sounds awesome.'

'No, not paintball. Pheasants. Think of a group of middle-aged men standing in a field and firing randomly into a sky filled with birds, and you'll be pretty much there.'

Her mouth drops open in horror. 'What, they're shooting actual live birds?'

'Yup. The birds are bred specially and released in the summer months. They then live in the woods until the season begins. On a shooting day, the guns are stationed in a field and a team of beaters walks through the woods making noise and banging on trees, to drive the birds towards the guns.'

'But *why*?'

'It's a sport, and pretty lucrative for the landowners. Each gun will pay hundreds of pounds per day to shoot.'

'It sounds vile.'

'Yeah, well. This particular weekend is being run by my ex-husband, James, and he specifically asked for me. That's why Annabel wanted to talk to me in private, to see how I felt about it.'

'Are you going to do it?'

'I don't know. I need to think. I don't want to have anything to do with him, but Annabel wants me to do it, and that makes things tricky.'

'Sooner you than me,' she laughs.

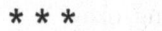

* * *

I'm still preoccupied with it when I meet up with Elliott after work. After our first impromptu dinner together, we sort of fell into a habit of meeting up once or twice a week after work before getting the train home. Sometimes we just meet for a drink, but more often than not we end up getting something to eat as well. To begin with, it was more of a kind of divorcees support group thing, where we'd take it in turns to talk about how awful our ex-spouses were, but it's grown into a genuine friendship, and recently we've challenged each other to sign up to a dating app. He's already in the pub when I arrive, and a glass of wine is waiting for me on the table.

'Give me the statistics,' I say, after I've swallowed my first generous mouthful. This is our standard greeting at the moment. We each have to tell the other how many matches we've had, and then analyse them.

'Three since last time,' he replies. 'A woman who completely adores cats but is allergic to them, an older woman who sounds like some sort of sexual predator, and a Hungarian who doesn't speak much English. You?'

'Five. Two sent me dick pics as soon as we were matched, so they're obviously out. One is a guy in his fifties called Leonard, and there was also a sort of fitness fanatic who messaged me wanting to meet for a workout in the gym followed by another in the bedroom. Yuck.'

'That still leaves one,' Elliott remarks.

I'm not sure what to say about the final one as, technically, there was nothing wrong with him. The reality is that I'm not really interested in meeting anyone; I'm only doing this to try to get Elliott out there.

'Yeah, he was just your typical no-hoper. Nothing happening there. I do have something else I'd like your opinion on, though.'

'Go on.'

I proceed to tell him all about our new client and the shooting weekend. He listens intently, which I've learned is one of his most endearing features. When he's listening, I sometimes think a bomb could go off and he wouldn't blink, because he's so focused on what I'm saying. His blue eyes lock on to mine, which I used to find a bit disconcerting, but I'm used to it now. When I've finished, he sits back, but doesn't say anything.

'Well?' I prompt him.

'It's a tricky one, isn't it? I can see why you're in knots about it. I guess that there isn't anyone else in your office with your level of experience in these things?'

'Well, I'm not exactly experienced, but I know what a shooting weekend is supposed to look like. I'm not sure any of the others do, and he specifically asked for me. What do you think that's about?'

'If we were being generous,' he replies, 'we'd see it purely as recognition of your particular skillset.'

'That doesn't work, though, because I'm sure there are agencies on his doorstep who do this kind of thing all the time. Why ring up a London agency, and ask specifically for his ex-wife?'

'I did say "if we were being generous",' he smiles. 'But, if it's any help, I agree with you. Something about this is fishy as hell. Any idea what you're going to do?'

'Not yet. I don't want to let Annabel down, but I get the feeling that this is a trap of some sort and I really don't want to fall into it.'

'Do you have to do it on your own? Can't you take someone else with you, as protection?'

I ponder his question. He might be on to something with that.

'You, my friend, are an absolute genius,' I tell him.

* * *

The next morning, I knock on Annabel's cubicle door and tell her that I'll do it, provided that someone else comes with me. After a brief team meeting, Emily bravely volunteers and the three of us congregate in the meeting room to thrash out the details.

'I'd like Emily to take the lead on this one,' I say to Annabel. 'I know James asked for me, and he's still getting me, but I'd like to be more in the background until we know what his ulterior motive is.'

'How do you feel about that, Emily?' Annabel asks.

'I'll be honest and say this is a long way out of my comfort zone,' Emily replies. 'I don't know anything about the countryside and, from what Sophie has told me about shooting weekends, it all sounds pretty barbaric. However, as long as she's there to support me, I'll give it my best shot.'

We all groan at her involuntary pun.

'That's settled then,' Annabel states. 'I'll write back to the client and say that we will take the engagement, but I can only spare you, Sophie, in an advisory capacity. I'll put in the usual flannel about all our personnel being extremely professional and that we have every confidence we can make his event a complete success. You can then follow up, Emily, and arrange the initial meeting. Okay?'

'Just one more thing,' I tell her. 'Make sure you get the money up front.'

'You really think he won't pay?'

'I think it's a significant risk, yes.'

'I don't think I can ask for all the money in advance,' she replies, after mulling it over for a while. 'What I suggest is that we do an initial consultation with him, followed up by a detailed proposal. We'll charge him a flat fee up front for the consultation, and I'll explain that this is standard practice for new clients. Then, if he's happy to go ahead with the event, we'll expect fifty per cent in advance, and fifty per cent within thirty days of completion. It's still a risk, but at least we won't be completely out of pocket if he doesn't pay.'

'We'll need an expense budget too,' I tell her. 'It's too far to go there and back in a day. I suggest that Emily and I drive down the night before, stay overnight in a hotel somewhere, conduct the meeting in the morning and come back after that.'

'Good point. Put together some numbers and let me have them by lunchtime if you can. Don't forget to include mileage if you're planning to drive down there.'

By the end of the day, Annabel has mailed the proposal to James, with costs included, and Emily has set up a meeting for early next week. Normally, it takes clients a few days to come back to us, but his reply was instant.

He's definitely up to something, and whatever it is involves me somehow. Even though I'm not going down on my own, and Emily is taking the lead, I'm deeply uneasy.

25

It's the day of our initial consultation with James. Any hopes I had that he would object to paying for it up front and thus get us off the hook proved unfounded when the money landed in the account the day after Annabel emailed him. Emily and I drove down yesterday afternoon and spent the night in a hotel in Exeter. Now that she seems to have got over her problem with me, she's actually very good company, and we had a very enjoyable evening together. As we get closer to the farm, though, I'm feeling more and more nervous and there's a nasty dragging sensation in the pit of my stomach. Emily is also silent this morning; she's already told me she's nervous about this event, so I guess she's gearing herself up for it.

I don't know what I'm more anxious about: seeing James again, seeing Becky (assuming they're still together), or seeing Rosalind. I haven't heard a peep out of Rosalind since blocking her number, and I have no desire to speak to her now. However, as I keep reminding myself, this is a *professional* engagement, and I need to keep it at that level. If that means being polite to my ex-husband, the woman who wrecked my marriage, and the mother-in-law from hell, I'll just have to grin and bear it. At least I'm not on my own.

I feel weirdly detached as we pass through the village. Everything is still the same as when I lived here and I see a number of people I recognise, but I'm also acutely aware that I don't belong here any more. After another five minutes, the familiar sign comes into view and I silently apologise to my car for the ordeal I'm about to put it through on the farm track. However, when I turn in, I have to do a double take to check that I'm in the right place. Instead of the broken lumps of concrete, with potholes hidden by the tall grass, the track is now smooth tarmac. Off to the left, I can see that the stables have been extended, and a huge horsebox with 'Lynton Farm Livery' emblazoned on the side stands in the yard. There are also other new buildings I don't recognise, and the whole place feels like it's been smartened up. As I pass our old cottage, I'm forced to pull into the side as another enormous horsebox with Becky behind the wheel trundles out of the yard. Despite my suspicions that she might still be on the scene, it's a surprise to see her in the flesh. I can't help wondering what the current set-up with her and James is, and if she knows about his little trip to Sussex to try to persuade me to come back. It's safe to say that she doesn't look at all pleased to see me, but she wasn't exactly welcoming the last time we met, so I'm not reading anything into that.

'I thought you said it was a dump,' Emily observes.

'It was. It's changed a lot since I was last here.'

I pull into a car park that has appeared where there used to be a bit of scrubland and some rusty bits of old farm machinery. Again, it's all smooth tarmac with delineated spaces and smart wooden fences. The main house has also received some attention, or at least a lick of paint on the doors and window frames. I feel like I've stepped into some sort of parallel universe as we climb out of the car and I lock it. A sign directs us to the farm office, where we've agreed to meet James. This was just a corner of the workshop with a tatty old chair and a battered computer when I lived here, but now it's a standalone wooden building that looks like one of those garden offices you see advertised in lifestyle magazines. My heart is thrashing with nerves as we push open the door and I come face to face with James for the first time since our confrontation at my parents' house.

He doesn't look any different. He's still handsome, and he smiles widely as he greets us, giving me the briefest peck on the cheek.

'Thank you both so much for coming,' he begins, as he directs us towards a large, squishy, leather sofa. I sink much further into it than I was expecting and I have to grab my skirt to stop it riding up. The last thing I need is to begin the meeting by flashing my knickers at him. It may seem odd to be protective of my modesty in front of a man who has seen me naked plenty of times, but I need him to know that there are strict boundaries now. I'm conscious of Emily having the same struggle with her skirt beside me, and I silently curse him for putting us in this predicament.

'We've made a few changes since you were last here, Sophie,' he says, making it sound as if I'm an infrequent visitor rather than an ex-wife who used to live here.

'I noticed,' I reply. 'The track is a huge improvement, and I see you've extended the stables. Are those your horseboxes too?'

'They are, and what a massive success they've been for us. It was Monica who worked out that we could significantly undercut the competition by using our own 'boxes.'

'Who?'

'Monica, Tony's girlfriend. Did you meet her?'

'Was she the woman who drove the milk lorry?'

'That's her. She came to us shortly after she got together with Tony. She's just as good as Becky with horses and, although we don't pay her anything like as much as she used to earn, she says the hours are much better. She's living with Tony in his cottage, so she doesn't exactly have a lot of outgoings. Anyway, she was the one who started us down the horsebox route.'

I'm intrigued, in spite of myself.

'How?'

'It's all about diesel,' James continues, leaning back in his chair as if he's about to dispense some incredible pearls of wisdom. 'The third-party boxes have to get from where they are to here, then take the horses to where they need to be, bring them back and then go back to their base. That's four journeys and four lots of diesel. See?'

'Yes.'

'Whereas our boxes start here. So they only have to make two journeys, saving a hill of money on fuel. That means we can charge less and still make a decent profit. We had to buy the boxes up front of course, and getting Becky through her HGV licence wasn't cheap, but it didn't take long for them to pay themselves back. We make our own cheese on site now as well. We sell it from our farm shop but I'm also in negotiations with a well-known supermarket chain and we hope to go national if that comes off.'

I'm starting to see why he asked for me. He's finally figured out a way to make the farm pay, and he's determined to rub my nose in it. Fair enough. If that's what he needs to make himself feel more of a man, I guess I can suck it up for a while.

'All of this must have taken quite a lot of investment. Did you win the lottery?' I ask.

'No. In a funny way, I have you to thank. Obviously, I didn't have the money to pay the divorce settlement, so I had to sell some land for development. It broke my heart to sell it, but it's probably been one of the best decisions I made, and it enabled me to put in the money to turn the farm around. It's a shame that some of the potential investors I approached earlier didn't share my vision; they could have done very well.'

'Yes, my father mentioned that you'd asked him for a loan.'

'Investment, not a loan. Anyway, it turned out that I didn't need him in the end. We've done just fine on our own.'

Unbelievable. He's completely re-written history, but now is not the time to challenge him. I have to remember he's a client.

'How did people locally react to you selling the land?' I ask.

'I'll admit that I wasn't very popular for a while. There was even a campaign in the village, with posters and stuff opposing the development, but they came round pretty quickly once I negotiated a couple of concessions from the developers.'

He's loving this. He's like the cat that got the cream, and I'm fighting the urge to slap his smug face.

'Oh yes?' I reply, keeping my voice neutral.

'I can't take all the credit, of course. It was Mum's idea, actually, but I negotiated it. As part of the condition of sale, the developers had to put in mobile phone masts and high-speed internet. When word got out that they'd agreed, the protests stopped overnight.'

'Well done you,' I say, with false admiration. 'So, tell us about this shooting weekend.'

As much as he's tried to sell himself as the successful businessman, it quickly becomes obvious that his good fortune is solely down to the common sense of others, and luck. The weekend is purely his idea and, in typical fashion, he hasn't thought it through at all. The meeting that I'd hoped would only last for the morning drags long into the afternoon, as we discuss meals, accommodation, transport, and all the other details that will make the difference between a triumph and a fiasco. The only high point is that he has had the main house redecorated inside as well, and it does at least look like the sort of place that could command the premium price the guests will need to cough up if James is going to stand any chance of making the event profitable. Emily and I take copious notes and try to keep my grandstanding ex-husband focused.

'God, he was annoying!' I exclaim, as we pull out of the farm track on to the road.

'I couldn't possibly comment,' Emily sniggers from the passenger seat.

'He's got no idea how expensive putting on an event like this is. I couldn't believe it when he said he thought the Co-op's own-label plonk would be perfect for serving to the guests. These people are going to be forking out a fortune for this weekend, and he was planning to give them a couple of pork pies and a splash of cheap red wine. I despair, I really do. And as for the camp bed idea, good grief!'

It's late by the time I get back to my flat, having deposited Emily at the station to catch her train to London. I'm dog-tired and tempted to work from home tomorrow, but I know Emily will need help and I'm meeting Elliott for a drink in the evening, so I climb into bed and try to get to sleep. It takes a while, as my brain is still digesting the events of the day. When I do finally fall asleep, I dream vividly and the only one I enjoy is one where Becky reverses a horsebox over James.

* * *

I'm unsurprisingly still a little groggy the next morning, so I order an extra shot in my coffee to try to get me going. Elliott isn't on the platform today, which is a shame, as I would really like to see him. Spending the day with James has given him back too much of my head space, and I would have liked some of Elliott's quiet humour to disperse it. Never mind, I'm seeing him later, and I have a proposal to put to him. He won't like it, but I reckon I can sell it if I'm careful.

Emily and I spend the whole day working on our ideas for the shooting weekend. I've been phoning suppliers to try to track down genuinely local ingredients for the meals, elevenses, and afternoon teas the guests will be served during their stay from Friday evening to Sunday afternoon. Authenticity is key, so generic produce won't do here. They will be expecting us to know the provenance of everything, especially any meat and game we serve. Emily was wondering about vegetarian options, and I've come up with a couple, but I'm fairly certain the type of people who enjoy standing in a muddy field blowing birds out of the sky are unlikely to be vegetarians. I've also had a long conversation with Ian the wine merchant and we've come up with a selection of wines that are complex enough to satisfy the most discerning palate, but not so expensive that they're going to wipe out any profit. Emily has been tracking down beds, linen, and all the other amenities that the guests will expect for a comfortable weekend. We're running multiple spreadsheets and the costs are mounting fast but, if James wants this event to be a success, he's going to have to invest in it. By the end of the day, we've documented it all and sent it to Annabel for review and approval.

I've definitely earned the glass of wine that I know will be waiting for me, and I'm looking forward to catching up with Elliott after being focused on James for the whole day.

26

'Please tell me you're joking.' Elliott's face is a mask of horror.

'No joke. I've booked us in for tomorrow night. It'll be fun, even if we don't meet anyone we like. And it's a Friday, so it doesn't matter if they're all awful and we have to drink too much to make it bearable.'

'But speed dating? That sounds like my vision of hell. What am I supposed to say?' he splutters.

'Look, I'm not sure about it either, if I'm honest,' I tell him. 'But we won't know if we don't try, will we? If it's awful then we don't have to do it again, but I just thought it might make a change from the apps. Maybe people will be nicer if we meet them in real life.'

'I'm not sure, Sophie. You know I'm not good with people I haven't met before.'

'Just ask them about themselves. People love talking about themselves. Please?'

He sighs. 'Okay. But promise me you won't make me do it again if I don't like it.'

'I promise.'

'I can't believe I'm letting you talk me into this. Distract me: tell me about your visit to the ex.'

'The headline is that he had to sell a piece of land to fund the divorce settlement, and he's obviously made a fortune on it because he's upgraded the stables and bought horseboxes, as well as a swanky new office for himself. He's even making his own cheese, would you believe?'

'So the hidden agenda was basically to show you how well he's doing and rub your face in it? Show you the prize you could have won?'

'I think so, yes.'

'And how did that make you feel?'

'Well, Mr Freud, it made me feel that my ex-husband is a complete arse.'

When we've finished laughing, Elliott steeples his hands and tries to look scholarly. 'I see. Would you care to elaborate?'

'It would be clever if any of it were his own idea, but it isn't. The only thing that was his idea was the shooting weekend and, without our intervention, that would have been a total disaster.'

'So you're doing it, then?'

'I don't really have a choice. At least Emily is taking the lead so I can stay in the background.'

'If what you've just told me is true,' he observes, 'there is precious little chance of that, I'm afraid.'

* * *

The speed dating is due to start at seven thirty, so I bang on Elliott's door at seven the next evening. I've ordered a taxi to take us to the venue so neither of us have to worry about driving. Even though I have no intention of meeting anyone tonight, I've made an effort, with white skinny jeans and a blue sparkly top. Elliott opens his door, and I'm relieved to see that he hasn't backed out, as he's dressed very smartly in pressed chinos and yet another light-blue shirt. His cologne is woody and spicy, and I suppress an urge to lean in and give him a good sniff.

'You look nice,' I tell him. 'They'll be fighting over you.'

'You scrub up pretty well yourself,' he replies. 'Are we really doing this? We could just go out to dinner instead.'

'We're doing this,' I tell him firmly. 'Come on, the taxi is waiting.'

The venue, when we get there, is not promising. It's a fairly run-down-looking pub, the kind of place my dad would have referred to as a 'boozer' back in the day. The patterned carpets are faded and sticky, and the wine Elliott brings me is sour and barely chilled. A woman with dark, spiky hair and blood-red lipstick takes our money and directs us to a table to collect our name badges, along with a piece of paper and a pencil. She must be sixty if she's a day, but her clothes and make-up are more suited to someone in their twenties. She's stick-thin, and even the super-skinny black jeans she's wearing hang loose over her legs. Her feet are encased in bright pink Doc Martens, similar to some of the pairs I've seen Bronwyn wearing. Her 'Hello Kitty' top strains over a chest that is suspiciously large compared to the rest of her body, and her nails are painted blood red to match her lipstick. She's terrifying, and she's openly sizing Elliott up, as if she's appraising cattle.

'Lovely to have some new faces,' she drawls at us in a husky voice that gives her away as a heavy smoker. 'I'm sure you'll be very popular. The ladies are going to love you and, if they don't, I might just keep you for myself.' She addresses the last sentence to Elliott, and I'm horrified to see her actually licking her lips, the tip of her tongue darting out like a snake's.

'Look on the bright side,' I tell him as we make our escape from her towards a motley-looking group of people that I imagine are our fellow speed daters. 'If all else fails, you've definitely pulled there.'

'Oh God, really?' He looks horrified.

'Relax. I'll protect you, I promise. One bucket of water is all it takes with her sort. I saw it in *The Wizard of Oz*, so it must be true.'

'Hmm. I don't know if that translates to the real world.'

At that moment, there's a terrifying screech from the PA system, and we turn to face our host, who is now holding a microphone.

'Good evening, ladies and gentlemen,' she rasps. 'Welcome to the night that could change your life for ever. Look around you. One of the people here could be your future life partner, and tonight is the night when your eyes will meet for the first time.'

'Unlikely!' one of the women roars. 'I've been coming for six months now and I haven't had so much as a flicker.'

'Shut up, Sandra. As I was saying, tonight is the night when you could meet the love of your life. In years to come, you'll look back and say, "If it wasn't for Davina and speedy dating night at the Prancing Horse, we'd never have found each other." Just remember to invite me to your weddings, okay? Now, in a moment, we'll go through to the function room, where the chairs have been laid out. Ladies, you'll sit in the inner circle, facing outwards. Gentlemen, you'll sit in the outer circle, facing inwards. You will have five minutes to get to know each other before the bell goes. When the bell rings, the gentlemen will move one chair to the left and the ladies will stay put. Do you all understand?'

'Yes,' the group calls out wearily.

'If you meet someone you'd like to get to know better, then write their name down on your card. Also, make sure you've put your name at the top of the card. I can't match you up if I don't know who you are, Bernard! If the person whose name you have written down has also written down your name, then I'll tell you afterwards and you can arrange to meet up. If you write someone's name down and they haven't written yours, then you must respect that decision and not pester them for a date anyway, Bernard. Has anyone got any questions before we begin?'

I glance at Elliott, but I can't read his expression. I have to admit that this probably doesn't rank as one of my best ideas. Quite a few of the speed daters are a lot older than us and, like Davina, some of the women are clearly sizing him up and liking what they see. They're almost predatory, and I begin to wonder whether we should make our excuses and leave before one of them pounces on him. However, before I get the chance to say anything, Davina throws open the doors to the function room and ushers us inside.

The kindest way to describe the function room is 'optimistically named'. It's more of a storage area, with boxes stacked here and there and random bits of lighting equipment lying around, probably from the last time this pub staged a live event sometime in the eighties. Two circles of grubby-looking chairs have been laid out in the centre of the room, and I realise my white jeans were a mistake. I make my way to the least disgusting-looking chair I can find and perch carefully. I notice that Davina has guided Elliott over to a station far away from me. The woman she sits him opposite has her eyes out on stalks. I only hope he keeps his sense of humour, otherwise it's going to be a very strained taxi journey home. I'm definitely going to need to eat plenty of humble pie whatever happens.

My first date is Bernard the stalker, as I've nicknamed him after Davina's opening remarks. He's probably nearly old enough to be my father, but still makes no bones about eyeing me up appreciatively as he talks. I learn that he works in one of the local supermarkets on the checkout, and he takes pride in remembering customers and what they buy. He regales me with a list of people and their regular purchases, asks absolutely nothing about me, and I'm mightily relieved when the bell goes and he moves on.

Al, who follows him, is short and wiry. Again, he makes no bones about sizing me up, and he obviously likes what he sees as his eyes light up. I can't say I feel the same, and I fear it's going to be another long five minutes.

'Why don't you tell me a little bit about yourself?' I begin. 'What do you do for a living?'

'Yeah, it's a little bit unconventional, as it goes. I'm what you'd call a professional gambler,' he replies and sits back, waiting for me to be impressed.

'That does sound interesting,' I lie. 'I don't know anything about gambling. What's the difference between a professional and an amateur?'

'Well, your amateur, he doesn't study the form like I do, see? I've got spreadsheets at home with all the horses I follow, cross-referenced against the racecourse, the going and their final position. So, although I don't actually place a bet as often as some other gamblers, my chance of success is much higher because I've factored everything in.'

I'm a little intrigued, despite myself. 'And does it work?'

He leans forward, conspiratorially. 'Of course it does. Last month alone, I made over five grand. And do you know the best bit?'

'What's that?'

'It's all tax-free. Her Majesty's revenue bastards don't get a single penny.' He settles back in his chair and puts his hands behind his head, incredibly pleased with himself.

'So you must live the real high life then. Swanky apartment, maybe a yacht?'

I've obviously hit a nerve, because he suddenly doesn't look so confident. 'It's complex,' he replies.

'How so?'

'Well, before I knew what I was doing, I made a few mistakes and ran up a few debts. Nothing serious, but you know what these credit people are like. I told them I only needed a little bit more time, but they sent the bailiffs round anyway and cleaned me out. So then I didn't have the money for my rent, and so I'm currently in, ah, family accommodation, just while I sort it all out.'

'I see.'

Luckily the bell goes before I have to say any more.

As the evening wears on and a succession of completely unattractive men pass me by, I realise that Davina is being very flexible with her definition of five minutes. I'm stuck talking to Keith about his views on immigration for nearly ten minutes at one point, and I realise that Davina is doing more than just hosting – there's some active matchmaking going on. Given that most of the people here are regulars, that must mean she's got her eye on either Elliott or me. Keith is still droning on, so I take the opportunity to glance over to where Elliott is sitting, in front of a woman displaying a large amount of cleavage. She's leaning forward resting her chin in her hand, giving him puppy-dog eyes. He looks terrified, as if she's about to eat him alive.

After what seems like an age, it finally ends. When Elliott got to my station, we barely had time to say hello before the bell rang, which just convinced me further of Davina's plan. The others all hand in their papers, and I notice her glancing down them as they do.

'You two have been very popular,' she drawls as we hand in our slips. 'Practically everyone wrote you down. Let's see who the lucky winners are, shall we?'

I notice that Elliott's slip is as blank as mine, and Davina wrinkles her nose with displeasure. 'What, nobody at all?' she asks. 'I think you're being a little over-choosy. If you don't want to spend the rest of your lives alone, you might need to learn to see people for who they are inside, rather than just looking at the surface. Keith and Barbara were particularly smitten. Are you sure you don't want to change your minds?'

'It's our first time,' I tell her, to try to defuse the situation. 'Maybe next time we'll be more...'

'Prepared,' Elliott interjects, saving me as my words dry up.

* * *

'Promise me you will never make me do anything like that again,' he says, once we're safely in the taxi on our way home.

'I promise. It was an experience, though, wasn't it?'

'I can't believe she thought I was a good match for Barbara,' he continues. 'That woman would make mincemeat of me!'

'Which one was Barbara?'

'The blonde one, wearing the tight V-neck top. She kept leaning forwards when she was talking to me, and I'm sure she kept pulling her top down to make sure I was in no doubt as to her intentions. If Davina hadn't rung the bell when she did, I suspect Barbara would have gone beyond mere cleavage to actual indecency. How did you get on?'

'Much the same. I just hope my jeans are okay. Remind me never to wear white jeans to a grotty pub again.'

By the time the taxi drops us off, we are at least able to make light of the evening, and we're laughing about some of the characters we met. Elliott has relaxed, mainly because I've had to promise several more times that I'll never do that to him again.

'I've got some wine in the fridge if you fancy a glass,' he tells me, as we climb the stairs. 'I noticed you barely touched yours earlier.'

'Ugh, it was horrible. Chateau Cat's-wee, I reckon. If you've got something to take the taste of it away, I'd be grateful.'

I follow him into his flat. I've only been in here a couple of times before, but it's totally Elliott. Everything is neat and in its place, and every surface is spotless. I plonk myself down on the sofa while he clatters around in the kitchen getting glasses and pouring the wine. When he comes out, he's also got some crisps and nuts in little bowls.

We clink our glasses, and he's right. This wine is a huge improvement on whatever they served at the pub.

'So, statistics?' I ask him, as he sits down next to me.

'Well, it seems that you and I were a huge hit, but I wouldn't have matched with any of them on an app, would you?'

'No. Definitely not.'

'To be honest, I'm not sure why I'm doing this,' he says. 'One thing tonight showed me is that I really don't have any idea how to talk to a woman, and that's the easy bit. If it started to get romantic, I would probably freeze. It's so long since I've kissed anyone, I think there's a good chance I've forgotten how.'

'That's patently not true,' I scoff. 'You have no difficulty talking to me, and I'm a woman.'

'That's different, though.'

'How?'

'Well, because it just is, okay?'

I can't help laughing at his discomfort. 'Kissing will be fine. It's just like riding a bike, you never forget.'

'I don't know. The idea of it frightens me. What if I'm no good?'

This is the wounded Elliott talking, and my heart goes out to him. From what I've heard of his ex-wife, she wouldn't have hesitated to put the boot into every aspect of him, including his sexual technique.

'I know! Why don't you kiss me and I'll tell you whether it's any good or not?' I say to him. I'm not sure where this has come from; it's probably the wine talking.

'Absolutely not!'

'Okay, then I'll kiss you, so you can remember what it's like. Nothing weird. No tongues or anything, just a simple kiss.'

I lean over, close my eyes and plant a soft kiss on his lips. I was right about his skin; it feels smooth against mine and I breathe in his cologne. I'm surprised how much I enjoy it, and he doesn't pull away, which is good.

'There,' I say. 'That wasn't so bad, was it?'

'No, it was nice,' he admits.

'Good. Now you try.'

Agonisingly slowly, he leans forward. When our lips meet again, he holds the kiss for a little longer before breaking away.

'How was that?' he asks.

'I liked it,' I reply, 'but I think you can afford to let it linger more. Like this.' I take his face in my hands as I press my lips against his. We stay there, without moving, for several seconds. I run my thumbs over his cheekbones and curl my fingers around the back of his neck. When we break away this time, my eyes don't leave his face. Something has clicked inside me. The fact that Elliott is attractive is not news, but the sudden reality of my attraction to him definitely is. From the look on his face, it would seem the feeling is mutual.

This time, we both lean forwards at the same time and, as our lips meet, I can feel my heart beating faster and my body starting to tingle. I slide my hand round to the back of his head to pull him closer into me. There's no doubt that he gets the message, as I can feel him opening his mouth. I do the same and our tongues touch for the first time. It's electric. I don't know what he's been so worried about; he's a fantastic kisser.

I have no idea how long we spend side by side leaning into each other but, after a while, the slightly awkward angle starts to hurt my neck. He obviously feels it too, because I'm aware of his hand on my hip encouraging me as I move to straddle him. This is much better, although my hands suddenly take on a life of their own, moving from his shoulders to his chest and then his shirt buttons.

27

We didn't have sex. Not quite, anyway. Things got pretty heated, but he didn't have any condoms and I'm not on the pill because there didn't seem to be much point with James. Despite that, we found ways to satisfy each other and it was better than normal sex in some respects. We took time to explore each other's bodies and discover what we both liked. I think we were both surprised by how natural and right it felt.

At least, that's how I felt last night. Now, I'm acutely aware that I'm in an unfamiliar bed with Elliott's arm draped across me. I'd really like to wriggle out and cross the hallway to my flat, where I can have a shower and brush my teeth, but I don't want him to wake up to an empty bed and think I've deserted him. I lie there, pondering my predicament. Elliott is still fast asleep, but I'm becoming increasingly aware of my bladder, and it's this that spurs me into action. I carefully detach myself from him and pull on my sparkly top. It's not quite long enough to cover my knickers, but it'll have to do. Modesty is the least of my concerns after last night. I leave the bedroom as quietly as I can and head for the bathroom.

Having dealt with the most immediate problem, my mind turns

back to the events of the previous evening. Do I have any regrets about what happened? No. In fact, I'm amazed that I didn't notice my feelings for Elliott earlier. Yes, he's quiet and reserved, but he's also kind and funny when he relaxes, and he's in pretty good shape physically, too. He made me feel desired, and that's a strong aphrodisiac for anyone. The memory of his hands and mouth on my body makes me smile. He was so keen to please me, and he did. One of us will need to buy some condoms today, though. There's definitely unfinished business there, and we have the whole weekend to attend to it.

I saunter into the kitchen in search of coffee, but quickly give up when I spy the coffee machine. It's a typical man gadget, all shiny chrome and incomprehensible buttons. I pour myself a glass of water instead and take the opportunity to have a good old nose around the flat while Elliott is still asleep. I've been in the sitting room before, and a quick browse of the bookshelves doesn't tell me anything I don't already know, so I turn my attention to the second bedroom. I know he uses it as a study, like me, but I've never been in there. I'm sure he won't mind, so I gently push on the door and turn on the light.

Whatever I was expecting to find in here, it wasn't this. My mouth drops open in surprise; I think I'd prefer to have discovered some sort of *Fifty Shades* sex dungeon than the scene in front of me. Suddenly, I feel as if I don't know Elliott at all. The whole room is a shrine to Nutsy the Squirrel. There are Nutsy posters on the walls, open boxes of Nutsy merchandise on the floor, and even a cardboard standalone Nutsy figure in the corner that's as tall as I am. There are four huge monitors above the desk, and a large computer underneath it. I don't get it. He's obviously got some completely bizarre obsession with Nutsy, and it's quite a turnoff if I'm honest, but how did I never spot this before? I don't remember ever seeing him play the game, and he's certainly never mentioned it. In fact, I remember that he pretended not to know what it was when he first saw me playing it on the train. Maybe he's ashamed of his obsession, and he creeps back here to play into the early hours. I'm completely confused. How could he have hidden this from me so successfully?

'It's not what it looks like,' Elliott's voice says from behind me, making me start.

'Sorry, I didn't mean to pry,' I tell him. 'I was just exploring while I waited for you to wake up and...' I run out of words. I turn to face him, but I can't meet his eyes.

'Are you okay? Are you having regrets about last night?' He's obviously picked up on my discomfort, but he's looking a little confused, as if there's nothing weird about having a whole room in your flat dedicated to a character in a mobile app.

'No, not at all!' I reply, far too brightly, and I can see from his expression that he doesn't believe me. 'I just didn't have any idea that you were so into Nutsy. It's a surprise.'

'It's not that I'm into him, so much as that I am him. He's been a part of my life for four years now. It wouldn't be putting it too strongly to say that he probably stopped me from going mad.'

Oh Lord, this is getting worse and worse. Maybe he's got some sort of Nutsy costume he dresses up in as well, and he selected me because he saw me playing the game and thought I might be a kindred spirit. I really will run for the hills if that happens. I'm generally pretty open-minded, but men who are obsessively into things normally associated with children, such as comics or cartoon characters, make me very uneasy. It's like a part of them has got stuck and they haven't managed to become complete adults. As I'm contemplating my predicament, Elliott's words sink in and I realise something doesn't add up here.

'That doesn't make sense, Elliott,' I challenge him. 'Nutsy hasn't even been out for a year.'

'You're right. It took me three years to write him.'

'You *wrote* him?' A wave of relief crashes over me. I remember my dad saying something about Nutsy being written by a guy in his bedroom. It just never occurred to me that it could be Elliott.

'Yes. When I first moved in here, I was a mess. I had work, obviously, and fighting over the divorce settlement kept me occupied to begin with. Once that settled down, evenings and weekends became like purgatory. I realised I needed a project to keep me occupied, otherwise I'd probably end up turning to the bottle. First, I had to learn how to develop software for both Android and iOS, which took quite a while, and then I started work on Nutsy. I never expected him to be as popular as he is; I really just did it as something to keep me sane. Are you sure you're all right? If you're having regrets...'

'I'm not having regrets about last night, okay? I really enjoyed myself, as you should know from, well...' I blush a little. 'But I'm very relieved to learn that you have all this stuff because you wrote him. I was worried that you were some sort of strange Nutsy obsessive.'

'God, no!'

'Why didn't you tell me about it? He's literally a massive success!'

'It's not something I broadcast. I haven't exactly hidden the fact that I wrote him; I just haven't advertised it. That hasn't stopped them tracking me down, though. I've been asked for interviews by all sorts of people. Here, let me show you.'

He turns on the computer and brings up his email program on one of the monitors. Sure enough, there are invitations from various computer magazines, bloggers, and even a couple of TV stations.

'That's amazing, Elliott,' I tell him. From being worried that he was a secret weirdo, I'm now full of admiration.

'I'm pretty chuffed with him, I admit. The problem is that it's gone a bit too far recently,' he says. 'All this stuff,' he indicates the boxes, 'gets sent to me by companies that want to make Nutsy merchandise under licence. I don't have the first idea how to go about that sort of thing. I imagine they would make it and I'd get a commission, but how am I supposed to know how much to ask for? I've also got some company in the Far East emailing me now, wanting to buy the rights to Nutsy so they can translate him into other languages, especially Chinese, Japanese, and Korean. They've offered me fifty million pounds. That's mad, isn't it?'

'It sounds to me like you've created a monster,' I tell him.

'He is getting a bit out of control, that's true. To begin with, it was fun to see how many people were downloading the app, and I enjoyed reading the reviews and seeing how much they liked it. Then the money started to come in, slowly at first. When it was picked up by some of the major bloggers, that's when things really started to happen and now it's pouring in, way more than I could ever have dreamed.'

'But that's good, isn't it?' I ask him.

'I guess so, but it's taken me a bit by surprise,' he replies.

'Hang on, that doesn't make sense either!' I exclaim, as another realisation hits me. 'If you're rich, what on earth are you doing renting a two-bedroom flat by Sevenoaks station?'

'Good question. I did go and look at a couple of swanky houses. They were very nice, but they just offered a bigger space for me to rattle around in. I'm not a particularly ostentatious person. I briefly considered fulfilling every teenage boy's fantasy and buying a Ferrari, but I realised I'd feel like a tit in it as soon as I got to the dealership and sat in one. I never thought I'd say this, but it's only when you have money that you realise all the things it can't buy you. Yes, I could fly first class to the Caribbean and stay in a top-notch resort, but what's the point if I'm just going to be there by myself? I'd love to give a chunk of it away, and I've got a pile of begging letters from various people and organisations who have also found out who I am, but I just don't know how to prioritise them or who to believe. I don't want to be taken in by some gold-digger or fall victim to a scammer, so I haven't done anything. All this money is just sitting in my savings account and I don't have the first idea what to do with it. The bank keeps writing to me, offering investment options and so on, but what if I unwittingly end up with shares in a company that sends children down mines or something? I'd never forgive myself. So, I just carry on as normal and try to pretend that everything is the same as it always was. I know I sound ridiculous, but I haven't talked to anyone about the money side of it. You're the first.'

He looks genuinely sad and my heart goes out to him.

'I can help you, if you want,' I tell him.

'How?'

'Well, if you need someone to come to the Caribbean with you, I'm sure I could force myself.'

'You're all heart.' At least he's smiling again.

'Relax, I was kidding. It seems to me like what you need is some good, impartial advice from someone who's been where you are and knows the right people. I'm going to go home, have a shower and get dressed, and then we're going to go on a little road trip, okay?'

Elliott looks less than enthusiastic. 'I'd rather hoped, you know...'

I'm so focused on his revelations about Nutsy that it takes me a minute to work out what he's talking about. As the penny drops, a smile spreads across my face.

'Well, you'd better put some clothes on and nip to the pharmacy then, hadn't you?'

***

I can tell that Bronwyn is struggling to contain her curiosity when Elliott and I walk into the café together just over an hour later. I hope she doesn't spot my post-coital glow, but it's hard not to grin like a Cheshire cat. Our repeat performance was everything I could have wanted it to be. After breakfast, we're going to head off to East Sussex, where Dad is waiting to talk him through his options.

'I'm going to have to bail tonight, I'm afraid,' I tell Bronwyn when I go up to the counter to place our order.

'Got a better offer, have you?' she grins. 'Does it involve elusive Elliott? You are a dark horse, Sophie, that's for sure.'

'I'll tell you all about it another time, I promise.'

'You'd better!' she laughs. 'This is a story I can't wait to hear. Now, go and entertain your new friend while I get your orders on.' She emphasises the word 'friend' and grins mischievously, before skipping away towards the kitchen.

I study Elliott as I walk back to the table. What is our relationship? Given what we've just done together, I've kind of assumed we're an item now. But we haven't said anything about it, and I feel suddenly insecure.

'Elliott,' I say, when I sit down, 'can I ask you a question?'

'Of course.'

'You and me. Are we a thing?'

'What do you mean?'

'Are we, you know, dating now?'

'Would you like us to be?'

'I'm not a one-night stand kind of girl. Or even a one-night-and-the-following-morning stand kind of girl. If you're not ready for more, you need to tell me now.'

His blue eyes lock on to mine. 'Sophie, I'd love us to be a thing, as you put it. I know it's a risk and we've both been hurt before but

I've been attracted to you ever since that first day when I saw you on the train. When you moved in opposite me, I couldn't believe how much I looked forward to seeing you on the platform each morning.'

'You have a really funny way of showing people you're attracted to them, you know that? I'd hate to think how you would have been towards me if you hadn't liked me,' I laugh.

'I guess I was scared of being hurt again, and my confidence was in the bin. It was only when you invited me to have dinner with you that first time that I began to think we could be more than neighbours.'

'But what about the dating app? Why did you sign up to that if you were secretly interested in me?'

'Because you sounded like you wanted to get out there again and I wanted to be a good friend and support you.'

'But that's what I was doing for you!'

'Why? What gave you the impression that I was ready to be "out there"? I nearly got smothered by busty Barbara, for goodness' sake. I should get danger money for that!'

I burst out laughing at the memory.

'Look, I know we're both wary, but I trust you and I'd like to see where this could go,' he tells me, when my giggles have subsided.

'I trust you too,' I reply.

I'm still smiling stupidly at him when Bronwyn brings our coffees.

'Elliott, do you know Bronwyn?' I ask. 'Bronwyn, this is Elliott, my boyfriend.'

Elliott blushes crimson as Bronwyn squeals with delight and envelops us both in a massive hug.

'You guys look so good together,' she gushes. 'I just know you're going to run and run. Wait till I tell Daisy and Katie, it'll make their weekend!'

'Is she always like that?' Elliott asks, once Bronwyn has disappeared again. The noise from the kitchen indicates that she's wasted no time in sharing the news with Daisy.

'She's lovely, if a bit in-your-face. Expect a Saturday invitation, as they'll want to get to know you properly, I'm sure. Don't worry, I'll protect you,' I add, registering the look of terror on his face.

'Thanks,' he replies. 'I think I might need it.'

28

Elliott has been largely silent on the drive to Uckfield. I think he's a bit anxious about what he's let himself in for. I've explained that my father is a successful businessman with a number of companies, but I've been pretty vague on the details. One of the things I've enjoyed about getting to know Elliott is that he doesn't have any idea about my background. Unlike James and his family, Elliott has got to know me as Sophie the next-door neighbour, rather than Sophie the daughter of a billionaire. I'm aware that's all about to change but again, unlike James, Elliott doesn't exactly need any more money. He's struggling to cope with what he's got. I just hope that Dad can help him to start to make some sense out of it all.

'Here we are!' I tell him brightly, as I turn into the drive and punch the number into the keypad. Thankfully, I'm up to date with the codes again, so the gates open straight away.

'Oh, wow!' Elliott exclaims when the house finally comes into view. 'Which bit do your parents live in?'

'Umm, all of it,' I reply.

'Bloody hell, Sophie! I know you said your dad was successful, but this is a bit more than that. You could have warned me.'

'Yeah, well. As someone said to me earlier today, I haven't exactly hidden it from you, I just haven't advertised it.'

'Yes, but... oh, God. I should have worn a suit or something,' he says, looking down in horror at his shirt and jeans.

'Why? They're just people, Elliott. Trust me, you're fine as you are.'

'They'll probably take one look at me, decide I'm some sort of no-hoper, and immediately forbid you from having anything more to do with me,' he moans.

'Umm, where would you like me to start unpicking that?' I reply. 'One: the main reason we're here is because you have all this money you don't know what to do with, which kind of rules out the no-hoper element. Two: this isn't the Victorian era and my parents don't get to dictate who I go out with, and three: you look absolutely fine and they'd think you were some sort of weirdo if you pitched up in a suit anyway.'

He looks distinctly unconvinced as I pull up on the gravel in front of the house. The front door opens just as we're unfastening our seatbelts, and Margot comes striding out.

'Welcome home, Miss Beresford-Smith. Mr and Mrs Beresford-Smith are expecting you and your guest in the withdrawing room.'

I love Margot, but I really wish she wouldn't do this. Every time I bring someone to the house for the first time, she insists on being very formal. I'm also amused by her assumption that I've changed my name. The reality is that I've been meaning to do it, but there are so many forms and whatnot that I just haven't got around to it yet.

'Hello, Margot,' I reply. 'This is Elliott. Elliott, this is Margot, my parents' housekeeper.'

'Delighted to meet you, sir,' Margot says, and I swear I detect the tiniest hint of a curtsey. God bless her, she does like to see the niceties observed, even if I frequently have to suppress a giggle when she's like this. I practically drag Elliott into the house, and I'm aware of his eyes popping out of his head as he surveys the hallway.

'Is that you, Sophie?' my dad's voice calls.

'Hi, Dad!' I reply, grabbing Elliott's hand and tugging him in the direction of the drawing room. Unfortunately, he seems to be rooted to the floor.

I'm just about to hiss, '*Come on*,' at him under my breath when Dad strolls out into the hallway.

'Hi, darling,' he says, kissing me on the cheek. I can see him clock Elliott's hand in mine, and he meets my gaze and raises his eyebrows. I'm desperate to play it cool and not give anything away, but I can't help a small smile forming at the corners of my mouth, which I know he picks up on straight away. He's always been able to read me like a book, and frequently teases me that I'd make a terrible poker player.

'Dad, this is Elliott,' I tell him, dragging Elliott forwards.

'Delighted to meet you, Mr Beresford-Smith,' Elliott begins, releasing my hand and holding his out nervously.

'Call me Barry,' my father smiles, wrapping an arm around Elliott's shoulder and guiding him firmly towards the drawing room, where my mother is waiting.

'Elliott, this is Lisa: my wife and Sophie's mum,' Dad tells him.

'A pleasure to meet you, Elliott,' my mother tells him, before turning to Margot, who has silently followed us in.

'Margot, tell Donald our guests have arrived, will you?'

'Yes ma'am,' Margot replies and retreats, closing the door behind her.

'So, Elliott,' my father continues. 'My daughter informs me that you're the genius behind Nutsy the Squirrel.' Out of the corner of my eye, I catch Mum shooting me an inquisitive look, so I smile and give her an almost imperceptible nod. She replies with an equally discreet thumbs-up.

'Yes sir, umm, Barry,' Elliott replies, still looking like a rabbit caught in the headlights.

'I think you're terribly clever,' Mum adds, turning her attention back to him. 'I can't get my head around these phone apps. One of Barry's drivers installed a parking one on mine for me, but I can't work it out at all, so I either get Gerald to drive me or I just take my chances.'

'And how is that working out for you?' I ask her, with a smile. Mum wears her many parking tickets almost like a badge of honour.

'Four tickets last month,' she replies. 'One of them was terribly unfair, though. I only stopped for five minutes.'

'Rubbish,' my father counters. 'It was fifteen minutes and you were on a double yellow line! We challenged it and they sent the CCTV footage. They had you bang to rights.'

'Yes, well,' she huffs, 'it was still unfair. It's not as if I was the only person parked there.'

Dad turns to me, looking exasperated. 'The other car belonged to a blue badge holder,' he explains. 'Anyway, Elliott isn't here to learn about you single-handedly funding the local council. Sophie tells me that Nutsy has done very well, but you're not sure where to go from here. Is that right?'

'Yes,' Elliott replies.

'Great. Let's have a chat after lunch. In the meantime, you'd better tell me all about your intentions towards my daughter.'

Elliott immediately blushes crimson.

'Leave the poor boy alone, Barry,' Mum scolds. 'Don't worry, Elliott, he's playing with you. He thinks he's being funny.'

'Sorry,' Dad tells a mortified Elliott. 'It's just my way. Why don't you tell me a bit about your background and how you came to be in this fascinating predicament?'

'I'm afraid my background is very ordinary, Barry. My parents lived in council accommodation in Orpington. In fact, my mother still lives in the same house that I grew up in. My Dad moved out when I was three, and we haven't seen him since, so it was just Mum and me for most of my life.'

'Nothing wrong with that,' Dad assures him. 'Lisa and I both grew up in council flats in London. I think you might find you and I have more in common than you think.'

I watch transfixed as, over the next hour or so, my parents very gently grill Elliott. It's so subtle that I doubt he knows what's going on, but I reckon they manage to squeeze more information out of him over lunch than I have since I've known him. I learn that he adores his mother, who obviously made a lot of sacrifices to ensure she could provide him with everything he needed while he was growing up. He's tried to buy her a nicer house as a mark of gratitude, but she refuses to move, saying that all her friends are around her and she'd only be lonely. He does make regular deposits into her bank account though, for which she scolds him, saying she doesn't need his charity. She knows about Nutsy, but not how much money Elliott has made from him. To quote Elliott, she's just pleased that her boy is doing okay particularly after Nikki pretty much took him to the cleaners. It's obvious that there's no love lost there.

'What a charming young man,' my mother observes after we've finished our coffee and Dad and Elliott have disappeared into the study. One other side effect of the conversation over lunch is that Elliott has finally started to relax, so I hope he'll be able to talk openly and frankly to Dad now.

'Isn't he?' I agree.

'How long have you two been an item?'

'Umm. Not long. Since yesterday, actually, although we only made it official this morning. I've known him for a while, though. He lives in the flat opposite mine.'

'I'm glad for you,' she observes. 'He certainly seems a more promising prospect than the last one.'

'We've only just started seeing each other! It's a bit early to be talking like that, Mum.'

'You could do a lot worse, that's all I'm saying.'

* * *

It's getting dark by the time Elliott and Dad reappear. I've read the Saturday paper from cover to cover and, after a prompt from Mum, had a long conversation with Gerald about the Land Rover, which looks completely unrecognisable. The light-blue bodywork is completely dent free and even the death rattle has gone; I wouldn't say it purrs exactly, but it certainly sounds a lot healthier than when I had it. I can't help noticing how he strokes it as he talks about it, and Margot confirms that he's like a man in love. She tells me that he often takes it to off-road events, bringing it home caked in mud, but that he then spends hours meticulously cleaning it until it shines like a new pin.

'How did you get on?' I ask Elliott, as the gates swing closed behind us and I turn back towards Sevenoaks.

'It was brilliant! Thank you so much for introducing me to him. I've got masses to think about, but at least I can see a way through now.'

'Good. I'm really pleased he was able to help.'

'Oh, he's done more than that. Depending on what I decide to do, he's given me names of people that can represent me and make sure I get the best deal.'

'And do you know what you want to do?'

'I think so. Your Dad told me I basically had three options where Nutsy was concerned. I could do nothing and just let things carry on as they are now, although he made it pretty clear he didn't think much of that as a plan. I could sell the rights, although he told me there was no way I should accept the opening bid. He advised me to get some professional negotiators involved, who would probably demand double as an opening gambit, before settling somewhere between the two figures. He quite rightly pointed out that, if they're offering fifty million, they're expecting to make a whole lot more than that otherwise it simply wouldn't be viable. So, the negotiators' job is to figure out the maximum the buyer is prepared to pay and agree on that. He called that the "spend a couple of million but make twenty in return" option.'

'And the third?'

'The third is potentially the one with the biggest return, but only if I'm prepared to give up everything else and focus solely on Nutsy. Basically, I'd have to pay to get the game translated myself, negotiate contracts for the merchandise, work with agencies around the world to promote him, and so on. It would be a full-time job and a lot of travel but, if I do it right, I stand to earn much more than I'd ever get from selling him.'

'Which one do you like best?'

'Oh, I think I'll sell him. I get what your dad was saying about the potential financial returns if I dedicate everything to Nutsy, but there's much more to life than money.'

I smile. 'Such as?'

'Well, I've just started going out with this amazing woman, actually, and I'd like to be around to see where that goes. And anyway, I'm still going to end up with more money than I'll ever know what to do with.' He places his hand on my thigh as he leans across to kiss my cheek, and it's all I can do to keep my concentration on the road.

'There's no such thing as "more money than you know what to do with"!' I exclaim, trying to ignore the almost crippling desire I feel for his hand to be about two inches further up my thigh than it is now. 'I'm surprised he didn't tell you that.'

'He did, actually, but I couldn't really get my head around it.'

'It's simple,' I tell him, as I reluctantly remove his hand from my lap, squeezing it tightly so he knows I'm not rejecting him. Far from it, I just want to make sure we get back safely, and then I have plans for not just his hand, but the rest of him too. 'You make a few million and you buy yourself a nice house somewhere and the Ferrari you said you felt like a tit in. Or maybe you make several million and get yourself a private jet and a yacht. There are always bigger houses, more houses, faster cars, better jets, and larger yachts. There will always be something you can't afford. If you're happy with your lot, then it's not a problem. If you're greedy or prone to envy, it means you'll never be content, no matter how much you have.'

'Yeah, I get that, but, as I told you this morning, I'm not an ostentatious person.'

'You aren't an ostentatious person now, but money changes people, Elliott.' I turn to him in the darkness. 'Please don't let it change you.'

'I won't, I promise. Or if I do, I'll try to make sure it only changes me in good ways.'

'Talking of which, did he give you any ideas on the charity stuff?'

'Yes, loads. He told me a bit about what he does and how he doesn't like to work with big charities because he can't see where his money is going. Did you know he goes and helps out at a soup kitchen for the homeless every week?'

'He told you that?'

'Yup. Every Thursday he gets up especially early and joins a group of volunteers that take a vanload of hot food to the Strand in London. They dish out the food, offer advice on benefits and so on.

None of the other volunteers know who he is, or that he pretty much bankrolls the organisation behind it. Pretty cool, huh?'

'He must have really taken to you to tell you about that,' I say. 'Apart from the fact that he doesn't want to come across as Lord Bountiful, which he says would be patronising, there's a security issue too. The only people who know are either people he trusts, or people who need to know as part of their work.'

'He was really passionate about it. He explained to me how complicated a problem homelessness is, and how some charities simply focus on getting people off the streets and into flats, but that they're often incredibly lonely when that happens, and they frequently end up back on the streets because that's where their community is. There are also huge issues around mental health and addiction that have to be addressed in many cases. He was telling me about a scheme he runs to help the homeless into work. Even though the success rate is fairly low, it gives people the opportunity to help themselves and get a sense of purpose, which makes it worthwhile. I think it might be something I'd like to get involved in as well.'

'Yeah. I remember when he first told me about that. I didn't get it, because most of what he does is all about the return being greater than the investment, and this completely flies in the face of it. He said to me, "People always say you can lead a horse to water but you can't make it drink. That's true, but you can't even give the horse the choice if you don't build the bloody well!"'

Elliott laughs. 'I can hear him saying that.'

'So, what now?' I ask.

'Baby steps,' he replies. 'I'm going to need to book some time off work to sort all of this out, but that shouldn't be a problem. HR are always on at me for not taking my holiday allowance, so they'll be delighted. Once I've organised that, I'll contact some of the people your father mentioned and get the ball rolling. Even though nothing has changed yet, I feel so much happier now that I've got the beginnings of a plan. In fact, I think we should celebrate!'

'Oh yes? What did you have in mind?'

'We could stop and get a bottle of Champagne, and then we could get fish and chips from over the road to go with it.'

I can't help but laugh. 'I can see how this isn't changing you!' I tell him.

'Also, I wondered...'

He has suddenly run out of steam and looks uncertain again.

'What?'

'Well, I wondered if you might like to stay the night again.'

'Are you suggesting what I think you are?' I can feel him blushing furiously, even though it's dark.

'Er...'

I turn to him and grin. 'I'd love to.'

29

Emily and I are on our way back to Devon for the shooting weekend. Normally, this is the point of an event where the adrenaline starts to kick in, because all the planning is going to turn into action and we'll find out what, if anything, we've forgotten and have to fix on the hoof without the client noticing. Today, I just feel low. It's not because I'm second fiddle on this event; Emily has walked me through it several times and I think she's done an excellent job. It's because I'm going to be stuck on the farm for several days. Everything has somehow come together in a perfect storm to trap me. I wanted to bring my car, but Annabel pointed out that it would be Emily's responsibility to resolve any issues and she might need transport to do it, so we're bouncing along in her Fiesta. It's slightly hair-raising, because her attention seems to be focused more on singing along to Ava Max at full volume than it is on the road. We're not even on the M5 and we've already had a number of near misses.

What this means, besides my frazzled nerves, is that I have no means of escape once we get there. I did toy with the idea of bringing my car anyway, but I think Emily would have seen that as a snub to her, and I don't want to upset her now that we seem to be getting on so well. Even worse, rather than the hotel we stayed in last time, Emily and James have agreed that we'll stay in a couple of the attic rooms in the main house on the farm.

'It saves accommodation costs and we'll be on site twenty-four hours a day to deal with any issues,' Emily explained. While I can see that her solution is practical, it does mean I'll be face to face with my old life for five days and, if James continues with his grandstanding, it's possible I may beat him to death with a shovel.

My mood isn't helped by the fact that I haven't seen much of Elliott for the last few weeks. He has taken time off from his job and is busily working with the negotiators on the deal to sell the rights to Nutsy. He's much happier, there's no doubt, and I'm pleased for him, but I miss him too. He calls me every day when he's away, but it's not the same as having him here. After a shaky start, he's fitted in well with the Saturday-night gatherings; I was a little reluctant to share him to begin with, but I quickly realised that dropping out of a friendship group because I had a new man was not the right thing to do. What's particularly galling is that I'm going to be away for the whole weekend when he's home, and he'll probably have disappeared again by the time I get back. I unlock my phone and open WhatsApp to send him a message.

Halfway to Devon and missing you like mad. xx

The ticks go blue immediately and his reply comes a few seconds later.

Nearly as much as I'm missing you, then! Hope it goes OK. xx

He did take me to meet his mum last weekend, which was unbelievably awkward to begin with. She was lovely, but kept apologising for the size of her house and insisted on giving me my tea in a tiny china teacup. It turned out that Elliott had told her about meeting my parents and she'd convinced herself I was some sort of princess. When I explained that I actually lived in the flat opposite him and preferred my tea in a mug, things improved dramatically. She's a lovely woman but she's definitely no pushover and she's fiercely protective of her son. She didn't have a good word to say about Elliott's ex-wife and I think even he was a little uncomfortable about the strength of some of her views. I liked her enormously, and I hope she approved of me by the end.

I'm pleased to see that the yard is full of removal trucks when we arrive. Men are unloading the furniture we've hired and carrying it into the main house. James is also nowhere to be seen, which is a bonus. As Emily is parking, a manoeuvre that seems to take several attempts even though hers is currently the only car in the parking area, another lorry rolls up with the name of a linen company on the side. In spite of everything, my spirits start to lift as my focus kicks in. Leaving our bags in the car, we make a beeline for the main house, and we're soon engrossed in checking items off the list as they arrive, ensuring that the hired furniture is going to the right places, and counting sheets, duvets, and towels to make sure we have the correct number.

'I've ordered two extra sets of bedlinen and towels,' Emily tells me as I start to count, 'in case anyone has an accident.'

'Good thinking,' I reply. 'What about mattresses? If someone gets blind drunk and wets the bed, it might have soaked in by the time anyone realises.'

'Yes, I ordered two extra mattresses, for exactly that reason. Let's hope we don't need them.'

By late afternoon, the house looks incredible. The bedrooms are all made up, with large fluffy towels, bathrobes, and good quality linen on the beds. Each room has a bouquet of flowers, and

Emily has got little scent spritzers that activate periodically to provide a pleasant fragrance. Each bathroom has a complete set of toiletries, and we have spares if we need them. The chinaware and cutlery have also arrived, along with enough wine and spirits to ensure even the hardest drinker can't empty the cellar. There are extra units in the kitchen ready for the chefs who are arriving tomorrow, and temporary fridges and food preparation areas have also been rigged up in a tent attached to the back door. I take pictures of everything and send them to Elliott, and he replies with a series of thumbs-up and heart emojis. We're just going through the checklist one more time before heading off to the pub for dinner when James strolls in.

'Evening, ladies. All set for the kick-off?' he asks.

'I think so,' Emily replies. 'The guests are due to start arriving tomorrow late afternoon, and the house team will be in charge of showing them to their rooms, unpacking, and so on. We've got pre-dinner drinks and canapés being served in the drawing room at seven o'clock, followed by dinner at eight. At some point, you'll give your welcome address where you'll explain the format of the weekend. Have you decided when that will be?'

'During the drinks reception,' James replies. 'No point in doing it after dinner, none of them will remember it.'

'Good point,' Emily refers back to her checklist. 'We have eighteen guests booked in, of whom nine will be shooting. There are two vegetarians. Dinner tomorrow is poached local trout with a watercress sauce, followed by venison with a selection of vegetables, spotted dick and custard for dessert, with a cheeseboard to finish. The vegetarians will obviously have a different starter and main, but I don't have the details of that yet.'

'Spotted dick and custard?' James questions. 'That doesn't sound very upmarket to me.'

'The chefs have elevated it.' Emily replies. 'The custard is actually crème anglaise, and the spotted dicks will be constructed so that they look like slices of Swiss roll. We tried it, and it's really good.'

'Hm. Okay. And the cheeseboard?'

'Your cheese will feature prominently as requested, alongside other British cheeses.'

'Fine. And on Saturday?'

'After a cooked breakfast, you and I will accompany the shooting party. The non-shooters will be offered a day trip to Exeter, which Sophie will be organising.'

Emily is sounding confident, but James doesn't look too pleased.

'I'm not sure about that one, Emily,' he says. 'It might be better to have Sophie accompany the guns, as she does at least have experience with shoots.'

I don't think so.

It's bad enough being stuck here, the last thing I want is to be dragged round muddy fields by my ex-husband and a load of boorish idiots. I'd much rather be window-shopping in Exeter, thank you very much.

'I don't think that will be necessary,' I tell him, quickly. 'Emily is the lead organiser for this event and, as such, should be with the main party. Experience with shooting isn't as important as experience with people. We need to ensure your guests' every need is met, and Emily can only do that if she's here.'

I see the flash of irritation pass across James' face, but there's no way I can put up with spending two whole days in his company with no means of escape. At least Emily doesn't have any history with him. I feel a bit bad about exposing her to the cold, muddy reality of a shooting weekend, but it is her gig and I did help her choose suitable clothing. It would be a shame if she didn't get the benefit of it, wouldn't it?

'Fine,' James replies with a certain amount of bad grace. 'We're shooting pheasants tomorrow. We aren't allowed to shoot game on Sundays, so I've organised clay pigeons and a competition. We'll wrap up in time for tea, and then the guests will leave after that.'

'Perfect,' Emily replies. 'And have you got everything organised for the drives?'

He'd better have. It's the only area where we haven't had any input. If the weekend flops because he can't get his birds up or the beaters can't find them, that's on him, but I know our reputation will suffer by association. Emily is still looking unruffled, which is to her credit, given that she's never done anything like this before and it was only last week that I was explaining to her that clay pigeons weren't an item of crockery.

'Don't you worry your pretty little heads about that,' he says with a wink. 'It's all under control. Just make sure your parts run like clockwork, okay?'

Patronising bastard. He never used to be like this, but I think it's all part of the showing off that he can't seem to help these days. I wonder how Becky puts up with it, if indeed she does.

Thinking of women associated with James reminds me of a question I've been meaning to ask.

'Are we expecting to see your mother at any point over the weekend?' I ask. 'After all, we've taken over her house.'

'I wouldn't have thought so, no. She moved out when the renovations started. She's actually living in our old cottage. I did it up for her, and now she says she can't understand why she didn't move sooner.'

That's only a partial relief, as it raises another question.

'So where are you living, if you don't mind me asking?'

'Here. I was in the master bedroom, but obviously that's been taken over for the weekend, so Becky and I are up in the staff quarters with you.'

Oh great. I know it shouldn't matter that he's still with Becky, and it doesn't, but that doesn't mean I want to pass them on their way to the only bathroom up there, or listen to whatever they might be getting up to.

* * *

By Friday evening, the car park is filled with the obligatory selection of luxury SUVs. The guests are exactly as I had predicted: loud, crude, and competitive. The women are a mix of long-suffering first wives, glamorous trophy wives, and a couple that I'm sure are probably mistresses. One of them looks young enough to be her partner's daughter, but the way he's pawing at her leaves the true nature of their relationship in no doubt. The women are also sizing each other up, albeit much more subtly than the men. The guns have all been taken down and locked in the gun safe and the wine is flowing freely enough that there are more than a few flushed cheeks in the room. James is actually doing a reasonable job as host and Becky is by his side, laughing dutifully at his jokes and looking much more glamorous than I've ever seen her in a black floor-length dress. She's evidently unhappy about me being here, because her eyes narrow in displeasure every time she sees me. Tough luck, sweetheart, I think. You should have talked your boyfriend out of it before he hired me. I pretend to be checking something on my phone and take a candid photo of her, sending it to Elliott with the caption, 'Introducing Becky...' His reply makes me smile.

I love her already. After all, if it wasn't for her, I'd never have met you xx

Emily was a bit wide-eyed when the guests first started to arrive – she's never come across people like this before – but she seems to be settling back into her rhythm and is currently supervising the waiting staff to make sure that everyone's drinks are kept topped up and the canapés keep circling. The chefs are getting ready to plate up, so we need to start ushering the guests into the dining room. I try to catch James' attention to let him know that he needs to do his speech now, as dinner is practically ready. Emily and I are dressed the same as the waiting staff, in white blouses and black trousers. I don't know whether it's the lack of give in the material or the cut, but mine are quite tight across my thighs and bum, and they keep digging into my crotch. I'm just pulling the legs down my thighs for the umpteenth time to alleviate the discomfort when I finally catch James' eye. He's watching me adjust my trousers and grinning wolfishly.

I really, really don't want to be here.

30

After breakfast the next morning, Emily and the shooters clamber into a trailer behind one of the farm tractors to be taken to the field for the first drive. I experience a momentary pang of guilt, as poor Emily is miles out of her comfort zone and looks it. Thankfully, I'm soon able to forget all about her as the ladies and I board the minibus to take us to Exeter. The atmosphere is less competitive today than it was last night; a pecking order appears to have been established and various little alliances have formed. The only person who doesn't seem to have made any friends at all is the very young one, who I've learned is called Catriona. When the minibus deposits us in the centre of Exeter, all the ladies immediately bustle off in their groups, leaving her behind. I had hoped for a quiet day of pottering about, but she looks so forlorn that I take pity on her.

'You can hang around with me if you like,' I tell her. 'I know the city fairly well, so I'm happy to be your tour guide.'

'Are you sure?' Her big blue eyes are filled with gratitude. 'I'm not sure the others like me very much.'

'That's because they're jealous of your youth,' I tell her, as we set off. 'You're also a threat, because they sense their husbands eyeing you up, and that makes them insecure.'

'Wow. I never thought of it like that,' she tells me. 'How do you know all this stuff?'

'Years of working with people,' I reply. 'In my work, a little amateur psychology goes a long way. It helps a lot if you can pick up on difficult dynamics, because then you know who holds the power, who is likely to cause trouble, and so on. As soon as Bill walked into the sitting room with you on his arm last night, I could see their feathers were ruffled.'

'I did notice that the men were much friendlier than the women,' she observes.

'That's because the men see you as a prize. If Bill can snare someone like you, they reason, then maybe they can as well. I suspect a number of them were forcibly warned off you in the bedrooms last night. Ah, here we are. I thought we'd start with a coffee, if that suits you. They do a lovely slice of carrot cake in here as well, if that's your thing.'

I have to confess I'm not being one hundred per cent altruistic here; buying her a coffee (and probably lunch) makes the cost something I can charge to expenses. I do genuinely feel sorry for her, though, and I'm more than a little curious to find out what on earth she sees in an oaf like Bill. She's very attractive and would have no difficulty finding someone closer to her own age to go out with. I guess she could have an Electra complex, but even then, she could do a lot better than Bill. He's enormously overweight and, based on what I heard of his conversation last night, unutterably dull.

'So, how did you and Bill meet?' I ask nonchalantly, as I place a mug of hot chocolate and a slice of coffee cake in front of her. I've just got a coffee and a chocolate chip cookie that I have no intention of eating. I'll have a couple of small bites just so that she feels like I'm keeping her company.

'I know what you're thinking,' she replies, a little defensively. 'What's someone of my age doing with someone so much older than me?'

'Well,' I reply, carefully, 'you are a slightly unusual couple, you have to admit.'

There's a pause before she speaks again. 'If I tell you,' she asks, 'will you promise not to tell the others? They hate me enough as it is.'

'I won't breathe a word to them,' I tell her.

'Okay. I'm Bill's sugar baby.'

'I'm sorry, you're his *what*?'

'I'm his sugar baby. Surely you've heard of it?' My silence obviously gives the answer, as she continues. 'Do you know how expensive it is to go to university? Even ignoring the tuition fees, which are covered by the loan, you've got accommodation, food, bills, books, and all the rest of it. My parents can't afford to cover the cost of those things, but that's where Bill comes in.'

'So, he gives you money towards your uni fees, and in return you give him—'

'It's not prostitution,' she says firmly, and her eyes are blazing defiantly. 'He gives me certain gifts, and in return I have dinner with him sometimes and accompany him to things like this.'

'But you're sharing a room.' I'm trying really hard to keep the judgemental tone out of my voice, but I'm not sure I'm succeeding. 'Doesn't he have, you know, expectations? He was very hands-on with you before dinner, I noticed.'

'It's not a cash-for-sex relationship; that's not how it works. When you enter into a relationship with a sugar daddy, you both have to be very up front about what your boundaries and expectations are. I belong to a website for sugar babies, and it was all made very clear when I signed up. He also signed up to the same website, so we both know exactly what is expected. I'm not exploiting him; his eyes are wide open and he knows this is a time-limited thing. Lots of my friends are sugar babies too. Some of them choose to have a sexual relationship with their sugar daddies and some don't. It's entirely our choice. Bill knows that I'm not a done deal. I might choose to have sex with him sometimes, but it's not a given that every encounter will end in the bedroom.'

I'm mesmerised. 'But how do you, you know, if you're not in love with him?'

She laughs. 'Easy. It's not quite close your eyes and think of England, but it's not a million miles away either. A bit of lube helps and, between you and me, he doesn't last very long.'

'How do you stay safe, though? What if he turned out to be some sort of stalker, or he became obsessed with you?'

'I admit that's a risk,' she replies. 'But I'm very careful what I tell him about myself, and he knows not to try to pry. He doesn't know where I live, because I always meet him at hotels or other public places. He doesn't have my main mobile number or even know my real name. I've got a crappy pay-as-you-go phone that he has the number for, so I can just throw it away and he wouldn't be able to contact me any more if things started to get out of hand or I didn't feel safe.'

'I'm sure he could find out those things, if he really wanted to.'

'He probably could, but why would he? The people who sign up to be sugar daddies get a kick out of being benefactors to people like me. It makes them feel good, so if I dropped off his radar, there are any number of other sugar babies out there who would be willing to take him on.'

'Do your parents know?'

'God, no! Can you imagine? They'd hit the roof. But this is the thing. I'm not stupid, and I thought about this long and hard before

I signed up. If I got a job in a burger bar or something like that, I'd have to work way more hours than I can afford to, just to pay the bills. My college work would suffer and, if I'm going to succeed later in life, I really need a good degree. Bill isn't the most exciting man in the world and he's no Greek god, I'll grant you. But he's kind and we both know what we're doing.'

'Is he married? What about his wife?'

'I have no idea. It's none of my business, the same way my life is none of his business.'

I don't know whether I'm appalled by her or whether I secretly admire her, but I have to admit Catriona is great fun to spend the day with. Whatever the morals of her relationship with Bill, she's clear-eyed about it, and it's not my role to judge her. By the time we set off to the rendezvous point for the minibus, she's firmly established herself as my favourite person in the group. Thankfully, the other cliques have also had an enjoyable time, from what they tell me, so they don't appear to mind that I've taken her under my wing for the day.

* * *

It's still light when we get back to the house, but it's not long before I hear the sound of the tractor crossing the yard bringing the guns back. I walk out to meet them and Tony gives me a cheery wave from behind the wheel. The men are all in high spirits, and they've obviously had a good day too if the number of corpses hanging from the bar in the game cart is anything to go by. As soon as the tractor stops, James jumps down from the trailer and helps them all down, laughing and patting them on the back as if they're his oldest friends rather than paying customers. I have to admit, grudgingly, that he's playing his role to perfection.

The last person off the trailer is Emily, and straight away I can tell that something is very wrong. Her face is white as a sheet and she seems unsteady on her feet. James helps her down gently and I rush over.

'Slightly squeamish, this one,' he laughs as he hands her over.

'I'll get her inside. Tea has been set out and the staff are ready to pour, so we shouldn't be needed for a while.'

I rush her through the house and up to her bedroom.

'Please don't ever make me do that again!' she sobs, as soon as we're alone. 'It was brutal. Those poor frightened birds didn't stand a chance. How could people do something like that for sport? I've never seen anything so cruel, and they were just laughing and congratulating James on the size of "the bag" the whole time.'

'If it's any consolation, I think they die pretty much instantly.'

'That's not true, though. There was one, it fell out of the sky and it was just lying on the ground, flapping its wings and trying to get up until one of the dogs got to it. I think I'm going to be sick.'

Hastily, I grab the only receptacle in the room, a metal bin, and position it under her head. I'm only just in time, and she vomits several times. I feel awful. I should have known that Emily would never have been able to cope, but I was so busy selfishly avoiding my husband that I never thought what the potential impact on her might be.

'I'm so sorry,' I say, as I hold her trembling frame. 'I should have gone instead of you.'

'No, it's my fault,' she replies, catching me by surprise. 'I was so busy trying to be the big-shot organiser that I didn't think it through. If you'd have offered to go in my place, I would have refused. I can't do it again, though. If I wasn't a vegetarian already, that would have been enough to persuade me.'

'We'll find a way,' I reassure her. 'It's only clays tomorrow, but maybe neither of us need to be there. From what you've described and what I saw, James has that part of it pretty well under control.

Why don't you do the spa day with the ladies, and I'll hang around here in case I'm needed?'

The look of relief in her watery eyes is all the confirmation I need. 'Just one thing,' I tell her. 'Look after Catriona, will you? The other women have taken against her a bit.'

'I've got a theory about her,' Emily replies, as she wipes her mouth with a tissue and takes a sip of water from the glass next to her bed. 'I reckon she's rented.'

'I'm sorry?'

'You know, an escort. Paid for the weekend to make him look good.'

'Interesting theory,' I reply, and leave it at that. When I get back to my room and check my phone, there's a message from Elliott.

Thinking of you. How's it going? xx

I smile and type out my reply:

Discovered one of the 'wives' is a sugar baby. Poor Emily completely traumatised by the shoot and vomiting in her room. Just another boring day in the office, really. You? xx

I can see he's typing, and his reply arrives a few seconds later.

Wow! Sounds interesting. I can't really compete with that. I'm having pasta for dinner and that's probably the most exciting thing that's happened today. xx

I'll tell you all about it when I see you next. xx

Can't wait xx

By the time dinner comes around, Emily has recovered and we're back to our double act. The guests are tucking into rib of beef from James' own herd, the wine is flowing freely, and even Catriona looks like she's enjoying herself. The men are regaling their partners with exaggerated tales of their shooting prowess, and James is lavish with his praise, stroking their already inflated egos. It's all going very well, and I take the opportunity to grab a plateful and head for the butler's pantry to eat it undisturbed.

I'm sitting on a box and only a couple of mouthfuls in to the amazingly tender beef, silently wondering if there's a spare glass of red somewhere to help wash it down, when I become aware of another presence in the room. I look up to see James standing there with an unpleasant look on his face.

'Well, this is quite the turnaround, isn't it?' he sneers. 'You're not so hoity-toity now, are you? You're just a skivvy, a servant, my *employee*. Just think, if you hadn't deserted me, you could have been out there enjoying the high life with me instead of skulking around in the servants' quarters, grabbing whatever scraps we decide to leave for you.'

I'm incensed, not only because he's completely wrong, but also because our current situation makes it look like he's right. Every fibre of my being wants to tell him exactly where he can stick his ideas, but thankfully I'm stone-cold sober and just about able to maintain my professionalism. I set my plate aside and stand up, so at least he's no longer looking down at me.

'I have to point out that I'm not your "employee", as you put it. I'm a contractor whom you've hired to perform a particular job. It's my role to stay in the background unless I'm needed. I'm very pleased that your event is going well, and—'

My words stop abruptly when he grabs my face, leans in, and kisses me. It's not a tender kiss; he's crushing my lips with his. I can smell the sourness of the wine on his breath as his other hand reaches around to the back of my head to pull me harder against him. His tongue is trying to force its way into my mouth. There's nothing loving here; this is about dominance and power.

He breaks off just as suddenly, and I can already see his cheek reddening where I've slapped him.

'Don't you ever, *ever*, do that again,' I tell him, and my voice is shaking with rage. 'If you so much as come near me, I'll slap a sexual assault complaint on you so fast your feet won't touch the ground. Do you understand?'

'You wouldn't dare,' he snarls. 'It's your word against mine, and all I have to do is complain about you to your boss and you'll be out of a job. I'll tell her you wouldn't leave me alone, that you were harassing me and trying to get me back.'

'I wouldn't do that if I were you,' Emily's voice says from behind him. 'I saw everything, and I'm more than happy to back Sophie up. I suggest you get back to your guests, and we'll look forward to a glowing review, okay?'

James stands there pouting and moving his mouth, as if searching for a comeback, before turning on his heel and stalking back towards the dining room.

'Are you all right?' she asks.

'Thanks to you, yes.'

'Don't sweat it. I owed you one for not dobbing me in to Annabel when you first came back. Shall we see if there's a glass of wine anywhere? I reckon you need a bit of mouthwash, probably even disinfectant. Wine is a disinfectant, isn't it?'

'You're rapidly becoming one of my favourite people in the world,' I tell her.

31

The next morning, James is understandably wary of me and raises no objection to running the clay pigeon shoot on his own. Emily has gone off with the ladies, so I decide to go for a walk, as there isn't really anything I need to do for the moment, and I don't want to hang around the house in case I bump into Becky. I also need some time alone to process what happened last night. As I walk down the drive towards the stables, I fish my phone out and take advantage of the improved mobile coverage to call Elliott.

'How are you holding up?' he asks.

'I could be better,' I admit. 'James tried to kiss me last night.'

'Seriously? What a scumbag!'

I fill him in on all the details. 'Don't worry, I slapped him so hard I think his cheek is still tingling,' I tell him. 'I just don't know what to make of it. What did he think he was doing?'

'I suspect it's what I told you before. Although I'm sure the shoot and the income from it are important, the underlying motive was always about you.'

'Go on.'

'He's determined to prove that you would have been better off if you'd stayed with him. I think he's hoping you'll spend the rest of your life regretting walking away from your marriage, especially now that the farm appears to be a success. When he saw you dressed like a member of the waiting staff, eating off your lap, it was practically his wet dream. There he is, lord of the manor, and you're his servant, as he put it. The kiss was all about him having power over you. He probably hoped you'd be into it, so he could be the one to reject you this time.'

'You seem remarkably calm about the fact that some other man tried it on with your girlfriend,' I observe.

'I don't like the idea, of course I don't. But I'm not going to get all Neanderthal about it and threaten to beat James up. Apart from the fact that it sounds like I'd probably come off worse than him, you're not some object to be fought over and owned. You're a free agent, and you make your own choices. I want you to choose me every time, and I hope you will. But I don't own you, and I hope I'll never treat you like a possession.'

'You are the most amazing man. Of course I choose you!'

'And I choose you too. I can't wait for these negotiations to be over so I can spend more time with you.'

'Me too,' I tell him. 'Me too.'

I'm grinning from ear to ear as I replay our conversation in my head after we've hung up. Elliott may feel that he'd come off worse in a fist fight, but in my mind he's twice the man James could ever be. It's just a shame I didn't meet him first, but then maybe I needed to be married to James to appreciate Elliott fully. I'm no believer in karma, but sometimes things happen for a reason. I'm nearly at the end of the drive when I spot a familiar figure walking towards me and the smile leaves my face.

'Good morning, Rosalind,' I say as she comes to a halt in front of me.

'Hello, Sophie. I heard you were working here this weekend. Shouldn't you be back at the house, doing something?'

'No. Everything is under control, thank you.'

'I see. So you decided to have a poke around, did you?'

'I was just getting a bit of fresh air.'

'I expect you were surprised to see all the changes James has made since you left. He really has done terribly well, and Becky is *such* a support to him. I'll admit that I wasn't sure about her at first, but she really is a charming girl and they make a lovely couple, don't you think?'

I know she's deliberately trying to wind me up, but I'm determined not to rise to it.

'I'm just glad he's happy and the farm is thriving,' I tell her.

'Of course you are. Don't take this the wrong way, will you, but I think the fact that Becky grew up around here is an advantage. She doesn't have the trouble fitting in that you did, you see.'

She really is doing her best to rile me, and I force myself to keep calm. I can't help having a little pop, though.

'It does sound like it's all worked out for the best,' I reply. 'Maybe, now that he has some spare cash and doesn't need to sell other people's possessions to keep himself afloat, James will be able to afford fertility treatment and the farm will have the heir I know you're so keen on. I also hope, for Becky's sake, that his infidelity issue turns out to be a one-off and not the beginning of a pattern, like his father. Or maybe, because she understands how things work around here so much better than me, she'll just put up with his sexual incontinence, like you did.'

I've hit a nerve, I can tell, as the faintest flush of colour appears on her cheeks.

'I've never said that what James did to you wasn't wrong,' she begins.

'Look, Rosalind,' I interrupt, 'I'll be perfectly honest with you.

It's water under the bridge as far as I'm concerned. I'm only here because James insisted that I come. Why did he do that, do you think?'

'He knew you were good at your job.'

'You know that's nonsense as well as I do. There are any number of event planners who could have organised this weekend for him, but he specifically asked for me.'

'Yes, but you know how the country works. Someone who'd never lived in the country wouldn't have a clue how to organise a shooting weekend.'

I laugh. 'Come on, Rosalind. You can't have it both ways. I can't be the poor city girl who struggled to fit in and the only person in the South of England who knows how a shooting weekend works.'

I can see her struggling for a riposte, so I decide to press home and deal my killer blow.

'Don't you see it?' I ask her. 'He can't bear the thought that I don't need him any more. He wanted me to come here and see what he's done, because he thought that I would be impressed and regret my decision to leave. But I don't. I don't even regret the seven years I wasted on him, because it's helped me to understand the qualities that are important to me in a man, and I'm sure you'll share my happiness when I tell you I've met someone who has those qualities.'

The gloves are truly off now, and her mouth is pursed in displeasure.

'You're delusional,' she replies archly. 'You're past history and we're better off without you. James only has eyes for Becky.'

'Of course he does. Which is why he tried to kiss me last night. Now, if you'll excuse me.'

I step around her and continue down the drive. I can feel her eyes on me, but I don't care. I have nothing more to say to her or her son.

32

When our time to leave finally comes around, after lunch on Monday, I'm exhausted and relieved in equal measure. The weekend has been a huge success, and we sent each of the guests away after tea yesterday with a brace of plucked and gutted pheasants in an ice box. The rest were collected by a couple of local butchers, one of whom will be including them as part of a game pie that James will sell in the farm shop. James has continued to stay well clear of me since our encounter in the butler's pantry, although I have caught him watching me a few times. The furniture lorries all appeared again this morning, and we've counted everything once more to make sure nothing gets left behind. A couple of glasses were broken, but I'm not expecting a bill for those, and everything else is undamaged. Given the amount of alcohol consumed and the rowdiness of some of the guests, I reckon that's a minor miracle.

Emily looks done in, and I'm slightly worried about sharing a car with her back to London, but she insists she's fine. We call Annabel on the way and update her, leaving out the whole sexual harassment incident for now. James has already been on the phone to her to say what a success the weekend was, and she fully expects another booking soon.

'I would be very surprised if he makes another booking with us. Would you do it again if he did?' I ask Emily as we're belting along the M5.

'As long as I didn't have to go on the shoot or have anything to do with the dead birds, I reckon I could handle it,' she replies. 'The hospitality part of it was fun, even if I never got to the bottom of what was going on with that Catriona woman.'

'Now that the weekend is over, I can probably tell you. Bill is her sugar daddy.'

'You're kidding! I've heard the term, but I never knew it was an actual thing!'

I tell her everything that Catriona told me, and we spend a happy hour raking over the questionable morality of it. One thing we do agree on is that she must have the constitution of an ox to be able to tolerate sex with him. Emily does a couple of impressions that leave us crying with laughter.

'I don't think it could have gone any better, in spite of James,' I tell her, once we've finished talking about Catriona and generally unpicking the events of the weekend. 'You should be very proud.'

'I had an excellent mentor. Can I ask a question?'

'Go on.'

'What did you see in him? James, I mean.'

'I honestly can't remember. I'm sure he wasn't like that when I fell for him, though.'

'Do you think he still holds a candle for you? There's obviously something going on there.'

'I don't think he can help himself. In fact, I'd be surprised if he and Becky last the distance, despite what his mother says.'

'When did you see her?'

'Yesterday morning. I bumped into her when I was out for a

walk. She wasted no time in telling me that Becky fits in much better than I ever did, and basically did everything to run me down.'

'I'm no expert, but you seemed to understand how things work around here pretty well. Better than I do, anyway.'

'Don't worry, I'm not going to let her get to me. She's nothing to me, and her opinions don't matter either. I think I got that point across.'

'I bet you did. She's probably terrified of you now.'

'I doubt it!' I laugh.

'You're pretty ferocious when you need to be.'

'I'm not sure she's the type to be scared of anyone. Anyway, she's not my problem.'

* * *

I don't think I've ever been so pleased to see my flat as when I walk through the door that evening. I did knock on Elliott's door, but there was no answer, so I've obviously missed him. I'm surprised by the force of my longing for him. He's so totally different to James in every way, and every one of those differences makes me love him more. I have no idea where we'll end up, but I've got a really good feeling about him. After unpacking and putting on a load of washing, I decide I don't want to be alone for the evening, so I call Bronwyn, who answers on the second ring. Katie will be at uni, so I know she's on her own.

'I've been thinking about you,' she tells me. 'How did it go with the ex and everything?'

'If you're free, I was thinking of getting some fish and chips. You're welcome to join me. I've even got a bottle of wine in the fridge, I think.'

'That sounds very tempting, but I've already got a shepherd's pie in the oven. It'll easily stretch for two, though. Why don't you come over?'

Five minutes later, I'm standing outside her door clasping the bottle. I can't help smiling when she greets me, as she's wearing a pair of overalls so covered in paint it's difficult to tell what the original colour of them was.

'Sorry,' she says as she stands aside to let me in. 'I've been painting all day today and I haven't got around to getting changed. Let's get a couple of glasses, and then I want to hear all about it.'

The shepherd's pie is delicious and, by the time I've filled her in on Catriona and the sugar daddy set-up, James' sexual advances, and Emily's trauma, the bottle is nearly empty.

'Are you going to tell Elliott what James did?' she asks, as I'm getting ready to leave.

'I already have. He was really nice about it, actually.'

'I thought he would be. Honesty is always the best policy, don't you think? If you hadn't told him, it would only have come and bitten you at some point in the future.'

'You're probably right. I can't tell you how much I'm missing him. I think he's away all week.'

'Bummer. It's funny how he's started having to travel so much for work all of a sudden, isn't it?'

'I think it's a temporary thing,' I tell her. 'Just until he's wrapped up the project he's working on.' I love Bronwyn, but I'm not going to tell her about Nutsy, as she's not the most discreet person in the world and I'm not sure Elliott is ready for the whole of Sevenoaks to know who he is.

As I climb the steps towards my flat, I'm looking forward to collapsing into bed. This weekend has really taken it out of me, and I've never been more grateful for Annabel's rule about time off in lieu. It's just a shame that Elliott isn't here to share it with me.

The stairwell light goes out just as I'm pushing the key into my door and something catches my eye. There's a strip of light below Elliott's door. The tiredness falls away instantly and my heart starts beating hard. Could it be?

I knock gently on his door and the banging in my chest intensifies when I hear footsteps on the other side. The door opens, and there he is. He looks just as tired as I was feeling until a few moments ago, and there are bags under his eyes, but his smile is as dazzling as ever.

'Hello, you,' I say, as he wraps his arms around me. 'I knocked earlier but you weren't here. I thought you'd gone already.'

'That's bad timing. I only popped out for half an hour or so to get some bits and pieces and a bottle of Champagne to welcome you back with. I was beginning to wonder whether you'd got held up somewhere. I was just about to text you to see where you were.'

'Sorry. I didn't want to be on my own so I had dinner with Bronwyn. If I'd have known you were here I'd have been straight over. What time do you leave?'

'I'm not going anywhere. It's done,' he replies. 'we've agreed the figure and now it's up to the lawyers to do their thing. I've missed you so much!'

'That's good,' I reply into his chest. 'I've missed you too.'

'Would you like to come in?'

'Yes, I think I'd like that very much.'

ACKNOWLEDGMENTS

This is my first all-new book for Boldwood and I couldn't be more grateful for all the support I've received. Thank you to my fabulous editor, Tara, who not only improved the story with her carefully thought out suggestions and comments, but also rescued me when I had a mini meltdown during the edits. I'd also like to thank Claire, Jenna, Nia, and Amanda for all their support and encouragement. Boldwood feels like a family, and I'm privileged to be a part of it.

This is one of those books that has left me with an interesting internet search history, everything from the legal machinations of the divorce process to sugar daddies and babies. However, I also have to thank some real people who helped me with my research! Simon, thank you for answering my divorce-related questions. I got in a bit of a flap trying to work out how much milk a dairy farm might hold in its tank, so thank you to Sal for rescuing me there. Thanks also to Phil, who patiently explained to me why 'How much does a tractor cost?' wasn't a simple question to answer. Huge thanks to my family for being so supportive and encouraging, giving me time to hide away and write.

As always, I'm very grateful to Frances, Mandy, and Robyn: thank you for being my alpha and beta readers, and for your wise input. Finally, I have to thank our dog, Bertie, who happily puts up with me working out plots with him when we're out walking.

MORE FROM PHOEBE MACLEOD

We hope you enjoyed reading *Let's Not Be Friends*. If you did, please leave a review.

If you'd like to gift a copy, this book is also available as an ebook, digital audio download and audiobook CD.

Sign up to Phoebe MacLeod's mailing list for news, competitions and updates on future books.

https://bit.ly/PhoebeMacLeodNews

Explore more heartwarming romance from Phoebe MacLeod.

Fred and Breakfast

Phoebe MacLeod

ABOUT THE AUTHOR

Phoebe MacLeod is the author of several popular romantic comedies. She lives in Kent with her partner, grown up children and disobedient dog. Her love for her home county is apparent in her books, which have either been set in Kent or have a Kentish connection. She currently works as an IT consultant and writes in her spare time. She has always had a passion for learning new skills, including cookery courses, learning to drive an HGV and, most recently, qualifying to instruct on a Boeing 737 flight simulator.

Follow Phoebe on social media:

twitter.com/macleod_phoebe
facebook.com/PhoebeMacleodAuthor
instagram.com/phoebemacleod21

Boldwood

Boldwood Books is an award-winning fiction publishing company seeking out the best stories from around the world.

Find out more at www.boldwoodbooks.com

Join our reader community for brilliant books, competitions and offers!

Follow us
@BoldwoodBooks
@BookandTonic

Sign up to our weekly deals newsletter

https://bit.ly/BoldwoodBNewsletter